A changed man . . .

The viscount and Jem obligingly turned while she took off her stockings. Standing up, she stepped into the water, lifting her skirt to ke...

Warrington look... ...by the display of the la... ...at feel wonderful, miss...

"Oh, yes," said A... ...he cold water. She smile... ...ed Jem run through the water with the dog chasing after him. "I am glad to see Jem enjoying himself."

The viscount nodded. A memory from his childhood came to him and he thought of himself wading in the fishing stream at his father's estate. "I remember when I was very young and I had a rat terrier. Boodles and I had many a good run in the stream. I also remember how my nanny would scold me for getting wet and muddy."

"Your nanny?" said Antonia. "So now I am hearing something of your mysterious past, Jack Bradford. You had a nanny."

"I confess I am at present less prosperous than I once was," said his lordship.

"It seems we've both come down in the world," said Antonia with a rueful smile.

"Perhaps so," said the viscount gazing into her blue eyes, "but I don't know when I've had a happier moment than being here with you. . . ."

Gentleman Jack

Margaret Summerville

A SIGNET BOOK

SIGNET
Published by the Penguin Group
Penguin Putnam Inc., 375 Hudson Street,
New York, New York 10014, U.S.A.
Penguin Books Ltd, 27 Wrights Lane,
London W8 5TZ, England
Penguin Books Australia Ltd,
Ringwood, Victoria, Australia
Penguin Books Canada Ltd, 10 Alcorn Avenue,
Toronto, Ontario, Canada M4V 3B2
Penguin Books (N.Z.) Ltd, 182–190 Wairau Road,
Auckland 10, New Zealand

Penguin Books Ltd, Registered Offices:
Harmondsworth, Middlesex, England

First published by Signet, an imprint of Dutton NAL, a member of Penguin Putnam Inc.

First Printing, March, 1999
10 9 8 7 6 5 4 3 2 1

1

It was scarcely past dawn when a stylish carriage pulled up in front of a redbrick town house in a fashionable London neighborhood. Climbing out from the passenger compartment of the vehicle was a somewhat disheveled-looking young man in evening clothes. He stood staring about the quiet street for a moment before making his way unsteadily to the front entrance of the residence.

As he approached the door, it was swung open to reveal a butler with graying hair and a solemn expression on his face. The servant nodded obsequiously. "Good morning, my lord."

John Augustus St. George Fortescue, Viscount Warrington, scowled in greeting his butler. "It's a damnable morning, Bishop."

"Indeed, my lord," murmured the servant apologetically. He paused. "Would your lordship be wanting breakfast?"

"Good God, no. I'm going to bed and I don't wish to be disturbed for anything less urgent than a fire."

"Very good, my lord," said the butler, nodding again. Watching his employer as he mounted the stairs, the butler reflected that the viscount must have had another unlucky evening at cards.

A prudish man, Bishop didn't approve of his young master's wild behavior. Warrington often stayed out all night, gambling, drinking, and consorting with what the butler called "females of an improper sort." However, the butler had been in service for over thirty years and was well acquainted with the habits of titled gentlemen. What had originally shocked him as a young servant no longer caused him to so much as raise an eyebrow.

In fact, despite his master's profligate ways, Bishop considered the viscount one of his better employers. Warrington was usually an amiable gentleman, except for an occasional foul mood or flare of temper. And more important, he acquiesced to the butler in all household matters, showing a lack of interest in anything of a domestic nature. Yes, one could do far worse than having Lord Warrington as an employer, thought the butler philosophically as he made his way back to the servants' hall.

Warrington walked haltingly toward his bedchamber. The effects of no sleep and too much wine were taking their toll and as the viscount continued along, he failed to see a bucket that the parlor maid had left in the hallway. Hitting the pail with his foot, the viscount overturned it, and the dirty water sloshed up on him. His lordship's loud oath brought the parlor maid scurrying down the hallway toward him.

The maid, a girl of sixteen, with carroty red hair and freckles, gazed in horror-stricken silence at her employer. Warrington stared ill-temperedly at her. "Did you leave this accurst thing here . . . ? What is your name, girl?"

"Betty, m'lord," said the maid in a strangled voice. "I'm so sorry, milord. I was just going to take the bucket downstairs when Mary said Cook needed me to . . ."

Warrington waved his hand impatiently. "I don't want to hear your excuses. 'Twas a damned half-witted thing to do, leaving a bucket about the place. By God, I could have tripped over it and broken a leg. I should have you sacked, my girl. By God, I should!"

"Oh, I am sorry, m'lord!" cried Betty, bursting into tears.

"Stop your blubbering and clean this up!" snapped the viscount, who then continued unsteadily on his way.

Betty hurried to do so, stifling her sobs as best she could. She would spend the rest of the day worrying about her fate, even though the viscount forgot her and the incident as soon as he got inside his bedchamber.

His valet, Finch, who had been awaiting his master's arrival, was appalled at his lordship's unkempt appearance. The viscount's wavy, dark brown hair looked wild and unruly, and there was dark stubble on the young gentleman's handsome face. Warrington's cravat was untied and his coat had a crumpled, slept-in look about it.

Finch helped his lordship take off his coat, while stifling a yawn. Finch, an ambitious young man, had been quite pleased to get the situation as valet to Warrington, a gentleman who would one day be an earl. However, his employer's late nights were making him think regretfully of his former service to Sir William Fitzwalter, an elderly baronet who always retired by nine o'clock.

Warrington kicked off his shoes and plopped down on the huge canopied bed, still attired in his evening clothes. Finch eyed him questioningly. "Would your lordship want a bath?"

The viscount closed his eyes. "No, Finch. I've got the most wretched headache. I'm just going to get some sleep."

"But wouldn't your lordship want to change out of your clothes first?"

"Hang my clothes," muttered the viscount and he was quickly fast asleep. Finch regarded him for a moment and then, with a shrug, he left the room.

Hardly two hours had passed when the door to Warrington's bedchamber opened and Bishop entered the room. Staring down at his master's recumbent form, he hesitated. "My lord," he said finally. When there was no response, he spoke in a louder voice. "My lord."

Warrington opened his eyes and regarded the butler with a somewhat befuddled expression. "What?" He sat up suddenly and then clutched his head and winced. "What time is it?"

"It's eight o'clock, my lord."

"Eight o'clock in the *morning*?" returned the viscount, fixing a bleary-eyed expression of annoyance on the servant.

"Yes, my lord," said Bishop.

"Great God, man, there'd better be flames licking about the house for you to wake me up," said Warrington, lying back down and placing a pillow over his head.

"No, my lord. But Lord Gravenhurst is here to see your lordship."

The viscount took the pillow from his head and gazed up at the butler. "My father here now? What the deuce does he want?"

"I couldn't say, my lord, but his lordship seemed most anxious to see you."

Warrington groaned. "Well, I can't see him now. Tell him I'm indisposed and I shall call upon him later."

Bishop appeared skeptical. "Indisposed, my lord?"

"Yes. Tell him I can't be disturbed by anyone."

The servant nodded. "Very well, my lord," he said in a dubious tone, leaving the room.

The viscount placed a hand to his forehead and groaned again. His head was throbbing and he felt perfectly dreadful. No doubt hearing about his father's unexpected call had exacerbated his condition, thought Warrington grimly. What could his father be thinking of to pay him a visit at such an ungodly hour?

Warrington and his father were not on amicable terms. Indeed, it seemed that every time that they met, they quarreled over something. The Earl of Gravenhurst was a serious-minded man who was dismayed by his son's extravagance and self-indulgence. Those in society who knew them both always marveled that the straitlaced earl could have produced such a son.

The door to his room was opened once again and the viscount looked toward it, expecting to see his butler. "What the devil is it now, Bish . . ." The words died on his lips as he beheld the furious form of his father standing before him. "Father," he said.

The earl, a handsome man of five-and-fifty, stormed over to the windows and drew open the drapes. He then turned to face his son, who was blinking in the bright sunlight. "How dare you refuse to see me!" said Gravenhurst, folding his arms in front of himself.

Warrington frowned as he sat up in bed. "Didn't Bishop tell you that I'm not well, Father?" he said. "I think I'm coming down with something. I fear it may be contagious, sir."

"Contagious? Bah!" exclaimed the earl. "You are just feeling the effects of another drunken night carousing about town! By heaven, look at you. You are a disgrace, Warrington!"

"Is that what you have come to tell me, Father?" Warrington said irritably.

The earl, who was growing rather red in the face, directed a disgusted look at his son and heir. "I've come to tell you that I've heard about your losing two thousand pounds in one of those damned gaming hells."

The viscount shook his head. "I fear your spies are wrong, sir. That is gross exaggeration. It was scarce eighteen hundred."

"Only eighteen hundred? Well, that makes me feel so much better," said Gravenhurst sarcastically.

"Come, Father," said Warrington, "surely that is a measly sum to you."

"Measly sum?" cried the earl. "Well, my boy, if you keep losing these 'measly sums,' you'll be the ruination of me. I suppose you spent all of last night gambling away more money."

"Not *all* of last night," said the viscount with a slight smile. He didn't elaborate on what else he did that evening since it involved a voluptuous actress.

The earl shook his head. "By God, sir, you may find this amusing, but I do not! You are four-and-twenty, Warrington. You must begin to act responsibly and quit this rakehell life of yours. It is time that you married and settled down."

Warrington grimaced. "Not this again, Father. I have no wish to 'settle down' as you call it."

Gravenhurst ignored this remark. "Yes, a wife is what you need, Warrington. A fine, well-bred young woman like Lady Sophie Parkenham."

"Are you still trying to foist her upon me?" said the viscount wearily. "You know I don't have any interest in Lady Sophie." Warrington tactfully omitted mentioning the fact that he found the prospect of marriage to Lady Sophie appalling. She was a dull young woman with a peevish temperament and a host of unpleasant relations.

The earl frowned. "Yes, I know that you prefer females of a vulgar sort, light skirts and actresses and their ilk. You would never even look at a respectable woman like Lady Sophie."

Warrington scowled. "Well, I'm sorry to disappoint you, Father, but I won't marry the girl just to please you."

"I'm not surprised. You have never done anything to please me," said Gravenhurst.

The viscount shrugged. "Yes, I'm well aware of that, Father. Now if there is nothing further that you want to upbraid me about . . ."

"Indeed, there is," said the earl. "I was upset by another story I heard about you."

"Good Lord," said Warrington, "what gabblemongers have you been listening to?"

"That doesn't signify," said the earl gruffly. "I was told that you snubbed Robert Underwood at Vauxhall Gardens last week."

The viscount shrugged indifferently. "I don't see why I should be lending countenance to such a fellow."

"You have no business snubbing Underwood. He is a distinguished gentleman."

"A gentleman?" said Warrington, scornfully. "You are rather generous calling him that. After all, who was his father but a tradesman, a seller of boot polish?"

"A useless popinjay like you has no right scorning other men for making an honest living, something you could never do. You'd starve if someone didn't give you sums to fritter away. Yes, I'll wager you couldn't live a month without coming to me for money."

"Don't be ridiculous, Father," said Warrington. "I scarcely ever come to you for money."

"That is because you owe a fortune to your creditors. I don't doubt they're dunning you mercilessly, as well they should."

"What nonsense," said the viscount, although he knew very well that his creditors were growing increasingly bold about demanding payment.

"You are a spendthrift and a wastrel. You've never had two shillings in your pocket for more than five minutes before you lost them gambling. Yes, you wouldn't last a month without me giving you money. Yes, I'm sure of it."

The viscount regarded his father indignantly. "I'd last a month. Indeed, I'd last a year. I shall never again ask you for money, knowing how you despise me."

The earl laughed. "You'll never ask me for money? What a fool you are, Warrington. Within a month, you'll be crawling to me, begging for money to pay your debts."

"I shall be damned if I do," said the viscount hotly.

"Well, we'll see." He regarded his son thoughtfully. "You are a young man who cannot resist a wager. Let me propose one to you. I'll bet you that you cannot live for one month without plunging further into debt. Yes, this is the wager. You will live on a reasonable sum for a month, not gambling and not going into debt. If you can do that, I shall settle your existing debts."

Warrington eyed his father in surprise. "You would do that? And all I have to do is refrain from gambling and live on a reasonable sum for a month? Why, that sounds too easy."

"Easy, is it?" said the earl. "It would be easy for any sensible man, but for you, it will be impossible. You cannot resist gambling and you cannot live on a reasonable sum, even for a month."

"Indeed, I can," said the viscount. "But what, may I ask, do you consider a 'reasonable sum'?"

"I imagine fifty pounds would be more than generous."

"Fifty pounds!" exclaimed Warrington. "You must be joking."

"Fifty pounds is more than enough for anyone to live on."

"You expect me to live on such a pittance for a month?"

"Yes, and not incur any debt," said the earl. "And no gambling, mind you. Nor are you to use your name and rank to get special treatment. It is time you learned what life is like for people without your advantages."

Warrington frowned. His father, who was very progressive in his politics, was constantly railing on about all the poor unfortunates in the world. Warrington himself had no interest in such matters and never gave them a moment's thought. "And what would you have me do, Father?" he said. "Give up my title and my name?"

"Yes," said Gravenhurst, "for a month. And I don't want you staying with any of your relations or friends. No, you must leave town and go someplace where no one knows who you are. Then see if you can live on fifty pounds."

"Leave London?" said Warrington, horrified at the idea of being stuck incognito in some backwater for a month. Still, if his father would pay his very considerable debts, it would be well worth it.

"So will you do it?" said the earl.

The viscount nodded. "If you are serious about this silly wager, I shall be more than happy to oblige you. Indeed, it will be a simple enough matter for me to win it."

"But you haven't heard what I will demand if you lose."

"And what is that, Father?"

"If I win the wager and you gamble or incur more debts or resort to using your name to get yourself out of difficulties, you will agree to marry Lady Sophie Parkenham."

"What?" cried Warrington.

"Ah, so you're not so confident after all," said his father.

"No," said the viscount firmly. "I have no fear of becoming Lady Sophie's husband. I will win this bet handily. And if I do, will you cease hounding me about wedding the girl?"

The earl nodded. "Very well, we have a wager," he said, offering his hand to his son, who shook it. "It's a bargain then."

"Yes, I suppose it is, Father," said the viscount. "Is there any particular place you'd want me to go?"

"I don't care, so long as it's a place where no one knows who you are." Reaching inside his coat, the earl took a banknote from a pocket. "Here is fifty pounds. You are to leave at once."

"At once?"

"The sooner the better. Have your servant send word to me where you have gone."

"But I shall have to call on Mama and my sisters and . . ."

"That isn't necessary. I'll speak to your mother. It's best you don't see her or your sisters."

"Very well, Father," said the viscount.

"Then I shall leave you to make your arrangements. And we will see what happens in a month." The earl took his leave, looking rather pleased with himself.

When his father had departed, the viscount rose from his bed. "He will regret this wager," he said, feeling very confident. "How I shall enjoy showing him how wrong he is."

The viscount rang for a servant and Bishop quickly appeared. "Yes, my lord?"

"Fetch an atlas from the library."

"An atlas, my lord?" inquired the servant, with an uncharacteristic tone of surprise in his voice.

"Yes, you heard correctly, Bishop," said Warrington.

"Very good, my lord," said the butler, bowing and then leaving the room.

He returned a short time later with a large volume which he placed upon a table near the bed.

The viscount opened the book and, thumbing through it, stopped when he reached the map of Great Britain. "Let me see, where shall I go?" Closing his eyes, he stuck his finger down on the page. He then glanced at the spot where his finger rested. "Shropshire," he said. "Yes, that should suit perfectly. It will be devilish boring, but I shall rusticate in Shropshire for a month and win Father's absurd wager." And with that decision made, Warrington pushed away the atlas and went back to sleep off the excesses of the previous night.

2

Antonia Richards gazed out of the schoolroom window at the well-manicured lawns of Larchmont. It was the middle of May and the trees and grass were a brilliant green. The far meadow glistened gold in the sunlight, and in the distance were the low-lying hills of Shropshire.

Taking one last wistful look at the inviting spring landscape, Antonia turned her attention back to her pupils. Her charges, two blond little girls, were sitting in seats, frowning down at the slate boards in front of them.

Walking over to the oldest girl, she glanced down at the numbers on the slate. "Oh, dear, Harriet," she said, "it appears you need more work on your sums."

Harriet ill-temperedly pushed the board down on her desk, making a noisy clatter. "I hate sums!" she cried. "Arithmetic is so dreary, Miss Richards."

Antonia shook her head. "You think geography, history, and literature are dreary as well, Harriet," she said with a sardonic smile.

"Well, they are," declared the nine-year-old, pushing a blond ringlet from her forehead. "I don't know why we must learn such things."

Her sister, Annabelle, grinned. "It is so you won't be such a blockhead, Harry."

Harriet gave her seven-year-old sister a warning look. "Oh, do be quiet, you little worm."

"And you are a—" began Annabelle eagerly, but Antonia quickly cut her off.

"That is enough of that, both of you," she said. "Let us get back to our lessons."

Harriet, who had no wish to return to her arithmetic, burst out,

"But, Miss Richards, why should girls have to learn sums or geography?"

Antonia sighed. "So they can become educated young ladies, Harriet. You should be glad that you have such an opportunity. Many girls don't, you know."

Harriet put on a pretty pout. "My brother says he can't abide educated females."

"Well, it is fortunate for you, Harriet, that your brother isn't your governess," she said.

Annabelle giggled. "Geoffrey our governess? How very silly!"

Harriet ignored her and turned back to Antonia. "But gentlemen don't want to marry educated ladies. Why, look at you, Miss Richards! You know all sorts of things and what good has it done you? You're an old maid!"

"Harry!" cried her sister, glancing at her governess with an expression of dismay.

Antonia frowned slightly, but appeared unperturbed. "I suggest you return to your sums, Harriet," she said.

"But you can't wish to be a spinster, Miss Richards," continued Harriet, eyeing her governess with a superior expression. "I daresay it is because you are too bookish, for you are tolerable looking."

"That is enough," said Antonia sharply. "Return to your lessons, miss. I don't want to hear another word from you."

Harriet stared down at her slate, but made no move to continue with her work. Antonia suppressed a sigh. Being Harriet's governess was certainly a trial, she thought. Well, she told herself, at least the girl thought her "tolerable looking." A slight smile came to her face as she regarded her difficult pupil.

Despite Harriet's faint praise, Antonia was more than just "tolerable looking." Indeed, she was a very attractive young woman. While Antonia faulted her nose as being too short and her mouth too full for classical perfection, less critical observers thought her exceptionally pretty. Short and petite, she had fine blue eyes, a lovely pale complexion, and a wonderful smile. She was also blessed with a splendid figure that evoked considerable masculine admiration and dark curly hair that was much envied.

And while Harriet considered her governess to be firmly on the shelf, Antonia was scarcely more than two-and-twenty. She had also, Harriet might be surprised to learn, refused three offers of marriage. Having a romantic temperament, Antonia Richards had been unwilling to marry without being in love. Instead, she had chosen the arduous life of a governess. Looking down at her recalcitrant pupil, Antonia wondered if she'd made the right decision.

Harriet sat staring rebelliously at the slate, not moving a muscle.

"Do get on with your work, Harriet," said Antonia.

"I don't want to do this anymore. I'm tired of sums."

Antonia fixed a resolute look on her. "You will do your sums, Harriet, and then you may have tea."

"I don't want to!" cried Harriet in a fit of temper. "You can't make me!" And taking up her slate, she threw it on the floor.

Antonia crossed her arms in front of her and said severely, "Very well, Harriet. You can go stand over in the corner and there will be no tea for you today, young lady."

On hearing this, Harriet burst into loud, melodramatic sobs. At that moment, the girls' mother entered the room. Lady Mansfield was a rather plump, but decidedly attractive blond woman, who was dressed in a fashionable muslin dress. She frowned at Antonia. "What is the trouble, Miss Richards?"

"Harriet refuses to do her sums, Lady Mansfield," began Antonia. "She had a tantrum and threw her slate on the floor."

To Antonia's surprise, Lady Mansfield only smiled. "One can't blame the child, Miss Richards. I daresay Harriet is very tired. She has been working so very hard."

"That is no reason for her to behave in such a childish fashion," said Antonia.

"Really, Miss Richards," said Lady Mansfield, "I believe you expect too much of poor Harriet. Indeed, you don't have to be such a slave driver."

"I don't feel that Harriet is being overtaxed in her studies," said Antonia. "And she should do as she is told."

Lady Mansfield eyed the governess with an imperious look. "My daughter will do as *I* say, Miss Richards. And I think she has had enough schoolwork for one day." Harriet quickly stopped crying and she flashed a triumphant smile at Antonia. "Now come, girls," said their mother, "I'm going to take you into town to see the dressmaker."

Antonia's face reddened, but she watched in silence as Lady Mansfield led the two girls out of the room. However was she to command her pupils' respect when their mother undermined her authority?

Walking back to the window, she once more stared out at the grounds. She reflected that the life of a governess at Larchmont, an estate near the village of Cawley in Shropshire, was exceedingly difficult. Antonia had been employed by Sir Harold Mansfield and his wife for scarcely two months, but it seemed like an eternity to her. Lady Mansfield behaved toward her in a very condescending manner, treating her little better than a servant.

In addition to her dislike of the haughty Lady Mansfield, and her difficulty in controlling the unruly Harriet, Antonia had another problem that made her position here difficult. This was the fact that she also had to put up with the unwelcome attentions of Sir Harold's son, Geoffrey.

Going back to her desk, Antonia sat down. She didn't even like thinking about Geoffrey Mansfield. That gentleman was becoming more and more trying. From the time she had arrived, he had been paying far too much attention to her. And only two days ago, he had come upon her alone in the library. He had made bold, suggestive remarks and she had fled from the room, blushing deeply.

After that incident, she had considered giving her notice, but upon further consideration, she had decided against it. After all, she had nowhere else to go and no money.

Since her mother's death the previous year, Antonia had found herself in severely straitened circumstances. Her father had been a naval officer who was killed seven years earlier in the Peninsular War. Captain Richards had made several unwise investments over the years, leaving her mother and her in debt with little income except his rather meager military pension.

Captain Richards's father had disowned him when he'd married Antonia's mother, for the captain had chosen as his bride a lovely Italian opera singer whom he'd met in Milan. His family had vehemently disapproved of the marriage, but Antonia's father had been too in love to care.

After the captain's death, Antonia and her mother had managed to live a frugal existence, adding to their income by giving music lessons. But with her mother's death and the termination of her father's pension, Antonia was forced to seek other employment as a governess.

Although Antonia was unhappy at Larchmont, she desperately needed the position. She knew that if she gave her notice and attempted to find another job, Lady Mansfield would never give her a reference. Resting her head in her hands, Antonia sighed. It seemed she had little choice but to stay there, at least for the present.

She decided that she had better get back to work and correct the assignment that Harriet had written that afternoon. Taking up the piece of paper, Antonia began to read. It was a short essay the girl had written on Charles I, and Harriet's sloppy handwriting and disjointed sentences made the paper difficult to follow. It appeared that Harriet's knowledge about the unfortunate king was lamentable, though she seemed to relate the details of his beheading with considerable relish.

Pushing the paper aside, Antonia gazed at the window again. Getting up from the desk, she walked over and looked outside. Why should she stay cooped up in the schoolroom, she thought. After all, Lady Mansfield had decreed that her daughters had had enough schooling for the day. She had taken them off to the dressmaker and it would probably be some time before they returned. Antonia suddenly decided she should take advantage of such a fortuitous event and, quickly leaving the room, she went off to get her bonnet.

A short time later, Antonia was outside in the bright sunlight, taking the path that led from the estate's gardens to the far meadow. Walking about in the fine weather did much to improve her spirits and she began to hum a tune in a melodious voice as she continued along the path.

As she approached the stables, Antonia waved at a small boy who was sitting on one of the gates to the horses' stalls. The boy waved back, and jumping off the gate, he eagerly hurried over to her.

"Hello, Jem," said Antonia, smiling down at him.

Jem Perkins was a small, sandy-haired boy of nine years of age. He stared up at Antonia with a lopsided grin. "Good day, miss," he said. " 'Tis a fine day."

"Yes, it is indeed," agreed Antonia.

Jem was overjoyed at his good fortune in having Miss Richards to himself. An orphan, Jem had been put to work in the stables at the age of seven, cleaning out the stalls and seeing that the horses were watered and fed. It was a hard life for the boy, since the grooms were constantly barking orders at him and cuffing him on the ears if he didn't respond quickly enough.

Antonia had been one of the few people at Larchmont to show Jem any kindness. Hungry for companionship, the small boy was practically bursting with things to tell her. "I found a lark's nest in the meadow, miss," he said. "There are seven eggs in there."

"Are there?" said Antonia, smiling broadly.

"Aye, miss." Jem suddenly looked concerned. "I do hope the foxes won't get them."

"Oh, so do I," said Antonia, becoming equally serious.

Jem nodded solemnly. His face brightened again. "Godiva's going to have a foal," he said excitedly. "Ajax is the father, you know."

"Why, that's splendid," said Antonia.

Jem nodded. "Aye, Godiva's foal will be a right one." He abruptly pulled something out of his pocket. "Here, miss, this is for you." He put out his grubby hand and held out a small pebble. "It's all speckled and glittering, see?"

Antonia picked it up and studied it appreciatively. "It's beautiful, Jem. Thank you."

The boy beamed and was about to say something else, when a rider suddenly came cantering toward them on the path. Antonia frowned when she saw that the horseman was Geoffrey Mansfield.

Geoffrey pulled his mount up before them, and lifting his tall beaver hat, he smiled down at Antonia. "Miss Richards."

Antonia nodded. "Mr. Mansfield," she said in a tone that was scarcely civil.

The young gentleman wasn't deterred by the lady's lack of enthusiasm. Although his short stature was a constant bane to him, Geoffrey was quite confident about his appeal to the opposite sex. His curly auburn hair, light blue eyes, and classical features had caused some ladies to consider him a veritable Apollo.

Jumping nimbly down from his mount, he stood before Antonia. "A lovely day for a stroll, is it not?"

Antonia regarded him with an annoyed look. "It was until now, sir."

Laughing, Geoffrey was about to say something else when he noticed Jem standing there. "What are you doing here, boy?" he demanded.

"I was talking to Miss Richards, sir," Jem said bravely.

This answer didn't seem to please Geoffrey. He scowled menacingly at Jem. "You aren't supposed to be hanging about, boy. Get back to work or I'll give you a proper thrashing."

Jem needed no further words from his employer's son. Giving Antonia a furtive look, he quickly dashed off to the stables.

Antonia eyed Geoffrey with irritation. "Must you speak to him like that?"

"Oh, come. The little rascal is like all of his class, taking any opportunity he can to get out of work."

Antonia was about to say that Geoffrey had his nerve making such a remark since he himself had never labored a day in his life. However, she held her tongue and merely glared her disapproval.

Geoffrey shook his head. "You have a soft spot for that little ruffian, do you?" He paused and grinned. "Can you not find a similar spot for me in that heart of yours?" And with those words, Geoffrey fixed a lascivious gaze on the bodice of Antonia's dress.

Antonia reddened. "No, I cannot, sir," she said hotly, and then she started walking briskly away from him.

Geoffrey quickly followed her, leading his horse behind him. "Come, Miss Richards, don't fly into the boughs. I promise I won't speak a harsh word to the little miscreant again."

Antonia kept up her pace and he hurried in front of her, forcing her to stop. He smiled down at her. "I should enjoy a more leisurely stroll, Miss Richards. Why don't we take the path over to the woods?"

"If you will excuse me, sir, I have to get back to my duties," said Antonia severely. "Now do get out of my way."

Geoffrey continued smiling at her. "What duties, ma'am? I know your charges aren't at the house. I passed my stepmama's carriage just now. She had the two monsters in tow." He leaned closer to her. "So there is no need for you to hurry back."

"Indeed, there is," said Antonia fiercely. "Now get out of my way!"

"My dear Miss Richards," he said, "did anyone ever tell you what a charming little nose you have?"

"Excuse me, Mr. Mansfield. I must return to the house."

He reached out and took her arm. "There is no need to rush off."

She pulled her arm away. "Leave me alone, sir. I do not appreciate your attentions. And if you persist, I shan't hesitate in speaking to your father."

Geoffrey tapped his riding crop against one hand. "But I'm just trying to be amiable."

"Well, I don't find you so," said Antonia. "Now let me pass!"

Geoffrey paused a moment, and then stepped aside. As she walked by him, he tipped his hat and grinned. Antonia quickened her steps and in a short time was back at the house. Hurrying inside her room, she locked the door behind her. Odious, odious man, she thought. And sitting down on her bed, Antonia decided that there must be some way that she could leave Larchmont and find another position.

3

Two days after the interview with his father, Warrington was making his way to Shropshire. Since he had to disguise his identity, he was unable to take his carriage, emblazoned as it was with the family crest. The idea of going by public coach didn't appeal to the viscount, so he had decided to make the journey by horseback.

His lordship's servants were quite intrigued by their master's mysterious departure. They found it very odd that the viscount had set off on his horse for an unknown locale without even his valet accompanying him. It caused much gossip in the servants' hall as to what Warrington could be up to.

One of the footman suggested that perhaps his lordship was a spy for the government and had gone off on a secret mission to France. The young servant would have been quite disappointed to discover that his employer was not involved in some exciting espionage against Napoleon, but was leisurely following a route to the far from exotic countryside of Shropshire.

To his considerable surprise, Warrington was finding himself enjoying the journey. It was something of a novelty pretending he was an ordinary gentleman and not the heir to one of the oldest titles and richest estates in the kingdom. Of course his fashionable clothes and fine horse marked him as a man of means and wherever he stopped, he was always treated with great courtesy. While the food and accommodations usually weren't up to his usual standards, the viscount accepted the privations in good humor. In fact, he was beginning to relish his journey as something of an adventure.

On the third day, Warrington reached his destination. As he rode past undulating fields of grazing sheep, he decided that spending a month in Shropshire on fifty pounds would not be difficult in the least. After all, what could one possibly spend money on in such a seemingly dull place? It would be an easy matter to take up lodgings somewhere for the month. All he would have to do was endure the boredom of it. Then he would return to town and have the satisfaction of proving his father wrong.

Coming to an intersection of roads, the viscount pulled up his mount and studied a sign that posted the directions and mileage to two villages. Warrington patted his horse's neck. "Well, my girl, which shall it be? Owen's Hill or Cawley?" The bay horse didn't express an opinion, but his lordship decided to take the road leading to the village of Cawley, which was only five miles distant.

He hadn't gone very far when he suddenly spied a man sprawled on the side of the wooded road up ahead of him. Thinking that the fellow had been in an accident, Warrington spurred his horse ahead and then quickly dismounted. Walking over to where the man lay, he leaned over the seemingly lifeless form.

The man on the ground suddenly turned over and grinned up at him. Somewhat startled, the viscount abruptly backed away. "What the deuce?" he began. There was a chuckle behind him and he turned around to see a giant of a man aiming a pistol toward him. The man on the ground, who was smaller in stature than his companion, jumped to his feet and brushed himself off. "So kind of you to stop, sir," he said, smiling and running a hand through his unkempt black locks. "Now if you would be so good as to hand over your money."

Warrington could scarcely believe his ill luck to be taken in by two footpads on his arrival in Shropshire. "You damned villains," he muttered, but his words were cut short by the large man at his back, who chose that moment to poke the pistol into his back.

" 'Twould be wise for you to do as he says," the man said.

The viscount scowled, but reached into his pocket and produced his purse. As he handed it over to the man, he was glad that he had wisely hidden most of his money in a pocket inside his waistcoat. The shorter man, who had a long pinkish scar along his right cheek, opened the purse and looked at the coins inside. "That is a very good start, your honor. Now if you would give me that watch and fob and that ring you're wearing."

Warrington hesitated. The watch had been a present from his father when the viscount had reached the age of sixteen. Despite his strained relationship with the earl, he was loathe to part with it. However, after receiving another nudge from the pistol, he pulled out the watch and handed it to the robber.

"And the ring, sir. I warn you that my friend is quite ready to shoot you."

The viscount hesitated again for a moment, before pulling the ring from his finger and giving it to the man. "Very well, you have everything I own of any value," said Warrington, frowning. "Now be on your way."

The man with the nasty scar exchanged a glance with his companion. "This here fellow thinks he can order us about." The giant chuckled unpleasantly, and for the first time, the viscount began to be fully cognizant of the danger he was in. The shorter man, who was apparently the leader, continued to eye him. "That is a handsome coat you have, your honor. And I do fancy that hat of yours. And those fine boots, too. Take them off," he commanded roughly. "And that shirt and britches as well." The viscount eyed him in disbelief.

"I will do nothing of the sort."

The man smiled. "It's up to you, your honor. But I'd rather have that coat without a pistol ball through it."

Warrington hesitated again and then, swearing an oath, he began to take off his clothes.

"Take off all of them, sir, every stitch," said the robber, waving the pistol at him.

The viscount started to protest, causing the big man to slap him hard across the face. "Do as you're told!"

Warrington regarded him with a furious expression, but somehow managed to restrain his temper. He knew very well that resistance was futile. He had little chance against the two of them, especially with a pistol pointed at him. As he continued to undress, the viscount realized that he'd never been so humiliated in his life.

The leader, who was about three inches shorter than the viscount, picked up the various items of clothing and eyed them appreciatively. He then took off his own clothes, replacing his well-worn and stained garments with Warrington's excellently tailored and expensive ones. After putting on Warrington's boots and striding a few uncertain steps in them, the man finally placed the viscount's hat on top of his head. Although the clothes seemed rather ill-fitting on him, he turned to his friend with a satisfied expression. "Don't I look the proper nob?"

The giant nodded. "Aye, that you do."

Warrington stood there with his arms crossed in front of him. "You damned blackguards."

The shorter man shook his head. "Now, see here, your honor. 'Tis a fair trade. You can have my clothes." Warrington looked down scornfully at the scurvy garments heaped before him. The robber grinned. "Or perhaps you'd rather be left like you are," he said. " 'Twould be a fine treat for the local wenches to see such a fine, strapping fellow as yourself." The giant guffawed loudly and Warrington cursed under his breath. But taking up the clothes, he quickly put them on. He then glared once more at the two men.

The robber with the scar turned to his companion again. "Give me the pistol and go and get the fellow's horse." Warrington, who had been waiting for such an opportunity, watched as the big man handed over the gun and then obediently went to get the viscount's horse, which had strayed over to one side of the road.

When he saw the ringleader glance over at his friend's progress in retrieving the horse, the viscount lunged toward him, knocking the pistol out of his hand and delivering a sharp punch to his face. The man with the scar fell to the ground and the viscount hurried to pick up the gun. But, unfortunately, the large man reached the weapon before Warrington.

Snatching it up, he aimed it at his chest. Warrington stared up at the man, expecting him to fire at any moment. However, the giant glanced over at his leader as if waiting for instructions.

The scar-faced man got up off the ground, rubbing his jaw. "Give me the gun," he said. After taking up the pistol, he scowled at Warrington. "You'll regret that, your honor. By God you will." He turned to the giant. "Hold him, Tom."

The giant grabbed Warrington's arms and pulled them roughly behind him, causing the viscount to wince in pain. The man with the scar then delivered a hard blow to Warrington's midsection, causing him to gasp. He then hit him hard across the face and again in the stomach. He continued to beat Warrington until his hand grew too sore to continue.

The large man then took over, shoving Warrington to the

ground and proceeding to punch him with his huge fists. When the now nearly senseless Warrington struggled, the man banged his head against the ground until everything went black around him.

The scar-faced man, who had been enjoying seeing his friend beat Warrington, was distracted by a noise coming from the road. "Tom, there's someone coming!" They both stopped and heard the familiar rumble of a farm wagon.

"Damn," said the man with the scar. "Just some penniless farmer. Come on, we've plucked a fine pigeon here. No point in getting a scrawny chicken. Drag him over behind that tree there and let's be off."

As the giant lugged the viscount's inert body out of view behind a large oak tree, the other man took the reins to the viscount's horse. The two men then quickly disappeared into the woods.

After some moments, the farm wagon came lumbering along the road. Its occupant, a stout, middle-aged man, urged his large horse onward. Eager to get home, the man drove the cart along, unaware that Warrington was lying off in the woods, bleeding and unconscious.

4

That same afternoon Antonia was returning from an expedition to the village of Cawley. Since Lady Mansfield had taken her two daughters to visit their grandmother that morning, Antonia had had the luxury of having the entire day to herself.

Fortunately for Antonia, Geoffrey Mansfield had also gone off early with some of his friends to attend a horse race. As a result, Antonia had had a most enjoyable day. She had spent a leisurely morning reading and playing her cherished mandolin. Then, clad in a peach-colored pelisse and wide-brimmed straw bonnet, she had set off on foot for the three-mile journey to the village.

After perusing several shops in Cawley and stopping for tea at Mrs. Wiggan's, a pleasant establishment that boasted that lady's delicious muffins, Antonia reluctantly started back to Larchmont. It was another fine spring day and she sang as she walked down the quiet country road that led to the Mansfield estate.

While nearing the small patch of woods that bordered the stream running through Larchmont, Antonia stopped singing as she saw a brightly colored bird fly past her. Straining her eyes toward the trees, she stood for some minutes, attempting to see the creature again. Somewhat disappointed at failing to spot the bird, she once again started walking along the road. However, a moment later, she stopped again. She thought she had heard a noise. It had sounded very much like a moan.

The countryside was silent, except for the chirping of the birds, and Antonia was beginning to think that she had imagined the sound. She was almost about to start off again when she heard the same noise. It definitely sounded like someone moaning. Walking off the road, Antonia made her way into the edge of the woods. As she walked under the dark canopy of trees, she looked somewhat apprehensively around her. Her eye then fell upon the prostrate figure of a man who was lying at the bottom of a great oak tree.

Hurrying to the man's side, Antonia bent down over him. Viscount Warrington, his face bruised and bloody, was in a semiconscious state. He was muttering something incomprehensible. Antonia regarded him in alarm. His injuries seemed quite serious. "Sir," she said, "can you hear me?"

The viscount stopped muttering and opened his eyes. He stared up at her. "What?" he asked, a strange look on his face. He suddenly tried to raise himself up, but then he sank back down.

Antonia placed a gentle hand on his chest. "You must stay still." Reaching into her reticule, she took out a handkerchief and began to dab the blood from his face. Warrington kept his gaze upon her. Suddenly remembering his attacker, he looked wildly around him and once more attempted to get up. "Where is he?" he growled. "The damned villain."

"Hush," said Antonia, alarmed to discover that the stranger before her had apparently been the victim of a vicious attack. "He is gone." Warrington stared at her for a moment, then lay back down. Antonia held the handkerchief against his forehead and looked toward the road. "I must go and get help, sir. Larchmont is scarcely a mile and a half from here."

The viscount didn't respond, but lay quite still. Afraid that he had lapsed into unconsciousness, Antonia quickly got to her feet and hastened back to the road. Running most of the way, she was breathless by the time she reached the lane that led into Larchmont.

Racing toward the house, she was met by a wagon driven by one of the Larchmont servants. Pulling up the horses, the burly young man driving the vehicle regarded Antonia in alarm. "Whatever is the matter, miss?"

"Oh, Will," she cried, "you must come! There is a man injured down the road!"

" 'Twas there an accident, miss?" asked the servant in an excited voice.

"No, it appears he was beaten and left in the woods," said Antonia.

This information was especially thrilling to Will. "Beaten, was he?"

"Yes, and we must hurry," said Antonia. Will jumped down and assisted her up into the seat. By this time, one of the other servants, who had witnessed Antonia running down the lane, had hurried over to them.

"Miss Richards says there be a man injured back on the road, Daniel," said Will. "You come along with us." The man nodded and jumped into the back of the wagon. Will then urged the horses on and they were soon on their way.

As they neared the woods, Antonia pointed. "There! He is there by that large tree!" The servant pulled up the wagon, and after helping Antonia down, he followed her with Daniel tagging along behind.

Warrington was still sprawled out in the same spot and Will walked over and glanced down at him. The viscount lay very still, his pale face covered with blood. Will shook his head. "It does appear that he's dead, miss," he said.

Horrified, Antonia rushed over and gazed down at Warrington. To her relief, he suddenly opened his eyes and stared up at them.

Antonia quickly bent down to him. "You will be all right. We are going to take you to Larchmont."

Warrington fixed his intent dark eyes on her and managed to smile slightly. Antonia smiled back at him and then turned to the two servants. "Do be careful with him," she said. Will nodded.

"You take his feet, Daniel," he said, and the two men lifted the viscount up from the ground. Warrington groaned in pain and then once again became insensible as they carried him off and deposited him in the back of the wagon.

Antonia kept an anxious gaze on the viscount during the short trip back to Larchmont. At her instructions, Will drove the wagon up to the front of the Mansfields' impressive country house. Hurrying up the steps to the residence, Antonia was met at the door by the butler. "Oh, Grigson, there is an injured man. We must bring him into the house at once."

At that moment, Lady Mansfield, who had recently arrived back home, entered the hallway. "Good heavens, Miss Richards," she said, eyeing the governess with disapproval, "what is all the commotion about? I saw you running up the stairs just now like a hoyden."

Antonia turned to her employer. "There is a man out in the wagon, Lady Mansfield. I fear he's been badly beaten. We must bring him into the house and fetch the doctor."

Lady Mansfield raised her elegant eyebrows. Without another word, she went out the door and stared down at the wagon at the foot of the steps. The two servants were starting to take Warrington gingerly out of the back of the vehicle. Her ladyship eyed the viscount with a frown. The man appeared most unpleasant to her with blood all about his face and his clothes dirty, ragged, and foul smelling. "Wait a moment!" commanded Lady Mansfield sternly and the two servants looked up in surprise. "You will not bring that man in here!"

Antonia had come out of the door and was standing next to Lady Mansfield. She regarded her with an astonished expression. "But, he's hurt! He needs help!"

Lady Mansfield eyed Warrington with a disgusted expression. "He looks like a beggar. Take him to the back to the servants' quarters. The butler can find a place for him there."

"Should Grigson send for the doctor, Lady Mansfield?" said Antonia.

Her employer frowned again. "I don't know why we should have to pay to have a physician come here. I very much doubt that the man has a penny on him."

"But he is very badly hurt," said Antonia.

"Oh, very well. I suppose it won't do to have the fellow dying here. Grigson, have one of the servants fetch Dr. Carter." The butler nodded and went off.

"That is very good of you, Lady Mansfield," said Antonia.

"One cannot say I shirk my duties in aiding the unfortunate," said Lady Mansfield. "But I do think he might have been brought somewhere else. It isn't very far to the village."

Antonia, who did not trust herself to make any comment, remained silent.

"And since you are so concerned for the man, Miss Richards, I suggest you see to him. Have him taken to the servants' hall." And with those words and a scornful look at Antonia, she retreated inside.

Astonished at her employer's indifference to the injured man's plight, Antonia turned and descended the stairs. "We must take him to the servants' entrance, Will," she said. Will nodded and he and Daniel proceeded to put Warrington back into the wagon.

5

A short time later, the two servants had carried the viscount inside the house. Grigson ordered them to put the injured man in Jem's room, where there was a spare bed. The servants had to maneuver up a narrow stairway to the tiny room where Jem slept. There they deposited the viscount on the narrow cot. Looking about at the stable boy's small and Spartan room, Antonia frowned. So this was where poor little Jem lived, she thought.

Will regarded Antonia a little bashfully. "I think we should take off his clothes, miss," he said.

"Oh, of course," said Antonia. "I shall go and get some water." Taking one last look at Warrington, she left the room and made her way to the kitchen. After getting a pitcher of water and some clean cloths from the curious kitchen maids, Antonia started back to Jem's room.

As she walked down the hallway, she was met by Larchmont's housekeeper, Mrs. Clay. A pleasant-faced, matronly woman with graying hair, the housekeeper was quite eager to hear about Antonia's adventure.

"My dear Miss Richards," she said, hurrying toward her, "Mr. Grigson said that you found an injured man."

Antonia, who was quite fond of the housekeeper, stopped to talk to her. "Yes, I was on my way back from the village when I heard someone moaning in the woods near the stream. I fear the man was badly beaten by someone."

The housekeeper threw up her hands. "Oh, dear! And so close to Larchmont! I daresay one isn't safe anywhere nowadays." She paused and cast a concerned gaze on the governess. "And you were out walking alone, my dear! I don't think that at all wise.

Why, what if you had run into the ruffian who had beaten the man?"

"Thankfully I didn't, although I rather wish I had got a look at him so I might tell the constable. But the poor man! I do hope he will recover. And if he does, it will be despite Lady Mansfield. Why, she didn't want him brought in. And now he's in Jem's tiny room. It is scarcely the place for an injured man."

"Yes, Mr. Grigson did indicate her ladyship was none too pleased. I fear Lady Mansfield is somewhat lacking in Christian charity."

"I would say she is *completely* lacking such sentiments," said Antonia. "Now do excuse me, Mrs. Clay, but I really should be getting back to him."

After promising to keep the housekeeper posted concerning the man's condition, Antonia continued back to Jem's room. Tapping lightly on the door, she entered to find Warrington lying quietly in the small bed, a cover thrown over him and his clothes in a pile on the floor.

Daniel took the pitcher of water from Antonia and placed it on a small table next to the bed, while Will picked up the pile of clothes. "I'll see to these, miss," he said.

Antonia smiled at him. "Thank you, Will. And you, too, Daniel." The two servants nodded and then left the room. Taking a seat on a small stool at the head of the bed, Antonia looked down at the viscount's face. Despite the blood and bruises, it was obvious that he was a very handsome man. Wondering again who he was, Antonia began to gently wipe off his face.

Warrington lay still for some time, but then he suddenly turned over, throwing a bare arm outside the cover. Muttering some words, he then opened his eyes and stared up at Antonia with a look of surprise. She smiled down reassuringly at him. "You'll be all right. We have sent for the doctor."

The viscount continued to gaze up at her with a befuddled look. He tried to say something, but his jaw was so painful that it was an effort to open his mouth.

"You mustn't worry. You are at Larchmont, Sir Harold Mansfield's home."

Warrington didn't reply, but seemed content to regard her with a somewhat stupefied expression. There was a knock on the door and the butler entered the room. "The doctor is here, Miss Richards."

Antonia nodded and turned back to the viscount. "I'll leave you to Dr. Carter," she said, quickly getting up from her seat and leaving the room.

It was some time before the doctor left the room. Antonia, who had been waiting outside in the hallway, was quite relieved when Dr. Carter reported that the young man would recover. He continued to say that he had been very fortunate in escaping without any broken bones or more serious injuries. However, a rib or two might be cracked and he did have a slight concussion.

His patient was disoriented and unable to speak lucidly, said Dr. Carter, but that was to be expected considering the nature of his beating. The doctor assured Antonia that rest was the best remedy for the man.

When the doctor left, Antonia opened the door to Jem's room a crack to see the viscount lying there peacefully, his eyes closed. After quietly shutting the door, she retreated back down the hallway.

Warrington awoke early the next morning. Still in considerable pain, he groaned as he shifted his tall frame in Jem's too-small cot. Glancing about the room, he noted the cramped and dingy accommodations. His eye then fell upon a small form huddled under a blanket on a bed in the corner. A boy was lying there, fast asleep.

A sharp pain in his head made the viscount wince. "Where the devil am I?" he muttered, addressing the sleeping boy. Jem only pulled his blanket over his head.

Frowning, the viscount tried to remember the events of the previous day. He had been robbed! Yes, the memory of his misadventure came back to him vividly. The blackguards had taken his money and clothes and had beaten him mercilessly. They would pay for their deed, he thought grimly. He would see to that.

Turning over, Warrington felt another stab of pain. Gingerly touching his sore ribs, he realized that he was fortunate to be alive. He remembered how he had been lying alone in the woods, thinking he might die there. Indeed, for a moment, he had thought he had died. There had been an angelic melody in the distance and

then a lovely dark-haired girl had appeared before him, like some
supernatural creature.

Warrington strained his memory, but he couldn't recall much
else that had happened. Everything seemed rather foggy after that
damned robber had knocked him out. He did seem to recollect
some large oafish fellow staring down at him and being jolted
about in a wagon. And then there was the lovely young woman
wiping his face and saying something about a place called Larch-
wood or Larchfield or some such name, owned by a Sir somebody
or other.

The viscount looked about the room. What was he doing here in
this shabby room? Didn't anyone know who he was?

No, of course they didn't, he realized. Indeed, it was clear that
whoever had taken him in hadn't even known that he was a gentleman. The viscount was momentarily offended. Yet it was true
that the robbers had taken his clothes, leaving him in shabby garments. Perhaps one couldn't blame them for not recognizing him
as a gentleman of quality.

Well, he would soon set them right on who he was. It would be
rather amusing to see the embarrassed reactions of his hosts when
he informed them that he was the renowned Viscount Warrington.
No doubt they would be horrified and immediately jump all over
the place to make amends. Yes, to think of putting him in this
wretched bed and dismal room with some sort of urchin.

"Boy!" said Warrington in a loud voice.

Jem opened his eyes and then pushed aside his blanket. "You're
awake!" he said, getting to his feet. "You are better. I must tell Mr.
Grigson."

"Mr. Grigson?"

"The butler."

"Then I'm in the servants' quarters."

Jem nodded. "This is my room. No one else would give up his
bed, so they put you here."

"So you were the only one who would give up his bed?"

Jem shrugged. "Oh, I hadn't a choice. But I didn't mind," he
added.

A slight smile came to Warrington's face. "Who is master
here?"

"Sir Harold Mansfield."

"Never heard of him," said the viscount. "Well, you are to inform this Sir Harold that . . ." He stopped in midsentence, his smile vanishing as he remembered the wager with his father. One of the conditions of the bet was that he not reveal is name or title to anyone. But surely his father couldn't expect him to abide by such a ridiculous demand under the circumstances, he thought. After all, he'd been robbed and nearly killed.

"Tell him what, sir?" said Jem.

Warrington's expression grew pensive as he considered the matter. His face darkened and he frowned again. He wouldn't be at all surprised if his father would hold him to the bargain. The earl wouldn't care one fig that he'd only barely escaped with his life. No, his father would say that he couldn't even survive a week without falling back upon his name and rank. And, the earl would certainly expect him to honor his pledge to marry Lady Sophie Parkenham.

"Damnation," said Warrington.

"What is the matter?" said Jem.

The viscount ignored him. He was in a hellish predicament, he thought. He had no money and no horse. Looking down at his bare chest, he frowned. "My clothes. Where are my clothes?"

"One of the girls is seeing to them. They needed washing and mending. But you must stay in bed until you're better. Would you be wanting me to tell the master something?"

Warrington hesitated. No, he couldn't reveal his identity. He'd have to do the best he could as an ordinary man buffeted by ill fortune. "Only that I appreciate his kind hospitality," said Warrington, trying to rise from the bed. "Oh, God!" he cried, as the pain in his chest cut like a knife.

"You mustn't move. 'Twas a bad beating you had, sir. Robbers, was it?"

The viscount nodded. "I'll see that the rogues hang," he muttered. "They stole my money and my horse as well."

Jem's eyes widened at the mention of hanging. "'Twas more than one, sir?"

Warrington nodded. "It was a pair of them."

The boy appeared thrilled with this information. "A pair of cutthroats," he said, seeming to relish the word. Then he looked slightly alarmed. "But they stole your horse?"

"Yes," said the viscount, "and I was damned fond of her."

Jem regarded him sympathetically. "I'm sorry for you, sir, losing your horse to them cutthroats." He paused. "But 'twas lucky that Miss Richards found you."

Warrington raised his dark eyebrows. "Miss Richards?"

"Aye, sir. Miss Richards found you lying in the woods and ran back to Larchmont for help. Will believed you to be dead at first. I reckon you looked a fright, all bloody and such. But Miss Richards will be pleased to know that you're better."

"And who is this Miss Richards?"

Jem's face brightened. "Oh, she is governess to the two young misses. She is a fine lady, too, as fine as her ladyship. But she don't act the great lady. I mean to say, she don't stick her nose up in the air like the mistress and think she's better than everyone. She is very kind to everyone, no matter their station. No, she's not like most of the quality, always lording it over everyone."

The viscount was rather amused at this remark. "Indeed?" he said.

Nodding, Jem tucked his shirt into his trousers. "Lord Almighty," he said, suddenly noticing the light streaming into the tiny window of his room. "It must be late. I must go or Mr. Samuels will box my ears for certain. I'll tell someone you're awake." He turned and hurried to the door. Opening it, he let out a glad exclamation. "Miss Richards!"

Antonia, who had been just getting ready to knock upon the door, smiled at the boy. "Jem, how is he?"

"Better, miss. He's awake and talking. He sounds quite right in the head."

The viscount, who had heard this remark, smiled again.

"Oh, I am so glad," said Antonia, very much relieved. Entering the room, she smiled down at Warrington. "You appear to be much improved. How do you feel?"

Although every bone in his body ached at the moment, the viscount said, "Much better." Staring up at her, he realized that she was the lady of his vague recollection. She was exceedingly pretty, he thought, noting her large blue eyes and dark curls.

Antonia was a trifle discomfited by his scrutiny. "I am very happy to find you better, Mr. . . . ." She paused. "I fear we don't know your name. I am Miss Richards."

"How do you do, Miss Richards?" said his lordship. "It seems I own you a debt of gratitude. The boy tells me it was you who found me."

"I'm just glad that I did so," said Antonia, who could not help but note that the stranger's bare shoulders and the portion of his muscular chest appearing above the bedclothes. He was a very handsome man, she found herself thinking as she looked down into his brown eyes.

"He said it was two cutthroats robbed and beat him, miss!" said Jem. "And they took his horse!" Although Jem would have liked to linger, he knew he must go to his duties. "Good day, miss," he said.

"Good day, Jem," said Antonia as the boy rushed off. Turning her attention to Warrington, she smiled sympathetically. "There were two men who beat you? That is dreadful, Mr. . . . ?" She regarded him expectantly.

Warrington was temporarily at a loss. What name should he give? He couldn't say his title and his given name, John Augustus St. George Fortescue, would hardly do either. After all, the Fortescues were one of the oldest noble families in the land. He must think of some other name and quickly. "My name is Bradford," he said, thinking of Nanny Bradford, the woman who had raised him. "Jack Bradford."

"I shall be happy to send word to your family, Mr. Bradford. I shall be happy to write to whomever you wish. Your wife perhaps?"

"Oh, I'm not married," said the viscount. "No, there's no need to write to anyone."

"But surely there is someone who will worry about you."

"No, no one at all," he said.

"Perhaps a neighbor," suggested Antonia. "I don't believe you're from this area."

"No, I was traveling through Shropshire."

"Where were you going?"

"Oh, I really hadn't any particular destination in mind, but I thought I'd stay in Shropshire for a time."

Antonia regarded him curiously, wondering about his background and station in life. His well-educated way of speaking was in contrast with the shabby clothes he had been wearing. Indeed, he spoke like a gentleman.

"Well, you must rest, Mr. Bradford. Dr. Carter has said you may have one or two cracked ribs. But he feels there are no other bones broken and you will recover very quickly. But you must stay in bed and allow yourself to heal."

"How long must I stay here?"

"Several days," said Antonia. "Perhaps a week or more." There was a sound at the open doorway and Grigson entered the room, accompanied by a stout, somber-looking, middle-aged man.

"Miss Richards," said the butler, "this is Constable Townsend. He has come to speak with the injured man."

"Do you feel well enough to talk to him, Mr. Bradford?" said Antonia, directing her question to the viscount.

Warrington nodded. He looked at the constable. "I should be grateful if you will do all that can be done to get my horse and money restored to me."

"We will do what we can," said the constable glumly.

A footman entered the crowded little room with a chair. "Place it near the bed for Mr. Townsend," instructed the butler. The servant did so, and then he and Grigson left the room.

The constable, who appeared rather red in the face from climbing the stairs up to Jem's room, seemed eager to sit down. But seeing Antonia had no place to sit, he hesitated.

"Oh, do sit down, sir," she said. "I assure you I would prefer to stand."

Nodding gravely, the constable sat down in the chair beside Warrington. He opened a small leather-bound notebook and took out a pencil. "I must ask you a few questions. Your name?"

"John Bradford."

"Where do you reside?"

Warrington hesitated. "London," he said finally.

"The address?"

The viscount hesitated again. "Actually, I had left town. I was going to take up residence in Shropshire."

"Your profession?"

"I don't really have a profession."

"No profession or trade?" said the constable, eyeing him with a frown.

"No, not at the present time," replied the viscount. "And what means I had were stolen from me by the accurst footpads. Indeed, everything I had is gone."

"And what was stolen?"

"My horse, my watch, a ring, money, and my clothes."

"How much money was taken?"

"Fifty pounds."

"Fifty pounds?" said Antonia, regarding him in surprise.

"Yes," said Warrington, realizing from her expression that she considered fifty pounds a very large sum, "it was all I had."

"And the horse?" said the constable, scribbling into his notebook.

"A chestnut mare fifteen hands. She has a white blaze and white stockings."

Townsend dutifully wrote this down. "And your clothes were taken?"

Warrington nodded. "And a damned good pair of boots. He left me with his own filthy rags."

"Would you describe your assailants?" said the constable.

"One was a big giant of a man and the other was shorter with dark hair and a long scar on his face."

Townsend nodded. "As I expected. The Scar and Ginger Tom."

"The Scar and Ginger Tom?" repeated the viscount.

"That's what we call them," said Townsend. "They've committed many a crime in this county. It will be only a matter of time before they're caught and brought to justice."

"A matter of time?" said Warrington. "They must be caught immediately. I've told you they took all my money. I'd like it back and quickly."

"They have eluded us for months. The Scar is a clever fellow," said Townsend. "And even if they were caught, there is nothing to say we'd recover your money, Mr. Bradford."

"Well, that is damnable," said the viscount. "You had best recover it. And I want to see those villains hang."

"I should like that as well," said the constable, rather irked by Warrington's demanding tone. "Be assured that all will be done to apprehend them. I regret the loss of your money, Mr. Bradford. Perhaps I might notify a family member or friend for assistance?"

The pain in the viscount's ribs seemed to worsen and he felt his head pounding. "As I told Miss Richards, there is no one to be notified."

Closing his notebook and placing his pencil into a pocket, Townsend rose from his chair. "I believe I have enough information for now. Good day to you."

Warrington nodded to him. When the constable had gone, Antonia sat down in the chair he had vacated. "I'm sorry to hear that so much money was lost," she said. "I had no idea it was such a sum."

The viscount suppressed a smile. He had never before thought of fifty pounds as a lot of money. He was accustomed to wagering that much or more at the drop of a hat. Yet it was clear that Miss Richards thought it was a fortune.

"And it was everything you had," she said sympathetically. "Oh, how dreadful. I must go to Lady Mansfield and explain what happened. You should be moved to a better room. This bed is so small and it is so dreary here. You must rest, Mr. Bradford. I shall visit you later when I am finished in the schoolroom." With these words, she departed, leaving the viscount to reflect that she had the most beautiful blue eyes he had ever seen.

6

After leaving Warrington, Antonia went to Mrs. Clay's room for breakfast. She and the housekeeper had their meals together and Antonia always enjoyed their conversations.

As usual, Mrs. Clay seemed very pleased to see her. "Good morning, Miss Richards," she said, directing a bright smile at the younger woman.

"Good morning, Mrs. Clay," said Antonia, taking a seat at a small table across from the housekeeper. "I have just been to see the injured man. His name is John Bradford. I am happy to report that he is much better."

Mrs. Clay poured the tea and handed a cup and saucer to Antonia. "I'm so glad to hear it. I was rather worried. Did he tell you where he is from?"

"London, it seems. But he told Mr. Townsend that the footpads stole fifty pounds from him."

"Fifty pounds!"

"Yes, and his horse and clothes. Those old clothes weren't his. He is very well spoken and gentlemanlike in his manner. I shall explain this to Lady Mansfield and ask that she allow him to be moved to a room in the house. He needs a larger bed and a more pleasant place to recover."

"You might try," said Mrs. Clay, rather skeptically. "But do tell me what you learned about the man."

Antonia began to tell her friend about her conversation with "Mr. Bradford," but she realized as she was speaking that she hadn't discovered much about him.

And upon further reflection after breakfast, Antonia considered that the injured man really didn't have a great deal to recommend him to Lady Mansfield. After all, he insisted he had no family and fifty pounds, while a goodly sum to Antonia, would seem a pittance to her employer.

Still, Antonia resolved to speak to her at first opportunity. After the morning lessons, when the girls were placed for a time into the care of the nursery maids, Antonia made her way to the morning room where she knew Lady Mansfield would be.

Entering the room, she saw that her ladyship wasn't alone. Seated on the sofa beside her was her stepson, Geoffrey. "Yes, Miss Richards?" Lady Mansfield said coolly. "I do hope you aren't here to complain about Harriet."

"Oh, no, Lady Mansfield," said Antonia. "I've come about the injured man."

"Oh, yes," said Geoffrey, leaning back on the sofa and adopting a bored look, "I heard about that. He's alive, I suppose?"

"He is much better," said Antonia. "He talked quite lucidly this morning."

"Then he does better than you, Geoffrey," said Lady Mansfield, directing a coquettish look at her stepson. "All you do is spout the greatest fustian."

Geoffrey grinned, evidently pleased at the comment.

"I wonder if your ladyship would consider moving Mr. Bradford to another room. The bed where he is is very small. And Jem has no place to sleep."

"Jem?" said Geoffrey. "Oh yes, he's your pet, isn't he?" He smiled at Lady Mansfield. "The boy is quite enamored of our Miss Richards."

Ignoring him, Antonia continued. "It seems that two footpads robbed him of his clothes as well as his money. They took fifty pounds and his horse."

"Fifty pounds?" said Geoffrey. "I thought he was a beggar."

"So did I," said Lady Mansfield. "He was so very dirty. What did you say his name is?"

"John Bradford."

"Bradford," said Lady Mansfield. "The name means nothing to me. Although didn't Lord Langdale have a tenant named Bradford?"

"Yes," said Geoffrey. "He was the one who poached rabbits."

"How would he have fifty pounds?" said Lady Mansfield. "What nonsense."

"I doubt he is the same man, Lady Mansfield," said Antonia. "He said he was traveling through Shropshire. He is from London and he speaks like a gentleman."

"Speaks like a gentleman?" said Geoffrey. "I note you do not say he *is* a gentleman. Anyone might speak like a gentleman."

"How true," said Lady Mansfield. "Why, my husband once had a valet named Jones. Hearing him speak, one might have taken him for a peer. Yet he was the son and grandson of servants, and Welsh besides."

Geoffrey nodded. "Who is this man then? A merchant or tradesman, I'll be bound."

"I don't know," said Antonia. "He said he has no profession at present."

"And he mentioned no family? No one to contact regarding his misfortune?" said Lady Mansfield.

Antonia shook her head. "No, ma'am. He said there was no one to be notified."

"Well, if he were anyone of consequence, he would have said who he was and who his family is," said Lady Mansfield.

"But he does appear respectable," persisted Antonia. "And I know that he would much appreciate a different room. Couldn't he be moved to a more comfortable bed? I'm sure he would recover more quickly."

"I don't see why we need to have him moved," said her ladyship. "Why, we know nothing about him except that he claims to have had fifty pounds. I won't have a stranger whom I know nothing about staying in rooms I need for guests. And I'm sure it is much more convenient for the servants having him where he is. And if he is so ungrateful to think us insufficiently hospitable to him, I shall have him taken to the village."

"Yes," said Geoffrey. "He could go to the vicarage. There's room there. Indeed, I don't know why we should be saddled with the fellow."

"So I suggest you return to your duties, Miss Richards," said Lady Mansfield.

Antonia, who feared the color was rising in her cheeks, took her leave. As she made her way toward the schoolroom, she told herself that both Lady Mansfield and her stepson were insufferable. It was amazing to her that they had so little concern for the injured man. To them anyone who wasn't a member of their snobbish little circle did not matter.

As she walked down the corridor, she saw Mrs. Clay coming toward her. "Oh, Mrs. Clay," she said, "I have just been to see Lady Mansfield. I asked her if Mr. Bradford might be moved."

"And what did she say?"

"She did not want him moved. I fear she didn't think him of sufficient consequence to occupy a bed in the house, save in the servants' quarters."

"I must say I'm not surprised," said the housekeeper. "Well, I shall speak with Mr. Grigson. Perhaps we might find him another bed. I've just been told that Mr. Samuels has sacked Edward the stable man. He has left Larchmont, so his room over the stable is vacant. We could move Mr. Bradford there."

"I'm sure it would be an improvement," said Antonia, pleased at the idea.

"It is a larger room and well ventilated."

"That sounds much better."

"I shall discuss it with Mr. Grigson and we will arrange it. Then I shall visit Mr. Bradford."

"That is good of you," said Antonia, greatly cheered at the idea of the young man being made more comfortable.

Mrs. Clay went off and Antonia continued on to the schoolroom. There she sat at her desk and started to look at the girls' compositions. Her mind soon wandered back to the injured man. She wasn't in the habit of forming *tendres* for young men she only just met, but she couldn't deny that she had felt something rather disconcerting when she had looked into his eyes. Sighing, she returned to the girls' papers.

After Antonia had left, Warrington had gone back to sleep. When he awakened later in the morning, he looked around the room. It seemed even smaller than before and it was airless and hot.

He was about to try to get out of the cramped cot when there was a tentative knock at the door. It was opened and a grandmotherly woman, wearing a white cap over her gray curls, appeared at the entrance.

Having hoped it would be Antonia, he was a bit disappointed, but the older woman smiled pleasantly at him. "Oh, good, you are awake. It is Mr. Bradford, is it not?" she said. "I'm Mrs. Clay, the housekeeper."

Before the viscount could reply, she turned back to the hallway. "Sarah, you can bring that in now." A plump, brown-haired girl entered the small room and placed a bowl on the small table next to the bed. Fixing a curious eye on the viscount, the maid stepped back and remained standing there. "That will be all, Sarah," said the housekeeper and the girl reluctantly left, casting a backward glance at Warrington.

"I have brought you Cook's herbal broth. An excellent tonic for most ailments." She paused and clucked her tongue as she studied him. "You poor man. I daresay, you are feeling quite wretched."

"I'm actually beginning to feel somewhat better," said the viscount, sitting up in bed.

"Good heavens, it is quite stifling in here," said Mrs. Clay, looking around the Spartanly furnished little room. "Miss Richards was right in thinking you should be moved. The men will help you to your new bed as soon as you have your broth." Taking up the steaming bowl, she handed it to him.

Warrington stared down rather skeptically at the bowl, but took the spoon and manfully sampled it.

"It will do you much good to eat it," said the housekeeper in a motherly tone.

While the viscount wouldn't have wished to serve the broth to dinner guests, he was so hungry that he had no trouble eating it. "I wonder, Mrs. Clay, if you could see about getting my clothes."

"Oh, your clothes," said Mrs. Clay. "I fear those you were wearing were in sorry condition. But we've found some things for you. One of the men will be in with them. And then they will help you to the room over the stables."

"Over the stables?"

"Yes, 'tis a very good room. Far nicer than this. And there are windows and you will have a fine view of the park."

So he was to have a room over the stables, thought his lordship. Well, at least it might be better than this. He ate more spoonfuls of broth. "I thank you for your trouble," he said.

"Oh, 'tis little enough. But I am so very glad to see you looking so much better. Are you in pain?"

"Some," said Warrington, "but it isn't bad if I don't move very much. I'm sure I'll be better very soon and will be on my way."

"You mustn't think of going until you are well enough. What a pity it was for you to lose your horse and money."

"Yes," said the viscount glumly.

"Well, let us not think of that," said Mrs. Clay cheerfully. "Perhaps you might think of someone you should write. So that you could go and stay with a friend when you are better."

Warrington frowned. He didn't know what he would do when he left here. He couldn't go and stay with a friend without losing his wager to his father. What he would do, he had no idea. "I hope that my horse and money might be restored to me."

"That would be wonderful," said the housekeeper. "But you mustn't worry. You must get well first. Now I must return to my duties. I shall visit you when you are settled in the other room. The men will be here shortly to assist you. I know you will be feeling better very soon."

The viscount could only murmur that he certainly hoped that she was right. Smiling, the always optimistic Mrs. Clay then left him to finish the broth.

7

Antonia spent the afternoon with her young charges. Since Harriet had been her usual disagreeable self, she was very glad when the girls left for their dinner, leaving Antonia free until later that evening, when she would once again take the girls for a short music lesson.

She sought out Mrs. Clay, whom she found in her room. "How is Mr. Bradford?"

The housekeeper smiled. "When last I saw him, he seemed much improved. That was at eleven o'clock. The room over the stables is much better for him. Why don't we go and see how he's getting on?"

The women made their way out of the house and to the stables, where they entered through a back door and climbed a narrow staircase that led to the upper story. Mrs. Clay knocked softly on the door at the top of the stairs before slowly opening it to peer inside.

"Come in," said a masculine voice.

"I didn't wish to disturb you if you were resting," said Mrs. Clay.

"Do come in," said Warrington, glad of any diversion. He was sitting in a wooden chair near the window. When he saw that Antonia had accompanied the pleasant older woman, he smiled at her and started to get to his feet. Antonia saw him wince with pain.

"Oh, pray, don't get up!" she cried.

"No, indeed, young man," said Mrs. Clay.

The viscount lowered himself slowly into the chair. He was now attired in a plain shirt and trousers. His unruly dark hair had been combed and he had had a shave. Despite the bruises on his face, Antonia thought he looked very handsome.

"You are doing much better," she said. "But do take care not to overtire yourself."

"I shan't do that. I've just been sitting here looking out the window. Do be seated, ladies." Warrington motioned to a bench, the only other piece of furniture in the room, and Antonia and Mrs. Clay sat down."

"I do believe you are looking much better, Mr. Bradford," said the housekeeper. "Would you like some books? I could have some brought to you."

"Yes," said the viscount, "that is kind of you. I am feeling better and would enjoy reading."

"Are you comfortable enough in here?" said Mrs. Clay.

"Well, this place is . . ." He glanced around the sparsely furnished room. "Larger."

"I do wish you could have had a room in the hall," said Antonia, "but Lady Mansfield . . ." She stopped, knowing it wouldn't do to criticize her employer. "Lady Mansfield thought it was more convenient for the staff if you were near the servants' hall. Mrs. Clay thought of this room, since one of the stable men just vacated it."

"How lucky for me," said his lordship with more than a trace of irony. "How kind of Lady Mansfield to be so hospitable to me. I shall be eager to meet her ladyship to express my gratitude."

"I shall be happy to convey your words to her ladyship," said Mrs. Clay. At that moment, one of the footmen popped his head in the door.

"I beg your pardon, Mrs. Clay, but Mr. Grigson must see you at once. He said it would take but a moment."

"Oh, I shall be right there, Timothy," said the housekeeper, getting to her feet. "But there is no need for you to leave, Miss Richards. Do stay with Mr. Bradford. I'll only be a short while. I'm sure he appreciates the company."

The housekeeper hurried out, leaving Antonia sitting there, feeling slightly awkward at finding herself alone with the viscount. His lordship, however, seemed very pleased at this turn of events.

"I am glad that you find this room is more comfortable," said Antonia.

"Yes, it is certainly that," said Warrington. "But am I correct in surmising that Lady Mansfield was none too pleased at having me as a guest?"

Antonia reddened. "I don't know what you mean."

"Well, here I am in a room above the stables. Of course, I can't blame her. She doesn't know anything about me. I suppose she fancies herself a grand lady."

"She is the wife of a baronet," said Antonia.

"And you think that a great thing?" said the viscount, who had long been accustomed to thinking of provincial baronets as being beneath his notice.

"Her ladyship thinks it is," said Antonia with a smile. "And Sir Harold's family is one of the oldest county families. Miss Harriet Mansfield, one of my charges, is forever reminding me of the fact."

"Good God," said his lordship. "I'd forgotten that you care for the brats in the family. And I don't doubt they are brats." When Antonia made no move to argue, he laughed. "So they are horrible, aren't they?"

"Only the elder," said Antonia. "The younger is very nice."

"And the mother?"

"She is very beautiful," said Antonia.

"But horrible like the elder daughter?"

"I should prefer not to comment," said Antonia, smiling again.

"I don't envy you having to make a living in such a way," said Warrington. "How long have you been a governess?"

"Only two months. But it isn't so bad, really. I have a nice room and eat very well. And Mrs. Clay has become a dear friend."

"Well, I thank Providence that I do not have to spend my days attempting to teach sums to children. Indeed, I have always detested the little monsters."

"You can't mean that."

"But I do."

"Then I hope you never become a schoolmaster."

"God forbid," said the viscount with a laugh. "I should do anything other than that."

"But what do you do to earn a living, Mr. Bradford? Oh, perhaps it is rude of me to ask. I know you told the constable you had no profession or trade."

Warrington was unsure of how to answer this question. He

could hardly pronounce himself a gentleman of leisure when he had said he had had only fifty pounds to his name. "I fear I haven't done very well at making a living. And that is why I am completely penniless. In fact, now that I think on it, I believe the only money I ever earned was that I won at cards."

"You cannot mean you are a gamester?"

The viscount smiled. "I confess I cannot deny it. I have a weakness for gambling that has gotten me into debt. But I was coming here to Shropshire intent on mending my ways. Of course, now that I have no money, I'm not sure how I shall live."

Antonia was very disappointed. It seemed that the young man sitting before her was a gambler and a wastrel. "You must find employment. There are many things an ambitious man can do."

"Are there?"

"One might go into law, for example. You appear to be an educated man."

"Do I? Well, I'm hardly that," said his lordship, who had been sent down after one term at Oxford.

"Perhaps you might start a business."

"Business?" said the viscount, trying to hide his dismay at the idea of a nobleman such as himself entering trade. "Indeed, I'd have no idea how to go about it."

"But you could find employment in a business and learn about it."

"Is that what you would do if you were a man?"

"Oh, I don't know. If I were a man, I'd write songs and operas."

"Well, I daresay that is something I could never do were I to live to be a thousand."

Antonia laughed. "I don't know whether I would succeed, but I should like to try. Or perhaps I'd go to sea like my father. He was a naval officer. Indeed, that is an idea for you. Many men make their fortune on the sea."

"I'd be miserable on a ship," said Warrington. "No, I'll not leave land for anything."

"There is the army."

"No, thank you. I have no desire for martial glory, I assure you."

Antonia regarded him in some frustration. Of course, she knew it was no business of hers if the young man seated before her had no ambition or idea of how to better himself. She didn't know why it mattered, but she found herself very much disappointed.

The viscount, who considered Antonia a very desirable female, found himself wondering about the possibility of becoming far better acquainted with the lovely governess. He smiled his most charming smile. "I have done little with my life thus far," he said. "And now I find myself injured, destitute, and without friends or family. I should be grateful for your advice, Miss Richards."

"I am hardly the person to advise anyone," said Antonia. "But I do know that one must earn a living in some fashion. Perhaps the vicar might have an idea. I shall ask him call on you."

"Oh, I shouldn't wish to trouble him," said Warrington, horrified at the idea of being visited by a clergyman. He changed the subject. "It seems your employers have some fine horses. There was a bay stallion that looked like a right one. I'm told your employer plans to race him."

"Yes, I suppose so," said Antonia, not very happy at this turn in the conversation. While she liked horses well enough, she thought that most of the young men she had known were far too interested in the creatures. Since Mr. Bradford had already admitted to being a gamester, she didn't welcome his apparent enthusiasm for horse racing.

"I'd like to see him run," said his lordship. "You wouldn't know who his sire is? No, I suppose not. I shall ask one of the lads."

At this moment Mrs. Clay returned. They sat talking for a short time longer, before the housekeeper announced that they must take their leave.

The next few days Antonia went about her duties. She was kept busy with the children, who seemed unusually cooperative that week. Even Harriet gave her relatively little trouble, a fact that she considered quite miraculous.

Whenever she had a spare moment, Antonia couldn't help but think about Warrington. While she knew that it was silly to allow the young man to occupy her thoughts, she couldn't help it. After all, she had been the one to find him and she felt a sense of responsibility toward him. It was only that, she assured herself, for she was far too sensible to form an attachment to a young man with a handsome face and little else to commend him.

Yet despite her determination to be impervious to his charm, Antonia couldn't deny that "Mr. Bradford" interested her more than any of the young men she had met before becoming a governess. She, therefore, thought it best to see little of him and rely on Mrs. Clay for reports of his progress. The housekeeper visited Warrington each day and was happy to find him improving rapidly.

One sunny afternoon, when the girls had gone to have tea with their nanny, Antonia was summoned to the drawing room to see Lady Mansfield. She found her employer seated on the sofa, eating bonbons from an ornate box on a table by her side.

"You wished to see me, Lady Mansfield?" said Antonia, approaching her ladyship and standing respectfully before her.

"Yes, Miss Richards," said Lady Mansfield. "It is about that man of yours, the one you found. I don't know his name."

"Mr. Bradford."

"Yes, Bradford. I'm told he is much improved."

"Yes, Mrs. Clay has said he is making excellent progress."

Her ladyship nodded solemnly. "Then I believe it's time he leave Larchmont. It is best that you tell him. You may do so now."

Antonia regarded her employer in surprise. "But, Lady Mansfield, I'm sure he isn't well enough."

"He's well enough to be moved."

"Yes, but I don't know where he is to go."

"That doesn't concern me," said Lady Mansfield. "Samuels needs to hire another groom and the man will need a place to stay. I don't mean we must toss this Bradford out this very minute. But in a day or two he is to be gone."

"But surely, Lady Mansfield, isn't there somewhere else where he could stay?"

"He has been here long enough," said her ladyship crossly. "Larchmont isn't a charity hospital, you know, and Cook has told me that the fellow has a hearty appetite. I'll have one of the servants take him to Cawley and he may seek assistance there. Now do go and see to the matter."

Knowing it was pointless to comment further, Antonia nodded. "Yes, Lady Mansfield," she said. She left the room and set off to convey her employer's message.

The sky was overcast and threatened rain as she stepped out of the house and walked toward the stables. She saw Jem as she neared the door of the stables. He looked tired and very dirty, but he smiled happily as he saw her. "Good day to you, Miss Richards," he said, tipping his cap.

"Good day, Jem."

"Were you wanting something, miss?"

"I've come to speak with Mr. Bradford. Her ladyship wished me to convey a message to him."

"I'll fetch him, Miss," said the boy, hurrying off. He returned a short time later with the viscount.

Antonia was pleased to find that Mr. Bradford appeared very much improved since the last time she had seen him. He walked without any difficulty and she noted that the bruises on his face had faded. "How are you feeling, Mr. Bradford?"

"Very much better, Miss Richards," said the viscount, directing a smile at Antonia. He thought she looked very pretty standing there in her plain gray dress with a woolen shawl wrapped about her shoulders.

"I'm so glad to see you look so much improved."

"I'm healing nicely. Indeed, I expect I shall be quite fit in a few days' time."

"That is excellent," said Antonia, a bit reluctant to deliver Lady Mansfield's message. Deciding it was best to get the unpleasant task over with, she continued. "I fear that I must convey a message from Lady Mansfield. It seems that the room where you are staying is needed for the new groom."

"I am to be moved again?"

"Well, Lady Mansfield felt it may be time for you to leave Larchmont. If you are well enough, of course. Perhaps in a day or two."

"You mean I'm being tossed out?" said the viscount, regarding her in surprise.

Antonia reddened. "It is only that the room is needed."

"I shall not soon forget this Lady Mansfield and her hospitality," said Warrington.

"She said she would have a servant take you to Cawley," said Antonia.

Warrington frowned. It appeared that he was faced with a dilemma. He had no money and no horse and he was determined not to reveal his identity or get help from his friends. But there were still three weeks to go before he could win his father's wager and return to town.

He had had the vague idea that he would stay at Larchmont, recovering from his injuries and perhaps attempting the seduction of the pretty governess who stood before him. Now what was he to do? If he went back to London, he'd lose the bet. The viscount was very sure that his father would have no sympathy for him. He'd have no choice but to marry Lady Sophie Parkenham.

"I had hoped I could stay here for a while longer," said the viscount.

Antonia shook her head. "I am sorry, but a new groom is being hired and this room is needed."

Warrington frowned again as he envisioned is father's exultant face. If only there were some way he could survive for three weeks longer. Suddenly a flash of inspiration hit him. "Has the groom been hired?"

"No, I don't believe so."

"I will take the job as groom."

"You?" said Antonia in surprise. "Have you ever done such work before?"

"I know a good deal about horses," said the viscount, rather evasively.

"I don't know," said Antonia skeptically. "But you might speak with Mr. Samuels about the position. He is a harsh taskmaster and expects a good deal from his men. And as you have no experience . . ."

"It will do no harm to ask the man," said his lordship, warming to the idea. "I shall see him at once."

With a pensive expression, Antonia watched him go off. While she knew very little about him, she had not judged him to be the sort of young man who would take well to such a job. Still, as Warrington vanished from view, she found herself rather hoping that he would obtain the position and stay at Larchmont.

8

Samuels had grave reservations about hiring the unknown and rather mysterious stranger who had appeared at Larchmont. Bradford seemed too much the gentleman in his way of speaking. His hands appeared unused to labor and he had no references. Indeed, he was vague about his past work experience.

The head groom wouldn't have considered taking Warrington on, except that the man to whom he had offered the job had taken a different position. So Samuels reluctantly hired "Jack Bradford," cautioning him that he'd best work hard and stay away from gin while on duty.

The viscount solemnly proclaimed that he would do so and Samuels set him right to work cleaning harnesses. As Warrington sat with his rags and saddle soap, diligently rubbing the harness, he smiled. It was certainly absurd to think of the Viscount Warrington laboring at such a task. Well, three weeks would pass quickly enough, and then he'd be back to town, victorious.

After a time, Samuels stepped into the tack room to find his new groom working diligently. The head groom critically eyed the gleaming leather harness that the viscount had finished. "Is that all you've done?"

"Yes," said the viscount, adding "sir" as an afterthought.

"Well, we haven't until Christmas. You'll have to work faster. I'll have no daydreaming and lollygagging. All four must be done and those two saddles as well."

"They must be done today?" said his lordship.

"Aye," said Samuels. "And they'd best all be as good as this one or you'll feel my boot."

While the viscount might have been expected to bristle at this warning, he suppressed a smile. Why, the fellow had praised his handiwork. Why, he'd be a groom of the first water in no time at all. The thought was very amusing. He managed to nod to Samuels, who left him at his work.

Some time later, Jem peered into the tack room to find the viscount polishing a saddle. "They say you're the new groom, Mr. Bradford."

"That is true," said the viscount, pausing to wipe his brow. He examined the saddle. There wasn't a spot of dirt on it and the leather positively shone.

While he viewed the saddle with some satisfaction, Warrington was beginning to lose his enthusiasm for the job. It hadn't been so bad cleaning the first harness, but the novelty had worn off by the third one. And he still had one last saddle to do.

"I hope to be a groom one day," said Jem.

"I'm certain you will be," said Warrington, putting up the saddle and taking down the other one he'd been instructed to clean.

Jem stood for a while longer, but finding nothing else to say, left Warrington to his work.

In the evening Antonia took her usual walk along the paths in the park behind the house. The weather was very fine and warm and the smell of flowering shrubs perfumed the air. The sky was darkening as Antonia walked along, humming to herself.

"Miss Richards," called a voice and Antonia turned to see Warrington standing there.

"Mr. Bradford," she said, assuming a tone of polite indifference. Antonia wasn't really pleased with the fact that the sight of the young man filled her with a strange sort of excitement.

"You mustn't waste a 'Mr.' on me, Miss Richards. I believe it is customary to address a groom by his Christian name. Jack will do well enough."

"So Samuels took you on then?"

"Yes. After I promised to work hard and avoid gin."

"That will be difficult for you, I suppose," said Antonia, with a smile.

"I have never been fond of gin," said the viscount. "As to working hard, I am none too fond of that either. But I shall endeavor to do my best. And not even Samuels could fault the way I clean a harness. I seem to have an aptitude for such work."

Antonia shook her head. "Something tells me that you aren't the sort of man to work long in service."

"Perhaps not," said the viscount, with a smile. "In truth I don't have any intention of staying long at Larchmont. There isn't much I like about the place." He paused. "Except you, of course."

Antonia hoped that the darkness would hide the fact that she was doubtlessly blushing. "I pray you do not say such things to me, Mr. Bradford."

"There is that 'Mr.' again. A lady such as yourself must address me as Jack."

"I am only a governess," said Antonia.

"Governess or no, you are a lady," said Warrington. "And a dashed pretty one."

"Well, I must be returning to the house," said Antonia, rather discomfited by the remark.

"No, I've disturbed your walk," said the viscount. "It is I who should go. Good evening, Miss Richards."

And with these words he was gone, leaving Antonia relieved yet rather disappointed at his hasty departure.

When Jem roused him from a sound sleep the following morning, Warrington was none too pleased. Yet, when Jem informed him that Samuels was looking for him and that he should have reported for duty some fifteen minutes ago, his lordship reluctantly rose from his bed and dressed.

Accustomed to sleeping all morning, the viscount wondered if he could endure the torture of getting up at such a ridiculous hour. The sun was only now rising in the eastern sky as he made his way to the stables.

Samuels took him to task for his tardiness, shouting that he would not tolerate "damned lazy slugabeds" and that if he were late once more, he'd be looking for another job. The viscount took the harsh rebuke with surprising equanimity. It had been a very long time since anyone had raised his voice to him, and receiving a tongue-lashing was a novel experience. After all, he told himself, if one took on the role of servant, he must be prepared to take some abuse.

As punishment, the head groom assigned him the task of cleaning out the stables. As he set to work, Warrington could not help but regard the situation with amusement. Here he was, the Viscount Warrington, heir to an earldom, mucking out stalls.

Samuels was surprised to see his new worker smiling as he went about his duties. The head groom didn't really know what to make of "Bradford," and he resolved to keep a close watch on the fellow.

After working for a couple of hours, the stable men paused for breakfast. Larchmont employed a staff of ten in the stables. They were mostly young men, although there were three older grooms who had been in service at the estate for more than twenty years. Most of them seemed amiable enough, but all were a bit reserved with the new man.

After consuming a meal of bread and butter and strong tea, Warrington and the others returned to work. The viscount was in the middle of cleaning out one of the horse stalls when Samuels shouted for him. "Bradford, saddle two horses, Mr. Geoffrey's black gelding and Lady Mansfield's gray mare. And be quick about it!"

Warrington, glad to have a break from his cleaning chores, put down his pitchfork and went to obey Samuels's order. When the horses were saddled he led them out from the stables.

Standing there in the stable yard were two well-dressed figures, a man and a woman. The viscount regarded them with interest. So this is Lady Mansfield, he thought, studying her. She wasn't a bad-looking female, he concluded, noting her plump, voluptuous figure and attractive face.

Lady Mansfield was attired in a close-fitting mauve riding habit with a fashionable hat perched atop her head at a jaunty angle. She was eyeing the gentleman who stood beside her with a flirtatious look and tapping her riding crop against her gloved hand. "Really, Geoffrey," she said, "what utter nonsense you speak."

Geoffrey smiled, but made no reply. His gaze had turned toward Warrington and the horses he was leading. He fixed an arrogant eye on the new man. So this must be the fellow they had boarded under their roof, he thought. Noting Warrington's height with resentment, he impatiently called to him, "Come on, man, do hurry! We've been cooling our heels here long enough."

Warrington, who had taken an instant dislike to his employer's son, made no reply. He brought the horses over to him, and then stood looking at Geoffrey. "Don't just stand there like an oaf," said Geoffrey, taking his horse's reins from him, "help her ladyship."

While the viscount had a sudden urge to plant a facer on Geoffrey's countenance, he only nodded and led the gray mare over to Lady Mansfield. He then wordlessly helped her up into the side saddle.

Unlike her stepson, Lady Mansfield was gazing at the new groom with a far more favorable eye. She hadn't realized that the man they had taken in was so handsome. Her gaze rested on Warrington's athletic physique, with his broad shoulders and well-muscled calves. She smiled at him. "You must be the man who was set upon by robbers."

"Yes, my lady," he said.

"You seem much recovered from your misadventure."

Somewhat surprised by the lady's friendly tone, he smiled his most charming smile back at her. "Thank you, your ladyship. It was good of you to take me in. I'm very grateful to you."

Noting that Geoffrey had mounted his horse and was now regarding her with disapproval, she smiled her most seductive smile at Warrington. "I was happy to do so," she said.

The viscount, who had received many such looks from members of the fair sex, was nonetheless surprised. He smiled in return. "You are very kind."

Lady Mansfield gave him another smile before turning her horse and starting off. Geoffrey, who seemed very perturbed at his stepmother's interest in the new groom, abruptly turned his horse and hurried after her, nearly knocking into Warrington in the process.

The viscount, who had stepped nimbly out of the way, watched them ride off, a disgusted look on his face. "He can't even sit a horse properly," he said out loud.

Samuels, who had heard the remark, commanded him to keep his opinions of his betters to himself and get back to work. As he went back inside, the viscount wondered whether he would be able to endure three weeks as a groom.

While the viscount was bending his back to his labors, Antonia was staring idly out the window of the schoolroom. She'd watched Geoffrey and Lady Mansfield ride off. How she envied her employer, she mused.

It wasn't that Antonia wished to go riding with Geoffrey. No, she certainly didn't envy her ladyship her companion. But Antonia couldn't help but think that it would be wonderful to do as she pleased, to go off riding on a fine May morning rather than to stay inside with her reluctant pupils. A gentle breeze blew into the room through the open casement window.

"Miss Richards," said Harriet in a peevish tone that made Antonia frown as she turned away from the window, "I have finished my sums."

"Have you?" said Antonia, walking over to the girl and looking down at her desk. To her surprise, she saw that Harriet had completed her work without any mistakes. "Why, that is very good, Harriet. Yes, that is excellent." Antonia smiled.

"And I have done mine," said Annabelle.

Walking over to her younger pupil, Antonia checked her arithmetic. "Why, you have done splendidly as well, Annabelle. You have both done very well."

"Then perhaps we might go out for a time," said Harriet. "You said that if we did well on our sums, we might go out."

"Yes, I did say so," said Antonia, as happy as the girls at the prospect of leaving the schoolroom. "We will have our natural history lesson. We'll collect some leaves."

"Leaves?" groaned Harriet. Then thinking it best not to complain, she changed her tone. "Yes, Annabelle would like that."

"Oh, I would," said the younger of the Mansfield girls.

"Then fetch your bonnets," said Antonia, "and shawls. There is a slight breeze."

They all left the schoolroom, happy at the prospect of going outdoors on such a fine morning. After getting her straw bonnet, Antonia met the girls in the foyer and they left the house.

There were a great many trees in the park and the girls had no trouble collecting leaves. Harriet grew bored with the activity very quickly. "I have a good many leaves, Miss Richards," she said. "Could we not take a moment to see Moonbeam?"

Moonbeam was Harriet's pony. While she had no enthusiasm for schoolwork, Harriet was quite mad about riding and she dearly loved her pony.

Antonia hesitated a moment before nodding. "Very well. I see no harm in a brief visit. But then we must return to the school-room."

"Hurrah!" cried Annabelle, who, like her sister, loved horses. She had a stout black pony named Peppercorn and she could scarcely wait to see him.

Antonia followed the girls toward the stables, wondering if she would see Jack Bradford. As they came into the stable yard, they heard a yell, and then the loud snorting and whinnying of a horse.

Harriet and Annabelle rushed to the fence to see a large white stallion rearing up on its hind legs. A red-faced man brandished a whip. "You white devil!" he cried. "I'll teach you your manners."

The man, a burly groom named Tom Dawson, drew back the whip and then snapped it at the horse. The leather bit into the horse's flank and it reared up and tried to kick him.

Shouting an oath, the man began to beat the horse with the whip. Antonia and the girls were horrified.

Suddenly Warrington appeared. Having heard the commotion, he had hurried out to see what was going on. Rushing over to the fence, the viscount called out to Dawson. "You fool, that's no way to treat him!" he cried.

Dawson scarcely heard him. The whip struck the horse again and the animal snorted and rushed toward the man, a murderous gleam in his eyes. Dawson barely managed to escape over the fence.

Warrington frowned at the man. "You'll ruin the creature with that sort of treatment."

Dawson's face darkened with irritation. He would have used a few salty oaths, but seeing Antonia and the girls, he restrained himself. "Caesar's a devil that needs a bit of the fight taken out of him. The whip's the only way."

The noise had caused several of the grooms and stable boys to appear outside to see what was happening. They all watched eagerly as Warrington stepped up to Dawson. "You'll only make matters worse," he said. "That animal's terrified and that whip is just frightening him more."

Noting the number of eyes upon him, Dawson folded his arms across his chest and directed a scornful look at the viscount. "I suppose you think you can control him. Just speak to him politely and the beast will do as he's told. Is that what you think?"

Warrington frowned, and without another word, he climbed over the fence. Jem, who was well aware of Caesar's wild temperament, cringed to see the viscount enter the paddock. "He's very dangerous, Mr. Bradford!" he cautioned.

"Are you daft?" cried one of the men. "You'll be murdered!"

Antonia called out to him. "Do come back!"

Glancing back at her, Warrington smiled. Then he turned his attention to the stallion, who was pawing the ground nervously with his front hoof.

The viscount began speaking to the horse in a gentle voice. "Now, lad, I won't hurt you. No one will hurt you." At first the horse continued to rear up and snort threateningly at him, but Warrington kept speaking in a low, soft voice and after a few minutes, the horse seemed to calm down a bit. "That's right, my lad. There's nothing to fear."

There was a dead silence in the stable yard as they watched Warrington and the horse. The onlookers caught their breaths as he walked slowly up to Caesar. He continued to talk to the creature. Caesar viewed him nervously for a time, but made no move to flee or attack.

The viscount kept murmuring to the stallion. Antonia's heart skipped a beat when Warrington confidently reached out to touch the animal. To her relief, the great beast made no move. "Good lad," said the viscount, patting the horse's neck.

"Well, I'm damned," said Samuels, who had witnessed the scene from a vantage point near the stable door. "Get back to work, all of you," he said, coming forward to disperse the group of onlookers who had gathered at the fence. "And you go on, Dawson. Bradford will see to Caesar. I'm glad I have one man who knows how to handle a horse."

Dawson, who was none too happy to have been shown up in such a manner, scowled at Warrington before stalking off. Jem, while happy to see Dawson get a setdown, felt ill at ease. Dawson was a lout and a bully who enjoyed terrorizing Jem. He didn't like to think that his newfound friend, Mr. Bradford, had made an enemy of the man.

Warrington gave the horse one more pat before coming back to the fence where Samuels was standing beside Antonia and the girls. "Few can handle the brute," said the head groom. "Do you think you can ride him? He's badly in need of exercise."

The viscount, who felt his ability as a horseman was second to none, nodded confidently.

"Then get a saddle and bridle and take him out for a ride."

Warrington was only too happy to oblige. Smiling broadly, he hurried off.

"Do you think it wise for him to ride Caesar?" said Antonia.

"He said he can, miss," said Samuels. "We'll see what he can do. But I doubt there's any cause for fear, miss."

Antonia, however, was not without misgivings as the viscount appeared. He put on the bridle and then saddle Caesar without the least difficulty. Then, hoping easily into the saddle, he began to walk the horse around the paddock.

Samuels opened the gate, and Warrington rode the white stallion out into the stable yard. It was clear to Antonia that Bradford was an experienced horseman. Caesar was soon trotting down the path away from the house. He eased him into a canter, and when the stallion had warmed up, he gave him his head and Caesar galloped effortlessly until they were out of sight.

The head groom looked thoughtful. Sir Harold had bought the stallion, hoping that the animal would win the upcoming Cawley Market Fair race. However, Caesar's performance had been disappointing. But perhaps with the right rider, there'd be a chance after all. Sir Harold would be very pleased to hear it.

"Oh, he is very fast," said Annabelle. "What a lovely horse. But I would like to see Peppercorn."

"Of course, miss," said Samuels, who was very fond of the younger Mansfield daughter. "I'll take you to the ponies."

Antonia took one final glance in the direction Warrington had gone, but she could no longer see him. Turning, she followed Samuels and the girls into the stable.

9

As Warrington galloped along the road toward the village of Cawley, he reflected that Caesar was a splendid animal. A good judge of horseflesh, the viscount was very impressed with the white stallion's speed and strength. He didn't doubt that Caesar could have great success as a racehorse.

The viscount was passionate about horses and racing and he would have loved nothing better than to own such a horse. As Caesar increased his speed, Warrington wondered if he might buy the animal. Once he was back in London and his father had settled his debts, he might do so. The idea pleased him very much.

When he had gone a good distance away from Larchmont, his lordship pulled the stallion to a halt and turned back. He doubted that Samuels would take too kindly to him being gone for so long and, besides, one shouldn't push Caesar too hard. He must be worked into proper condition for racing. Perhaps Samuels would allow him to work with him. If he could do so, the three weeks would fly by.

The viscount smiled as he rode back in the direction of Larchmont. Yes, perhaps it wouldn't be so bad. He could work with Caesar by day and in the evenings, he could see more of Miss Richards. Indeed, he wanted to see considerably more of that young lady.

As he continued on, Warrington thought about Antonia and his chances of becoming better acquainted with her. He was well aware of his appeal to the female sex and he had reason to suspect that she wasn't indifferent to him. His mind wandered to some pleasant fantasies, until he was distracted by the appearance of two riders.

A man and a woman had come out from a wooded path. He recognized them immediately as Lady Mansfield and Geoffrey. Warrington eyed them with interest. He found himself thinking that Lady Mansfield's riding habit seemed unusually rumpled. And wasn't her hat perched at a far less modish angle?

An experienced man of the world, the viscount drew his own conclusions. He had lived too long in society to be shocked at much, and it wasn't too surprising that a woman with a much older husband might be interested in a younger man.

When Geoffrey caught sight of Warrington, he frowned. "Damn and blast," he said. "It's that new fellow riding Caesar. What the devil is he about? This is accursed bad luck, him seeing us here."

"Don't be ridiculous," said Lady Mansfield, adjusting her hat. "He didn't see anything. And in any case, he isn't anyone we must concern ourselves with."

"You there," shouted Geoffrey, as Warrington rode up to them. "What are you doing on that horse?"

"Mr. Samuels told me to give him some exercise, sir," said the viscount.

Lady Mansfield was scrutinizing the viscount with an appraising gaze. He was a handsome man, she thought, and he could certainly sit a horse well.

"I doubt he wanted you to take him this far. Get back to the house."

"Yes, sir," said Warrington, happy to leave the pair of them.

As Warrington rode off, Geoffrey frowned. He didn't like the fellow. There was an insolence in his look that ill became a servant. What had got into Samuels to hire him? Well, he decided as he watched Warrington ride off, he'd have a talk with Samuels and see that this new groom be sent on his way.

But when Geoffrey returned to Larchmont, he found his father in great good spirits. Sir Harold informed him that he had excellent news. The new man whom Samuels had taken on was an expert horseman who could handle Caesar very well. Samuels had said that the new man, Bradford by name, would have a very good chance to ride Caesar to victory at the Cawley Market race.

The news had delighted Sir Harold. Geoffrey realized with some irritation that Bradford would have to stay at least until the race.

* * *

That evening Antonia sat in her room, reading a book. Although it was an interesting account of the author's travels in Greece, Antonia was finding it hard to concentrate. Her thoughts kept focusing on Warrington and how he had calmed the white horse.

Setting the volume aside, Antonia restlessly got up from her chair and went to the window. It was a lovely night, with the moon shining brightly and the sky full of stars. Suddenly eager to escape from the house, she wrapped a shawl around her shoulders and made her way downstairs.

As she passed the drawing room, Antonia caught a glimpse of Geoffrey Mansfield sprawled on a sofa and heard Lady Mansfield's distinctive laugh. Anxious that they wouldn't see her, she hurried past the door and down the hallway.

Leaving the house, she made her way toward Larchmont's walled garden. As she passed through the wrought-iron gate that marked the entrance, Antonia stopped and looked about her. There were sprays of white roses clambering about one wall and they seemed to glow in the moonlight. Smiling, Antonia strolled along the garden path and then took a seat on an old stone bench.

She sat there for some time, breathing in the garden's fragrant stocks and gillyflowers and staring up at the stars. Content in her solitude, Antonia was dismayed when she heard steps coming along the path toward her. Remaining very still, she hoped that she might not be detected here.

The steps stopped for a moment and then continued on. A figure appeared on the moonlit path in front of her and Antonia was surprised to find Warrington standing there. "Miss Richards," he said, smiling at her. "What good fortune to meet you here."

"Good evening, Jack."

Without as much as a by your leave, Warrington took the seat next to her. "This is a cozy nook you've discovered," he said.

His closeness was provoking disturbing sensations in Antonia, but she tried not to show her confusion. "Did you enjoy riding Caesar?"

"By heaven, he's a dashed fine bit of blood and bone," said his lordship. "And fast as the wind."

"Mrs. Clay told me that Sir Harold is very pleased. He and Samuels intend for you to ride him in the Cawley Market Fair race."

"Ride him in a race? Well, Samuels hasn't said a word to me about it. When is the race?"

"On Saturday next."

"But that's hardly time enough to prepare a horse for a race."

"I don't know anything about that," said Antonia. "Mrs. Clay said that Sir Harold had given up on Caesar since he was so hard to control. I do hope he isn't too dangerous for you to ride."

"Oh, he's not dangerous at all." Warrington smiled at her. "It is very good of you to worry about me."

Antonia looked down. "I'd worry about anyone riding a horse in a race. It's very dangerous." When she looked at him again, their eyes met and the viscount had a tremendous urge to take her into his arms and kiss her there in the moonlit garden. As he leaned toward her, Antonia jumped up from her seat. "I must be going in. Good night, Jack." She hurried off, leaving a very disappointed Warrington to watch her go.

10

There was a steady downpour the following day and Antonia had her hands full with her two charges. Unable to get their usual morning's exercise, the two girls were unhappy at being cooped up all day in the house. Harriet was in an especially bad humor and continually squabbled with her little sister.

Antonia was quite relieved when the girls were taken away by their nurse. Leaving the schoolroom, Antonia made her way toward Mrs. Clay's room, where the two ladies routinely shared afternoon tea.

As she walked through the halls, Antonia couldn't help but notice that there seemed to be a bustle of activity among the servants. Passing the drawing room, she saw several maids industriously washing the windows. And perched atop a ladder, a footman was carefully polishing the brass candelabra that hung from the ceiling. Two other footmen scurried down the hallway ahead of her, carrying a large, rolled-up carpet.

Arriving at the housekeeper's room, Antonia found that lady sitting on her sofa, the tea tray on the table in front of her. Mrs. Clay looked up. "Oh, good. I'm glad you're here, my dear. Sarah has just brought tea for us." She picked up the flowered teapot and began to pour.

Antonia took a seat on the sofa and glanced around her. Although the housekeeper's room was small and somewhat cluttered, Antonia found it quite charming. Mrs. Clay had a collection of dainty porcelain figures that sat on her mantel and her walls were filled with prints of Shropshire landscapes. Talented with a needle, the housekeeper also had numerous embroidered pillows scattered about the sofa and chairs.

Handing a cup to Antonia, Mrs. Clay smiled at her. "And there is a ginger cake, my dear."

"That is splendid," said Antonia, knowing that it was the housekeeper's favorite.

"There is none to equal Cook's ginger cake," continued Mrs. Clay as she sliced a generous piece for her young friend.

"Indeed there is not," agreed Antonia.

After taking a bite of the cake, Mrs. Clay leaned back on the sofa and sighed. "Ah, it is good to have a bit of rest. My dear Miss Richards, what a day it has been! I've not been so harried since the Christmas ball."

Antonia regarded the older woman with interest. "It did seem that the household staff was in a frenzy of cleaning."

The housekeeper nodded. "Oh, yes. Everything must be spotless!" She paused before she made her momentous announcement. "You see, Miss Richards, Lord and Lady Rochdale are coming!"

Mrs. Clay was somewhat disappointed that this news didn't seem to create an awed reaction in the governess. Antonia raised a quizzical eyebrow. "Lord and Lady Rochdale?" she asked.

"Why surely you've heard of them," said the housekeeper. "Lord Rochdale has a magnificent estate near Shrewsbury and is said to be an intimate of His Royal Highness. And Lady Rochdale is accounted to be a glittering light in London society."

Although Antonia wasn't overly impressed with this information, she attempted to show enthusiasm since Mrs. Clay seemed so thrilled at the prospect of such illustrious guests.

"Lady Rochdale is her ladyship's cousin. Lady Mansfield just informed me this morning that our guests would be arriving here Thursday. I do wish I'd had more notice. There is so much to do in such a short time."

Antonia put down her teacup. "But the house looks lovely as usual, Mrs. Clay. I don't think you need worry about a thing."

Although gratified by this remark, the housekeeper still appeared apprehensive. "I do hope you are right, my dear. I do so want everything to go well."

They discussed the company for some time and then Mrs. Clay finally changed the subject. "I'm told Jack Bradford put Caesar through his paces today."

"In the rain?"

"Of course, a little rain doesn't signify. Why, races are often run in the rain. Mr. Grigson was told by Samuels that Caesar did very well. Sir Harold is in an uncommonly good mood about it. I do hope Caesar will win. What a triumph for the master if he does. Lord and Lady Rochdale will be at the race and that will make victory so much sweeter."

Mrs. Clay paused to take a bite of ginger cake before continuing. "It may turn out to be very lucky that Jack Bradford came here. I've heard that it was quite remarkable how he calmed that dreadful animal."

"Yes, it was astonishing, Mrs. Clay. The horse was quite wild, thrashing about and making a commotion. Jack Bradford was fearless. He went up to the horse and the animal was utterly transformed."

"That is amazing," said Mrs. Clay. "He must have a gift. Well, it doesn't surprise me. He's such a charming young man." She smiled. "Perhaps too charming."

"What do you mean?" asked Antonia.

"Well, sometimes a young, handsome man can cause trouble in a household, especially where there are many young girls in service. Mr. Grigson fears that several of the girls appear smitten with him. There is something of the rogue about him, don't you think, my dear?"

Thinking of their meeting last evening, Antonia blushed. He had come very close to kissing her and she had come very close to allowing him to do so. "I don't know," she managed to say.

"Well, I think a girl would be a fool to lose her heart to such a man," said Mrs. Clay. "And we know so little about him."

Antonia, who was finding the conversation taking an awkward turn, put down her cup and saucer and got up from the sofa, "I mustn't keep you any longer, Mrs. Clay. I know you are very busy."

The housekeeper suddenly remembered the impending visit of Larchmont's lofty guests and an anxious look returned to her face. After bidding Antonia good-bye, she got out her list of tasks that had to be completed before Lord and Lady Rochdale's arrival and began to study it.

Returning to the schoolroom, Antonia frowned as she thought of Mrs. Clay's words. She suspected that the housekeeper knew of her interest in Larchmont's new groom. No doubt Mrs. Clay was right. It was quite foolish to lose her heart to Jack Bradford. But, Antonia was very much afraid that that was exactly what she'd done.

The servants in the stables at Larchmont were also caught up in the flurry of preparation for the visit of Lord and Lady Rochdale. Samuels was as determined as Mrs. Clay that everything be in perfect order for the arrival of those worthy guests. As a result, he was even more demanding of his men.

Warrington, however, had no problem with the head groom's testiness. The viscount's duties now encompassed only taking care of Caesar. He exercised the horse and worked with him throughout the day. Having taken on the role of horse trainer and jockey, his lordship was very happy. He could scarcely believe his good fortune to be involved in the sport he loved.

Warrington's star had also risen with his coworkers. All the servants at Larchmont, with the exception of Dawson, viewed him with admiration. They began to refer to him as "Gentleman Jack," due to his genteel manners and way of speaking. Jem, in particular, seemed to regard him as something of a hero.

The only negative feature of Warrington's next few days at Larchmont was the fact that the viscount saw very little of Antonia. She was occupied with duties as governess during the day and, in the evening, she felt it best to stay indoors to avoid further moonlight meetings.

On his fourth day on the job, the Rochdales arrived in a splendid coach drawn by six black horses. Most all of the servants were agog at seeing such esteemed members of elite London society and the servants' hall buzzed with excitement.

Warrington, of course, impressed his coworkers by his seeming indifference to the new arrivals. For the life of him, Warrington couldn't remember ever having met Lord and Lady Rochdale. He could vaguely remember hearing the name, but Lord and Lady Rochdale were not in the same lofty circle of society that he himself frequented.

However, the viscount knew that there was the possibility that the Rochdales would recognize him. Warrington was well aware that his face was familiar to just about anyone with connections in society. He, therefore, resolved to say out of Lord and Lady Rochdale's sight, and, as a mere groom, this wouldn't be difficult.

Antonia had been able to watch the guests' arrival from the schoolroom window. Glancing down at the front of the house, she had seen a well-dressed lady alight from the carriage. Following her from the equipage, was a stout, middle-aged gentleman, who Antonia decided must be the baron. A short, dark-haired lady, attired in a green dress and bonnet, exited the carriage next, followed by a tall gentleman in a bright blue coat.

"I do hope we will be able to meet them," said Harriet, wistfully watching as the company made its way inside the house.

"You will most certainly meet them," said Antonia. "But for now you must return to your lessons."

Although Harriet didn't look too pleased at the suggestion, she sat down at her desk without a complaint. That evening the girls were briefly trotted out before the company, but they were quickly ushered off to bed.

Harriet, quite miserable at being sent to her room, cried herself to sleep that night. The next day Harriet was even more difficult than usual. Antonia knew that she was distracted by the idea of the company from London, and she tried to make allowances. Yet, by the afternoon, Antonia's patience with her wayward pupil was wearing thin.

She was glad when one of the maids appeared in the schoolroom to announce that Lady Mansfield had requested she bring the girls to the drawing room to join the guests. Both Harriet and Annabelle greeted the news with cries of joy. They rose eagerly from their chairs and hurried to the door.

Antonia, who was curious about the guests, was glad of the diversion. "You must both act like young ladies," she cautioned, but neither Harriet nor her sister heard her. They had begun to chatter excitedly as they scurried down the corridor from the schoolroom. "Don't rush so!" called Antonia. "Both of you, walk!"

The girls slowed their pace and Antonia caught up with them. When they entered the drawing room, they found Sir Harold standing near the fireplace next to the short, dark-haired gentleman whom Antonia had earlier decided was Lord Rochdale. Lady Mansfield sat in an armchair chatting with her guests in an animated fashion. Geoffrey was seated on the sofa in between two well-dressed ladies, while a tall gentleman in a canary-colored waistcoat, stood across from them, absently twirling a gold quizzing glass. Mr. Fairfax Caufield fancied himself a dandy of the first water. He paid careful attention to his clothes and adopted a carefully cultivated attitude of ennui wherever he found himself.

On Antonia and the children's entrance, Caufield raised the quizzing glass and stared over at them. Antonia could not fail to note that he seemed more interested in her than in Harriet and Annabelle.

"Ah, here are your darling girls!" cried Lady Rochdale, a slender woman with red curls, who was attired in a morning dress of sprigged muslin.

"Do sit here by me, my dears," said the other lady, the dark-haired woman, attired in a stylish blue dress with a high collar and tight-fitting sleeves.

Harriet and Annabelle sat down on the sofa beside the guest, whose name was Mrs. Caufield.

Antonia felt suddenly rather awkward standing there. She retreated a little and then sat down in a chair away from the others.

"That is the children's governess, I suppose," said Lady Rochdale, casting a disinterested look in Antonia's direction.

"Yes," replied Lady Mansfield.

"I do hope you girls do not vex her too much," said Mrs. Caufield. "I fear I always plagued my governesses."

"My daughters are exceedingly well behaved," said Lady Mansfield.

Harriet smiled sweetly at her mother's remark. The conversation turned to the latest fashions and how a certain titled lady wore the most frightful old frocks in town. Mr. Caufield chimed in to deplore the lady's lamentable indifference to fashion.

Antonia, who could hear the talk from her vantage point, found herself thinking the company rather insufferable. They laughed and gossiped about a number of their acquaintances and seemed to have very high opinions of themselves.

"I heard you bought old Brimwell's horse, Mansfield," said Lord Rochdale, addressing Sir Harold.

Sir Harold nodded. "Yes, and Caesar's a right one."

"My dear sir, everyone knows the animal is a terror," said Mr. Caufield. "I can't imagine you don't regret your purchase."

Sir Harold smiled. "You are very much mistaken, sir. Caesar is a fine beast and as fast as lightning."

"Come, come, sir," said Lord Rochdale. "What does it signify if the animal is fast if no one can ride him?"

"No one can ride him?" said Sir Harold. "What nonsense. I'll show you what Caesar can do. I'll take you to the stables right now."

"My dear," said Lady Mansfield in a disapproving voice, "surely our guests don't wish to traipse out to see that horse of yours."

"I certainly do, Lady Mansfield," said the baron.

"Why, I should like to see him," said Lady Rochdale. "The weather is pleasant. Why don't we all go see the horse?"

"Yes, I think it a splendid idea," said Mrs. Caufield.

"If you wish," said Lady Mansfield, still none too happy at the idea.

"Could we go, Mama?" said Harriet, jumping up from the sofa. "We'd like to see the horse."

"Oh, very well," said Lady Mansfield. She looked over at Antonia. "Miss Richards will take charge of you. And after you see the horse, she will take you back to the schoolroom."

While Harriet didn't like this pronouncement, she was glad to have a respite from her studies and both of the girls were eager to accompany the ladies and gentlemen to the stables.

Lord Rochdale and Sir Harold took the lead, escorting their wives from the drawing room. Mrs. Caufield decided to stay indoors and her husband, who had no interest in horses, said he would remain with her. He did, however, walk Geoffrey to the door.

"A rather pretty little governess, Mansfield," said the dandy, smiling at Geoffrey. "What a lucky fellow you are to have her about. Most females of that breed are dowdy and pudding-faced."

"Don't get any ideas about the girl, Caufield."

The dandy regarded him with a sly smile. "Oh, I see. You've already gotten a claim on the chit. But what does your stepmama think of your interest in her girls' governess?"

"It is none of her business," said Geoffrey, scowling. "And it's none of yours either." The dandy chuckled and Geoffrey went out the door.

When the party arrived at the stables, Samuels hurried out to meet them. "We've come to have a look at Caesar," said Sir Harold. "Have that new man bring him, Samuels. I wish to show Lord Rochdale what he can do."

"Aye, sir," said the head groom, and then went off to find Warrington. The viscount was in one of the stalls, brushing down a bay mare, when Samuels appeared before him. "Jack, saddle Caesar and bring him out. Sir Harold and his guests wish to see him. And be quick about it!"

Warrington frowned. "The company?"

"The ladies and gentlemen who are the master's guests. Stop gaping and do as you're told."

The viscount nodded and left the stall to get Caesar. He had no wish to be seen by Sir Harold's London company. What if they recognized him? However, he had little choice, since Samuels began shouting for him to hurry up.

After putting the saddle on the large white horse, the viscount led the stallion outside into the paddock. Glancing over at the group congregated in the stable yard, Warrington was glad to see that none of the Mansfields' guests looked familiar to him. And it appeared they didn't recognize him either.

Noting Antonia standing with the two children, he smiled over at her. Antonia met his glance and smiled back. Taking her charges by the hand, she walked up to stand by the fence.

Lady Mansfield also smiled over at Warrington. Although she'd been annoyed at her husband for suggesting the excursion to the stable, the sight of the handsome young groom made her more amenable to the outing.

Unlike his wife, Sir Harold's attention was centered entirely on his horse. Regarding the magnificent animal with satisfaction, he turned to the baron. "So, what do you say of Caesar now, Rochdale?"

The baron eyed the horse for a long moment. "I admit he is a fine specimen," he finally admitted. "And he appears quite docile, but I've been told there isn't a man in the kingdom who could ride the beast."

"Is that what you were told?" repeated Sir Harold, smiling. He called over to Warrington. "Ride Caesar for his lordship, Jack."

The viscount nodded and then mounted the tall horse. First

walking the horse around the paddock, he then put the animal into a trot, followed by a canter. After taking several turns about the enclosure, Warrington pulled the horse up and brought it to an abrupt halt.

Sir Harold fixed a smug smile on the baron. "Well, sir?"

Rochdale shook his head. "It seems I was misinformed."

"Well, I confess Caesar was a troublesome beast," said Sir Harold. "But my new man here is a damned fine hand. I doubt there's a horse in the kingdom the fellow couldn't ride."

"Yes," said Lady Mansfield, smiling up at the viscount, "we are so lucky to have Jack working for us." The entire gathering gazed up at the viscount, who remained seated upon Caesar.

Geoffrey was irritated at all the praise being heaped upon the groom. Glancing over at Antonia, he noted that that lady was also casting an admiring look at Warrington. Frowning, he stepped forward. "I shall take Caesar for a ride myself."

Sir Harold looked at his son in some surprise. "What? You ride Caesar?"

Geoffrey's frown deepened at his father's obvious lack of confidence in his equestrian skill. Ignoring his father's words, he opened the paddock gate and stepped inside. "Get off of him," he demanded. "I'll take him now."

Warrington didn't move, but remained in the saddle. "I shouldn't advise it . . . sir. Caesar is—"

Geoffrey angrily broke him off in mid sentence. "I said get off of him," he muttered.

The viscount hesitated and then he dismounted. He held the stallion's head as Geoffrey put his foot into the stirrup and raised himself somewhat gingerly into the saddle. Caesar shifted nervously, but remained standing in the same spot. Geoffrey smiled in triumph. Staring down at Warrington, he said, "Let go of him."

The viscount obligingly stepped back and waited expectantly. If the damned fool wished to break his neck, he thought, he'd not try to stop him.

Geoffrey gave a sharp kick to the horse's sides. Caesar snorted and reared up on his hind legs. This abrupt maneuver startled Geoffrey, who was thrown from the saddle and landed in the mud some feet away. The viscount quickly stepped up to the horse and calmed him down.

Cursing, Geoffrey got up. His fine clothes and new boots were covered with mud. Annabelle, who had watched in horror as her brother had fallen from the horse, was relieved to see that he appeared to be all right. She suddenly giggled. "Oh, Geoffrey, you look so funny!"

"Yes," said Harriet, giggling, too, "you look like one of the pigs that was rolling about in the mud!"

"Harriet! Annabelle!" said Antonia sternly, but the two girls were now laughing merrily at this great witticism.

Geoffrey regarded his two half sisters with such a furious look that they suddenly grew silent. "You little brats," he began, taking a threatening step toward them.

Antonia pulled the girls away. "I believe it is time to go back to your lessons."

"But we've only just got here," protested Harriet.

"Take the girls into the house, Miss Richards," commanded Lady Mansfield. Antonia nodded and, taking Harriet and Annabelle by the hand, she led them away from the group.

Turning her attention back to Warrington, Lady Mansfield could not fail to note that the handsome groom was watching Antonia with more than usual interest. She frowned, but was soon distracted by her guests.

11

That evening Warrington returned to his room. Stretching out on his bed, he thought about Antonia. He'd been thinking about her more and more. He pictured her standing by the fence with the girls that afternoon.

His face grew thoughtful. He wanted her. There was no doubt of that and it was frustrating to think of her there at the house while he was here alone on his bed. Putting his hands behind his head, he stared up at the ceiling. Perhaps he should send a note to Antonia asking her to meet him in the garden that night.

He was considering this idea when there was a knock at his door and Jem appeared. "I've brought you something," he said, coming forward and extending his hand. " 'Tis a stone."

Sitting up on his bed, Warrington took the proffered gift. "That is good of you, Jem."

"I found it. I found this one, too." He took another stone from his pocket and handed it to the viscount. "I've never seen a prettier one. 'Tis so very smooth and pink. I found it in the woods." He paused. "I'm going to give it to Miss Richards. Do you think she'll like it?"

The viscount felt the smoothness of the stone and then he handed it back to the boy. "Yes, I'm certain that Miss Richards will like it."

Jem grinned. "I do hope so." He paused. "I wish I could have seen Mr. Geoffrey tossed from Caesar. That would have been a sight."

"I must confess that I derived a great deal of pleasure from seeing him land in the mud."

A lopsided smile appeared on the boy's face. "Aye, if only I could have seen it. I don't like him, you see, sir."

"You show good judgment. The man's an ass."

Jem grinned delightedly as he shoved the pink stone into his pocket. He then pulled out a number of other items.

"What have you got there?" said Warrington.

"Oh, things I found about the place," said Jem. "Feathers and stones and such." The boy was encouraged by the viscount's apparent interest and he began to show him his collection. Warrington was amused by Jem's enthusiasm as he began to talk about the wildlife around the estate.

"Miss Richards likes birds. I promised to show her the lark's nest after supper. I'll give her the stone then."

"You're going to show Miss Richards a nest? Could I go with you?"

Jem hesitated. While he was pleased at the viscount's interest, he'd been looking forward to some time alone with Antonia. "Aye, if you wish," he said finally. "I'm to meet Miss Richards in the meadow. I'll come back when it's time."

"Good lad," said the viscount, who thought it very fortuitous that Jem was providing him with a way of seeing Antonia.

The twilight was beginning to fall when Jem led the viscount past the stables and down the path which led to the meadow. The viscount looked ahead of them, trying to catch sight of Antonia. He was beginning to think that she wasn't there, when he suddenly spied her standing next to a poplar tree stationed at the edge of the field.

Jem called out to her and Antonia waved back. Surprised to see Warrington walking alongside the boy, she wasn't sure if the meeting with Jem was a good idea. She hadn't planned on seeing Warrington, and certainly spending more time with him was imprudent.

"Good evening, miss," said Jem, rushing toward her. "Mr. Bradford wanted to look at the lark's nest, too, so I said he could come along. 'Tis all right, isn't it?"

Antonia seemed to be mulling this over.

"Come, Miss Richards, you can't begrudge me the opportunity to see a lark's nest," said Warrington. "I very much want to see these baby larks of Jem's."

"Oh, very well," said Antonia, trying to appear indifferent. Why did he have to be so handsome and charming? she asked herself.

Warrington bowed low to her. "You are too kind, Miss Richards," he said. Then he offered her his arm. She took it and they began to follow Jem, who was quickly making his way on a narrow path through the meadow's tall grasses and flowers.

As they walked along, Antonia looked out across the landscape. The fading sun was casting a golden glow on the meadow and a number of butterflies and birds flitted among the wildflowers. "I do love this time of day," said Antonia, with a sigh. "It is a beautiful view here, isn't it?"

Warrington looked at her and nodded. "Indeed, I've never seen anything lovelier," he said in a low voice.

Antonia met his gaze and was somewhat disconcerted. "I didn't know that you were a nature lover, Jack," she said, trying to hide her discomfiture.

"Oh, yes, there is nothing I like better than scouting in the wild for a bird's nest," said the viscount with a smile. "Especially when I'm accompanied by such a charming lady." Antonia met his blue eyes again and could feel herself blushing. Remembering Mrs. Clay's words about Jack Bradford being a ladies' man, she suddenly looked away. She was glad when Jem turned around.

" 'Tis just over there," he whispered. They crept quietly up to a small scrubby bush and glancing down into the branches, they were able to detect the nest. In it were nestled seven small birds. Antonia, Warrington, and Jem all looked up and smiled at each other and then returned their gazes to the nest. After a brief time, Jem made a motion and they carefully backed off.

"That was wonderful, Jem," said Antonia. "Thank you for showing the nest to me." The boy beamed happily.

They began walking back along the narrow path. Jem was now occupying Antonia's attention, chattering on about this and that. Warrington frowned, wondering how he could get Antonia to himself.

When they neared the poplar tree, the viscount suddenly looked behind them. "What was that?" he said.

Jem followed his gaze. "What?"

"Why, it looked like a purple bird," said Warrington. "It had some sort of yellow spots all over it. It flew off toward that stand of bushes there."

"Purple with yellow spots?" Jem looked perplexed by this description, but he strained his eyes toward the bushes that were situated a good distance back. "I wonder what it was."

"Why don't you go investigate?" suggested the viscount in an innocent voice. "Miss Richards and I shall wait for you here by this tree." Jem nodded and dashed excitedly back into the meadow.

Antonia crossed her arms in front of her and regarded him skeptically. "A purple bird with yellow spots all over it, Jack?"

He appeared thoughtful. "Well, perhaps they weren't exactly yellow spots. Actually, I'm not sure now that there were any spots at all."

Antonia shook her head. "Poor Jem. Now he shall be off looking all over the place for a purple, yellow-spotted bird that doesn't exist."

"Yes, that is exactly what I had in mind," said Warrington, smiling. He looked at her and suddenly grew serious. "Miss Richards, I—"

Antonia met his intent gaze. Feeling herself in a dangerous position, she interrupted him with a light tone. "It does appear you know horses much better than birds, Jack. Lord Rochdale was quite amazed at your feat in riding Caesar today. It was foolish of Geoffrey Mansfield to try to ride Caesar."

"The man is no horseman," said Warrington scornfully.

"And he is a pompous, conceited. . . ." began Antonia. She suddenly stopped. "Oh, dear, I shouldn't say anything about him."

"And why not? He is pompous and conceited." Warrington grinned. "Indeed, you've been overly generous to him."

"Well, there is no point in speaking ill of someone."

"Isn't there? Good heavens, if no one were to speak ill of anyone, conversation would be deadly dull."

Antonia laughed. "Perhaps you're right. Still, I shall say nothing more about Mr. Mansfield, nor anyone else at Larchmont."

"Good, I don't think any are fit topic for discussion. They are quite unexceptional, the lot of them."

"I don't believe Lady Mansfield would agree. And you cannot mean that her ladyship's illustrious guests are unexceptional."

"I can indeed," said the viscount.

"But what of Lady Rochdale? Mrs. Clay has told me that she is a leading lady of fashion."

"Lady Rochdale? Utter nonsense. I've scarcely even heard of her."

Antonia laughed again. "I'm sure that will cut Lady Rochdale to the quick that Jack Bradford never heard of her. I suppose you are so well acquainted with London society that you know everyone of consequence."

"Why, yes, I suppose I do," said Warrington with a broad grin. "You cannot mean you doubt me? Surely you can imagine me cutting a dashing figure at Almack's?"

"Perhaps if you dressed like Mr. Caufield," suggested Antonia, with a mischievous smile.

"Caufield? You mean that popinjay in the horrible waistcoat? Egad, the fellow needs a new tailor."

Antonia burst into laughter. At that moment Jem returned. Breathless, the boy rushed up to them. "I didn't see it, Mr. Bradford," he said, looking disappointed.

"See what, lad?" asked Warrington.

"Have you forgotten the purple and yellow-spotted bird?" asked Antonia in an ironic voice.

"Oh, yes, the bird," said the viscount. "I had forgotten."

"But I did find this," said Jem, thrusting his hand forward. " 'Tis a musk rose, miss. 'Twas growing amid the brambles by the bushes." He eagerly pushed it up to her. "I picked it for you."

Antonia smiled. "Why, thank you, Jem, it's lovely." She lifted it to her nose and smelled it.

Warrington gazed at Antonia as she held the rose to her face. He again had the urge to take her into his arms and cover her mouth with his. What deuced bad luck that Jem should be there with them. He smiled slightly as he followed Antonia and the boy on the path leading back to the house.

12

The next morning Antonia was glad to learn from Mrs. Clay that Lady Mansfield and her guests had already departed on an expedition to view the remains of an ancient castle some ten miles away. Although she could scarcely imagine Lady Mansfield the sort who would enjoy rambling about an old ruin, Antonia was relieved that she would have no chance of seeing her or any of the guests that day.

Sir Harold had remained at home. Never a very sociable gentleman, the baronet had had his fill of company and was glad to retreat to his library for the day.

Unlike her governess, Harriet was upset that her parents and their illustrious visitors had gone off on the outing without her. As a result, she spent most of her time sulking and picking fights with her little sister.

When she could endure her pupil's ill temper no longer, Antonia suggested that they go out-of-doors. A walk would do them all good, she said and the girls were very happy to have the opportunity to go outside.

"Could we go riding?" said Harriet.

"Oh, yes," cried Annabelle. "I should so enjoy a ride! Peppercorn would love it."

"I don't know," said Antonia. "I'm not sure that your mother would wish you to go riding when you are to be at your studies."

"But Mama isn't at home," said Annabelle.

"I'm sure my mother wouldn't mind in the least," said Harriet. "A lady must be a good rider." She directed a superior look at her governess. "I daresay you haven't had much opportunity for riding, Miss Richards."

"But I daresay I have," said Antonia. "I rode a great deal when I was a girl."

"I bet Miss Richards is a good rider," said Annabelle.

Harriet's expression made it clear she thought this doubtful, and Antonia had an urge to strangle the unpleasant child.

"Could we ask Papa?" said Annabelle. "Could we ask him if we could go riding?"

"Oh, very well," said Antonia. "You may tell your father that I will allow it if he gives permission."

Harriet and Annabelle dashed out of the schoolroom. A short time later, one of the maids entered to inform Antonia that Sir Harold had given his consent for the girls to go riding and that they were in their rooms changing into their riding habits.

Antonia was very happy to have a break in her routine. After going to her room to fetch her pelisse and bonnet, she met the girls in the foyer and accompanied them to the stables.

There they were met by Samuels and Dawson, who was leading the ponies. Harriet and Annabelle mounted their diminutive horses and were soon off, accompanied by Samuels, who was riding a bay mare.

Antonia stood watching the girls for a time. Glancing around the stable yard, she wondered where Warrington might be. Then chiding herself for thinking of him, she started off on a walk.

Jem, who had been cleaning out a stall, caught sight of Antonia through a window. Why, Miss Richards was walking away. She'd been at the stables and he hadn't even known. He felt keenly disappointed.

Walking out of the stable, he saw Dawson and another of the grooms standing outside watching Antonia walk off. "Now there is a nice piece of skirt," said Dawson. "What a thought to have a wench like that."

Jem, astonished at this crude talk about his revered Miss Richards, grew livid. "How dare you speak so about a lady?" he cried.

"What's that?" said Dawson, turning in surprise.

"How dare you speak so about Miss Richards!" repeated Jem, his face reddening with fury.

"It's you, is it?" said Dawson. "Why, you little weasel. I'll teach you to listen when it is naught your business." The man lunged at Jem and gave him a hard slap across the face. Jem reeled back.

Dawson, who was happy to have an excuse to teach the boy a lesson, came after him. He hit Jem hard in the stomach and laughed to see the boy grimace and cry out in pain.

Dawson lifted his fist to strike again, but he was grabbed from behind and spun around. Dawson viewed his new adversary in surprise. Standing before him was Warrington. The viscount's fists were raised in a pugilistic stance and his face was frowning ominously. "Why, you cowardly bastard," he said. "To hit a boy who can't defend himself."

An unpleasant grin came to Dawson's face. "I've been hoping for this," he said. "A chance to show Gentleman Jack a thing or two." He raised his fists. "Come on then. I warrant you'll be sorry you took on old Dawson."

"I don't think so," said the viscount, regarding him with scorn.

Dawson, who outweighed Warrington by nearly fifty pounds, felt very confident that he would finally have the opportunity to put the man he regarded as his hated usurper in his place. He came forward, directing a powerful punch at the viscount's midsection. The viscount stepped nimbly aside. Then he threw out his fist with lightning speed, connecting sharply with Dawson's jaw.

The big man staggered back, surprised at the blow. The viscount's scornful little smile infuriated him and he rushed forward, a murderous gleam in his eyes. The viscount stepped out of the way just in time, tripping Dawson in the process. He fell heavily to the ground and Warrington heard shouts and laughter.

Looking around, the viscount saw that all the stable hands had come out to witness the fight. Dawson rose quickly to his feet and, bellowing with rage, charged Warrington. This time the viscount stood his ground and when Dawson came in range, he delivered a series of quick punches to his midsection, and then another to his jaw.

Dawson's face took on a stunned expression, and then he fell to the ground and stayed there. There were shouts and applause from the onlookers.

Warrington stood for a time, waiting to see if his opponent would get to his feet. When Dawson only lay there motionless, he turned his attention to Jem. "Did he hurt you, lad?"

"No, sir," said Jem, regarding the viscount with a look of admiration akin to awe, "I am fine."

"That's a nasty bruise on your face." He looked over at Dawson, who was starting to shakily rise to a sitting position. "He'll not bother you again. I'll see to that."

The other stable men gathered around Warrington, slapping him on the back and congratulating him on his pugilistic prowess.

When Antonia returned from her walk, she went back to the house to await the return of her pupils. Later that afternoon, when she went to join Mrs. Clay, she found that worthy lady eager to tell the story.

"There was quite an altercation in the stable yard this afternoon, Miss Richards," she said, as she poured Antonia a cup of tea and then handed her the plate of bread and butter. "Your Mr. Bradford fought with Dawson. And Dawson got the worst of it."

Antonia's eyes grew wide. "What happened?"

"It seems that Dawson was beating Jem and Bradford interceded."

"Oh, dear. Dawson was beating Jem?"

"You mustn't worry. The boy came to no real harm. And Dawson will live."

Antonia appeared shocked at this news. "And what of Jack Bradford?"

"I'm told he had hardly a scratch on him. The servants' hall is abuzz with the story. It seems Mr. Bradford is quite adept at fisticuffs."

Antonia frowned. She had a horror of violence and pugilistic combat filled her with revulsion.

After taking a drink of tea, Mrs. Clay continued. "Samuels was furious when he found out what had happened. He threatened to sack Bradford and Dawson. But when Samuels told Sir Harold, the master said that Bradford must stay. After all, he was to ride Caesar in the market fair race."

The housekeeper smiled. "I'm not accustomed to so much excitement, my dear. Indeed, having our guests is excitement enough for me. I do believe the visit is going well. Lady Mansfield seems pleased with everything."

"I am glad," said Antonia, knowing how important it was for her friend that the guests and Lady Mansfield be well satisfied.

They chatted for a while longer and then Antonia took her leave and retired to her room. There, she picked up her mandolin and tried a new melody that had been running through her head. Pleased with the tune, she picked up a sheet of paper and began to write down the notes.

Antonia saw very little of Warrington for the next three days. She spent most of her time with Harriet and Annabelle. Lady Mansfield, who was occupied with her guests, had no time for her daughters. She preferred that the girls stay out of the way of the company most of the time, so Antonia had been instructed to keep them well occupied with schoolwork.

This did not please Harriet, who had developed an infatuation for Mr. Caufield. Harriet thought it abominable that she was forced to labor at her boring studies when she might be having such an amusing time in the company of her mother and their charming guests. She was, therefore, even more peevish and vexatious than usual, causing Antonia to consider again whether it was time to look for another position.

Warrington kept busy with preparing Caesar for the race, which was now only two days away. He was determined that the white horse would win, and as the big animal ran consistently well, he grew more and more confident that they would triumph.

When the day of the race came, there was great excitement in the village of Cawley and the surrounding area. A great number of people came from miles around for the fair and there was a merry, festive atmosphere throughout the village. Crowds of people strolled about, visiting booths where food and all manner of merchandise were displayed, and admiring the livestock on display.

There were a great number of horses for sale, as well as many cattle, sheep, goats, and fowl. There was also a small traveling circus that featured a trick rider, acrobats, and a juggler.

The servants at Larchmont had been given time off to see the fair and none was more enthusiastic than Jem. He was excited by the throngs of people and the noise and smells.

He stood staring at the circus tent where a large sign proclaimed

PICKERING'S AMAZING CIRCUS, and debated whether he should
spend the pittance he had on a ticket, or on one of the delicious
sweets being sold in the booths.

Unable to decide, he went off to find Warrington. Ever since the
viscount had saved him from Dawson, Jem regarded "Jack Bradford" with unabashed hero worship. Finding the viscount in a serious discussion with Samuels, Jem held back, watching them.
Tethered close by was Caesar. The big stallion's coat was a brilliant white in the bright sun.

When the head groom walked off, Jem came forward. "Mr.
Bradford."

"Good morning, Jem," said his lordship in an amiable tone.

"Good morning, sir," said the boy, grinning broadly. " 'Tis a
fine day for the race."

"It is that," said Warrington, nodding.

"Don't Caesar look handsome? I know he'll win."

"He appreciates your confidence, lad," said his lordship, "but
Caesar isn't the favorite. Samuels has just now been telling me that
most think the big chestnut owned by a man named Wilcock will
win."

"Oh, that is a fine horse, but not so fine as Caesar," said Jem.

Warrington nodded. "I wholeheartedly agree, but the outcome
of a horse race, no matter how good the horse, is never certain. I
speak as a man with a long history of betting on horses who didn't
do as I expected."

Yet, Warrington knew that if he had money to wager, he'd
wager it on Caesar. Of course, even if he had any money, he was
honor bound to refrain from gambling.

The viscount knew that there was a good deal of money being
wagered on the race. For a gentleman of his lordship's habits,
being unable to bet anything at such a time was exceedingly trying.

"Oh, look, there is Miss Richards," said Jem, his face brighten-
ing at the sight of Antonia, who was walking with Harriet and
Annabelle.

Warrington smiled. It seemed like a long time since he had spoken with her. She'd been in his thoughts more and more, but he
hadn't been able to figure out a way to see her.

"Miss Richards," he said, doffing his hat as she and her pupils came up to them.

"Good day, Jack," said Antonia.

"Oh, doesn't Caesar look handsome?" said Annabelle. "He is the loveliest horse, isn't he, Harriet?"

Harriet glanced at the horse without much interest. She was wondering if Mr. Caufield and the others from Larchmont had arrived at the fair.

"I wish you luck," said Antonia, smiling at the viscount. "Sir Harold is hoping for victory."

"Oh, I know Caesar and Mr. Bradford will win, miss," said Jem, eager to enter the conversation.

"No one cares about your opinion, boy," said Harriet sharply.

"Harriet!" said Antonia. "You mustn't be rude."

"I may be as rude to him as I like," said Harriet haughtily. She cast a disdainful look at Jem. "He's only a stable boy." Harriet then walked off, not allowing her governess to reprimand her further.

Casting an exasperated look at the viscount, Antonia went after Harriet, with Annabelle following. Jem frowned, very disappointed that Antonia had left so quickly. He wasn't too upset about Harriet, for he had more than once received a tongue-lashing from the ill-tempered young lady.

Warrington was also disappointed in having so little opportunity to speak with Antonia. He thought that after the race he'd find a way to have some time alone with her.

Mr. Caufield cast a bored look in the direction of the horses who were being put into position for the race. A gentleman who hated the country, he wasn't too pleased at finding himself there at a village fair. He did not appreciate such rustic amusements, nor did he like horse racing very much.

He stood among the great crowd of people assembled to witness the competition. His wife was beside him, talking excitedly with Lady Rochdale and Lady Mansfield. Sir Harold and Lord Rochdale were nearby, discussing the horses in serious tones.

Antonia and the girls had joined the Mansfields to view the race. Annabelle chattered happily with her governess, while Harriet's attention was riveted on Caufield, who was some distance from her, standing next to her half brother Geoffrey.

Geoffrey, who found the race scarcely more exciting than did Caufield, took a pinch of snuff and then offered it to the dandy. "Gad, no, Mansfield," said Caufield, waving it away. "I don't approve of your blend of tobacco."

"Suit yourself," said Geoffrey, placing the snuff in his nose and inhaling. He studied the horses who were now lining up for the race. "For the most part, damned sorry-looking horseflesh."

"I don't claim to be an expert," said Caufield languidly. "One horse is the same as the next to me."

"Wilcock's chestnut is the one to beat," said Geoffrey, casting his eye on the big red horse that was favored to win. "I daresay I hope my father's horse wins or the old fellow will be in a devilish bad temper. Of course, if he loses, I shall have the satisfaction of seeing that fellow Bradford lose."

"Bradford?"

"The man riding the horse. He's one of our grooms. There's an insolence about him that I find intolerable."

Caufield looked at the white horse he knew to be Sir Harold's entry in the race. He fixed his gaze on Caesar's rider. "Why, damn me if the fellow isn't a lookalike for Warrington. Yes, the resemblance is unmistakable."

"Warrington?" said Geoffrey.

"Viscount Warrington. He's the Earl of Gravenhurst's son." He turned to his wife. "Doesn't the fellow on Sir Harold's horse look exactly like Warrington?"

Mrs. Caufield regarded the viscount with interest. "Oh, perhaps a little," she said.

"My dear, he could be his twin brother," said Caufield. "Indeed, it is quite remarkable."

"They are not that much alike," said Mrs. Caufield. "You are always seeing likenesses." She turned to Lady Rochdale. "He once claimed a boot maker in Surrey looked exactly like the Duke of Wellington. When I saw the man, I was very much disappointed. But I do confess that man is more like Warrington than the boot maker was like the duke."

Antonia, who heard the exchange between Mr. and Mrs. Caufield, smiled. So Jack Bradford resembled a lord? He'd be interested in hearing that. She stared at Warrington, who looked in her direction and smiled. He appeared calm and confident as he deftly handled his rather nervous mount.

All the horses were finally in position and they stood awaiting the start. The sharp report of a pistol signaled the race to begin and the horses raced off.

Caesar went immediately into the lead and the horses thundered by Antonia and the others. The big white stallion remained in front, increasing the distance between him and the rest of the horses as he galloped furiously ahead. Only the favored chestnut gained a bit as they raced across the course.

Warrington held the lead easily and Caesar reached the finish a good ten lengths ahead of his chestnut rival. Lord Rochdale clapped Sir Harold soundly on the back, while Annabelle jumped up and down with joy.

Sir Harold was very pleased to receive the silver bowl that was the winner's prize. He even shook Warrington's hand and said, "Well, done, Bradford."

The viscount was nearly as happy as his employer. He received the accolades of a great crowd of well-wishers, and was finally led away by several of his coworkers from Larchmont, who thought the occasion demanded alcoholic refreshment.

While Antonia would have liked to congratulate Warrington, she had no opportunity, due to the great crush of people surrounding him. Annabelle tugged at her hand, reminding her that they hadn't yet seen the puppet show, and Antonia obligingly escorted her young charges off in the direction of that entertainment.

13

When Antonia returned to Larchmont with Harriet and Annabelle, it was nearly five o'clock. The girls went to the nursery for tea, allowing Antonia to join Mrs. Clay in the housekeeper's room. While the two friends drank tea and ate cake, Antonia told Mrs. Clay all about the fair and the race.

The housekeeper was very happy to hear about Caesar's victory, for she knew how much Sir Harold had wanted to win the race. She listened as Antonia related details of the race, as well as everything else she could remember about the fair. While Mrs. Clay loved to hear about such excursions, she had adamantly refused to join the other servants in going to the fair. She preferred to enjoy such occasions vicariously through the stories of others.

After leaving Mrs. Clay, Antonia decided to take a stroll about the grounds. After fetching her straw hat, she made her way outside. The weather was still warm and fair, with a light breeze blowing.

While she was tempted to walk by the stables, Antonia resisted the urge. She didn't want Jack Bradford to think she was eager to see him. No, it was better to walk in the opposite direction, where a path led out through groves of trees and along a lovely pond.

The sun was sinking quite low in the sky as Antonia came toward the pond. She stopped to look at several ducks that were swimming there, ignoring her as they paddled across the water.

She noted a profusion of white and yellow wildflowers growing at the edge of the pond. Antonia could hear a warbler's melodious singing from the nearby orchard. Closing her eyes, Antonia breathed in the fragrant air and sighed.

Her reverie was broken by the sound of footsteps. Turning

around, she saw Warrington approaching. He was grinning broadly, clearly pleased to see her.

The sight of him engendered a now familiar quickening of her pulse, but she tried hard to calm herself. It was quite ridiculous to react in such a way at the very sight of a man, she told herself. She had to stop feeling like a silly mooncalf about him.

"Good evening, Miss Richards," said Warrington, eagerly coming up to her. He had been hoping for a moment alone with her for days and he could scarcely believe his good luck when he caught sight of her walking in the direction of the pond.

"Good evening, Jack. I must compliment you on your victory."

"It was Caesar's victory, not mine."

"Without you, there would have been no victory. I'm sure Sir Harold feels that way."

"I must say Sir Harold was rather good about it. He gave me five guineas. And I'm told that he isn't one to part with his blunt lightly, at least where his servants are concerned."

"Five guineas?" said Antonia. "Oh, I am glad. That was generous of Sir Harold, not that you didn't deserve that and more."

"Well, I was very glad to get the money," said his lordship. "But then Sir Harold wagered two hundred pounds on Caesar, so he could well afford it."

"Two hundred pounds!" cried Antonia. Since her annual salary came to thirty-eight pounds, this seemed an enormous sum. "I can scarcely imagine gambling so much." She gave him a meaningful look. "Surely it is ill-advised to do so."

Warrington felt it prudent to nod in agreement. "I'm sure you're right, Miss Richards."

"Now that you have some money, I expect you will be thinking of leaving Larchmont."

"Do you think I should leave?" said the viscount, fixing his gray eyes upon her blue ones.

Antonia looked down in some confusion. "I cannot advise you," she managed to say. "But you were going somewhere before you were robbed and injured. You had a horse and fifty pounds and, therefore, I cannot imagine you would wish to stay long at Larchmont, working as a groom."

"When I look at you, I don't think I ever want to leave Larchmont," he said in the suave voice he had often used on females. But as he said the words, he knew that they were true.

Antonia realized that she was dangerously close to falling into his arms. Suddenly, there was a shout. "You there! What are you about?"

They both looked over to see a most unwelcome sight. Geoffrey Mansfield was approaching along the path. "Good God," muttered Warrington.

Geoffrey came up to them, an angry look on his face. "What are you doing here, Bradford? I won't have you bothering Miss Richards. Now go about your business."

Warrington stood for a moment, considering what to do. "My duties are finished for the day," he said. "Miss Richards and I were having a conversation. That is all."

Noting that the viscount had omitted calling him "sir," Geoffrey bristled. "Of all the insolence. So you were having a conversation with Miss Richards, were you? It appears your victory has inflated your self-importance. You are not to speak to Miss Richard again, is that clear?"

The viscount hesitated. He was having difficulty controlling his temper.

"I do think you should go on, Jack," said Antonia.

"Yes, do as you're told. I shall see Miss Richards back to the house."

Warrington looked at Antonia. He could tell by her expression that she didn't want him to make a scene, so he nodded. "Very well. Good evening, Miss Richards." He then turned and started back to the house.

"That fellow is acting far above his station," said Geoffrey, frowning as he watched Warrington walk down the path until he disappeared behind a grove of trees. "I'm sure that everyone is aware that it was the superior horse that won today, not the superior rider."

"One cannot deny that he is a fine horseman."

"I won't call him a fine anything," said Geoffrey, clearly disgruntled by Antonia's remark.

"I must be returning to the house, Mr. Mansfield," said Antonia, eager to get away from him.

"Don't be so hasty," he said, reaching out and grasping her by the arm. "I said I'd escort you back."

She snatched her arm away. "That isn't necessary, I assure you." Antonia started quickly walking away from him.

He hurried after her, and this time he grabbed her more firmly by the arm. "Wait a moment, my girl."

She glared at him. "Release my arm, sir."

"Come, I've had enough of this missish behavior. Don't think I don't know what you're about, you and that groom. Harriet said you went out of your way to see him this afternoon. I'm no fool."

"How dare you!" said Antonia, her face growing red with anger and indignation. "Now let me go, Mr. Mansfield."

Holding her fast, he grinned. "Not until you're a bit more pleasant to me."

"I warn you, sir, I will tell your father of your infamous conduct toward me."

"My father is not here, madam. Indeed, we are now quite alone. And don't pretend that you aren't glad of it." And with those words he pulled her to him and crushed his mouth against hers.

Frightened and horrified, Antonia tried to pull away, but he held her firmly. When he finally took his lips away from hers, Antonia cried out. He quickly stifled her cries with another brutal kiss, while she struggled in vain to free herself.

Suddenly, there was a loud shout, "Let go of her!" Then two strong arms pulled Geoffrey off Antonia and shoved him to the ground.

Warrington stood over Geoffrey, his face purple with rage. Reaching down, he pulled Geoffrey to his feet. "You damned bastard," he said, directing a hard blow to his face.

Geoffrey fell backward, landing in an undignified heap on the ground. Seeing the murderous gleam in Warrington's eyes and having heard how he had beaten Tom Dawson, Geoffrey drew back in fear. "Keep away from me. I warn you."

The viscount, who had a strong desire to thrash his employer's son within an inch of his life, was restrained by Antonia. "No, Jack, stop! I beg you!"

"Are you all right?" he asked.

She managed to nod. "Yes."

Warrington returned his gaze to Geoffrey. "You're contemptible, Mansfield. Come, Miss Richards, I'll take you back to the house."

Geoffrey, terrified that Jack Bradford would hit him, kept silent. Watching the viscount take Antonia's arm and start off toward the house, Geoffrey vowed that Jack Bradford would soon regret his conduct.

As they walked back, Antonia leaned on his arm, "Oh, Jack," she said. "If you hadn't come, I don't know what I would have done."

"I hadn't gone far. I wouldn't leave you with him. Come, I'll take you to Mrs. Clay."

"Thank you, Jack," she said and the two of them returned to the house.

After leaving Antonia with Mrs. Clay, Warrington returned to the stables. He was well aware that his treatment of Geoffrey Mansfield was a serious matter and he would, in all likelihood, lose his job.

"Mr. Bradford!" Jem hurried up to him as he walked up the stairs to his room. "I must tell you something. It is very funny."

"I don't know if I'm in the mood for funny stories, Jem," said his lordship.

"You will like this. I heard it from Agnes in the kitchen. Betty, the parlor maid, heard Lady Rochdale tell the mistress that Mr. Caufield had said you looked exactly like a lord, someone he knew in London. That you might be his twin brother." Jem grinned delightedly. "I thought you would want to hear it."

Warrington frowned. "What was the man's name?"

"Mr. Caufield."

The viscount looked thoughtful. Caufield? He didn't know any Caufield. Or did he? The name was vaguely familiar. Of course, a good number of people knew Warrington by sight. He was a person of consequence, the heir to a great fortune and one of the oldest earldoms in the kingdom.

Jem continued. "And Agnes said Mr. Caufield came in when Betty was serving tea and Lady Rochdale started to laugh about him thinking a groom looked like a nob, and he said you were so very much like this lord someone that he must take another look at you."

"Caufield," muttered the viscount, trying to place the name.

Suddenly, he remembered. Yes, there was a man named Caufield whom he'd met occasionally. What bad luck that this Caufield had appeared at Larchmont. Warrington was irritated to think that the man could recognize him.

The viscount frowned. He'd have to leave Larchmont before Caufield had another look at him. No doubt it was prudent to leave in any case considering what had just occurred between him and Mansfield.

"I thought you'd think it funny, sir," said Jem, puzzled by Warrington's expression.

"Oh, it is funny," he said absently. "Jem, I must send a note. I shall need a pencil and a piece of paper."

"I saw a pencil in the tack room," said Jem, "and I know where there might be a scrap of paper. I'll fetch them for you, sir." Jem scurried off, eager to help.

He returned with a pencil and a rumpled old playbill. "I had this in my room," said Jem. "I found it."

"Good lad," said the viscount, taking the paper and writing a note on the back side of it. He then took three coins from his pocket and placed them inside the paper, carefully wrapping them up inside. "You must give this to Miss Richards. And to no one else. Do you understand?"

"Yes, sir," said Jem, taking the paper.

Warrington tousled the boy's hair. "Good-bye, Jem."

"Good-bye, sir," replied Jem, rather puzzled by his errand. He obediently went off to the house to find Antonia.

Antonia sat a chair in Mrs. Clay's room. The housekeeper had been very disturbed by Antonia's story. She was well aware that Geoffrey couldn't be trusted with women. There had been two housemaids who had to leave service during her time at Larchmont.

"Perhaps the matter can be smoothed over," said the housekeeper.

"I cannot stay at Larchmont, Mrs. Clay. I shall leave here and find another position."

"Are you sure that you must go?" said Mrs. Clay, alarmed at the prospect of losing her friend.

"I shan't live under the same roof with him," said Antonia. "Just seeing him is horrible."

"Well, don't make any hasty decisions tonight. You must rest and think about it in the morning."

"I don't believe there is anything more to think about. I shall give Lady Mansfield my notice in the morning and I shall leave Larchmont as soon as possible."

"But where will you go?"

Antonia shrugged. "I don't know. I shall think of something. But you mustn't worry."

"Well, I shall worry," said the older woman.

There was a knock at the door and one of the maids entered the room. "Begging your pardon, Mrs. Clay, but Jem is here looking for Miss Richards. He has a note for her and won't give it to anyone but miss."

"Have him come in, then," said Mrs. Clay.

Jem entered the room a bit shyly. Walking over to Antonia, he handed her the note. "'Tis from Mr. Bradford," he said.

Antonia unfolded the paper and found the three gold coins. She regarded the money in surprise. Taking up the note she read:

Miss Richards, by the time you read this, I shall have left Larchmont. It is necessary that I do so. My only regret is that I won't be able to see you again. Take the three guineas. It will help you leave this place.

Your obedient servant, Jack Bradford.

P.S. I shall also miss Jem and Mrs. Clay. Say good-bye for me.

The note stunned her. He was leaving Larchmont so suddenly, without even saying good-bye to anyone. While she tried to deny that her feelings for him were nothing more than a silly infatuation, the idea that she would not see him again filled her with dismay.

"Oh, dear, is it bad news?" said Mrs. Clay.

"Mr. Bradford is leaving Larchmont," said Antonia.

"Leaving Larchmont?" cried Jem.

"Yes, he said he will miss you, Jem."

"It can't be true! I must find him." Jem rushed from the room.

"And the coins?"

"Sir Harold gave him five guineas for winning the race. He's given me three to help me to leave here."

"That is good of him," said Mrs. Clay. "But this is very bad news. I fear that Sir Harold will take it very ill. Of course, I can understand why Jack Bradford has gone. One cannot tell what Mr. Geoffrey might do. He is such a dreadful man."

Antonia nodded. "He is odious." A shudder of revulsion passed through her as she remembered his lips pressed against hers.

Retiring to her room, Antonia bolted her door. When she got into bed, she lay thinking about the calamitous day. Now her entire world had been turned upside down and she would have to find new employment. Of course, it wasn't that she hadn't considered giving her notice numerous times. No, she hadn't really been happy at Larchmont.

Yet Antonia had hoped to have obtained another position before leaving. She had little money and she was unsure where she should go.

Her thoughts turned to Warrington. It seemed unbelievable that she would never see him again. Well, she reflected, it wasn't as if he had declared himself in love with her. If he had any intentions toward her, one couldn't say whether they were honorable. No, it was probably for the best that Jack Bradford was gone from her life. But as she lay there in the darkness, she was filled with a desolate sense of loss.

In the morning, Antonia had scarcely risen from bed when she received a summons from Lady Mansfield. When she entered the morning room to see her employer, that lady directed a particularly icy look at her.

Lady Mansfield was seated upon the sofa, attired in a fashionable dress of pale peach-colored muslin. "Miss Richards, I was very much alarmed by what I was told by my stepson last night."

"I cannot imagine what Mr. Mansfield told your ladyship."

"He told me that he came upon you and the man Bradford in a, shall we say, compromising position. When my son expressed his disapproval at such conduct, Bradford attacked him."

"That is untrue!" protested Antonia. "I was only talking with Mr. Bradford when Mr. Mansfield came upon us. It was your stepson who attempted to take liberties with me. Mr. Bradford came to my aid."

"I was told you'd tell this story," said Lady Mansfield. "In short, I do not believe you. And I don't wish to have my daughters under the tutelage of anyone so lacking in morals. I am dismissing you. You are to pack your things and leave Larchmont at once."

"But I am not at fault. Mr. Mansfield has been making advances to me since the first day I arrived here."

"That is enough," snapped her ladyship. "I won't have you slandering my stepson. I now know what sort of person you are. I do not wish to discuss this matter any further."

Antonia hesitated. She could tell by Lady Mansfield's expression that it would be useless to protest. "Might I at least ask a reference from your ladyship?"

"A reference? Don't be ridiculous. How could I recommend you to anyone?" She made a dismissive motion with her hand. "Now go. Grigson will give you your wages. I want you to be out of my house by midday."

"Very well, I am happy to go," said Antonia, her temper getting the better of her. "You've never liked me and I confess I have never liked you. And your daughter Harriet is a dreadful brat. I pity her next governess. As to your stepson, he is a lecherous blackguard and a liar."

"Get out!" cried Lady Mansfield, horrified by such insolence.

Antonia cast a disgusted look at her employer before turning to go. Furious, she hurried to her room and began to gather up her meager possessions.

14

Since Lady Mansfield had been very eager to have Antonia gone from Larchmont, she gave orders for one of the grooms to drive Antonia to Cawley, where she could take a stagecoach. After saying farewell to Mrs. Clay, Antonia climbed into a dogcart, carrying an old valise and her mandolin, and rode off to the village.

At Cawley, she was deposited in front of the Black Swan Inn to await the arrival of the stagecoach. However, when she inquired at the inn, she was disappointed to find that there was no coach to London arriving that day. She would have to stay at the inn until the following day or travel six miles to the town of Trudlow, where she could board an afternoon coach.

Antonia knitted her brows in concentration as she pondered what to do. She didn't relish staying overnight at the inn in Cawley, but how would one get to Trudlow? The idea of walking there while carrying a valise and mandolin seemed impossible.

Perhaps, she might find someone who might drive her to Trudlow, thought Antonia as she sat down at a table in the inn to consider the matter. She wished she had a clear plan as to what to do, for she dearly wished to get as far away from Larchmont as she could.

She had no family in England, or at least no one she could call upon for assistance. Most of her relations lived in Italy. And while she had a number of friends from her childhood days, she wasn't happy at the prospect of imposing on them.

Thank goodness that she had a little money, she thought, contemplating the coins she had carefully hidden in her valise. In addition to the wages of six pounds, seven shillings, which she'd received before her departure, she had the three guineas Warrington had given her. It would be enough to live on for a time, if she were very frugal.

After a time, Antonia rose from her chair and walked out of the inn. Setting her valise and mandolin down, she looked about hesitantly. While she stood wondering what to do, a familiar voice greeted her. "Miss Richards!"

Antonia turned around to find Jem standing before her, a broad smile on his face. "Jem!" she said, regarding him in surprise. "I didn't expect to see you here."

"When I heard they'd told you to leave, I thought I'll not stay at Larchmont a day longer. 'Twas bad enough that Mr. Bradford was gone. Last night I looked everywhere for him, but he was nowhere to be found. And this morning when I come down to the stables, Tom Dawson was waiting for me and he gives me a cuff on the head and says I'd best not cross him or I'll regret it and I was to know that Mr. Bradford wasn't there to protect me.

"And then to hear that you had been taken off to Cawley and would not return—well, miss, I couldn't bear life at Larchmont anymore. And so I run off. I'll find something else. Maybe in Trudlow. They say 'tis a bigger town. Mayhap there would be work there."

"I was thinking of going to Trudlow myself," said Antonia. "There is a coach stopping there this afternoon. But it is rather a distance. Six miles I'm told."

Jem's face lit up. "Could we not go there together, miss? I could carry your bag. And I should protect you from footpads and the like."

"I don't know, Jem. Indeed, I'm rather worried about you. Perhaps you are acting too hastily. You could talk to Mrs. Clay. Perhaps there is another job you might get at the hall away from the stables."

"Not for me, miss. No, I'm done with service at Larchmont. I'll find some other sort of job. But do let me go with you. 'Tis not so far a walk on such a day as this."

"Very well," said Antonia. "Why not? I don't like staying here. It is a fine day for a walk and the road is dry."

Jem eagerly snatched up the valise and mandolin, but Antonia took the instrument from him. "I can't have you carry everything and this isn't heavy."

They set off, with Jem smiling happily. He could scarcely believe his good fortune. There he was walking with Miss Richards and for six miles he would have her all to himself.

Warrington muttered a curse as he walked along the road toward Trudlow. It was midmorning and unseasonably warm and the viscount was not in the best of moods.

After leaving Larchmont the evening before, he had walked to Cawley, where he had spent the night at the Black Swan Inn in a bed even more uncomfortable than the one he had occupied at Larchmont. Then he had been told that no coach would pass through Cawley until the following day.

And so Warrington had set off on a six-mile hike to Trudlow. Such a distance would not have normally bothered the viscount, but the sorry pair of boots he was wearing was not suitable for walking. After three miles, his feet hurt and he devoutly wished there was some other way to get to Trudlow.

Warrington found himself looking back on the road from time to time, hoping that some vehicle would come along that might give him a ride. Yet, the road was little traveled and the drivers of the few vehicles that had passed him had given him suspicious looks before hurrying past.

The viscount continued on for a time, but soon stopped under a large oak tree to rest his feet. Sitting down beneath the tree and resting his back against it, he pulled off his boot to survey the blister that was forming on his foot. "Damn and blast," he muttered, tossing the boot to the side and stretching out his legs.

It was pleasant in the shade and the viscount sat there with a thoughtful expression on his handsome face. He hadn't wanted to leave Larchmont. Actually, he admitted to himself, he hadn't wanted to leave Antonia Richards.

What deuced bad luck that the fellow Caufield had shown up, he thought. He had had no choice but to get away or risk being recognized. Of course, it had seemed bad to run off without saying good-bye to Antonia. In all likelihood he would never see her again.

Warrington folded his arms across his chest and stared out at the road. It was probably for the best that he'd left. It wouldn't do for him to become involved with a respectable young woman. No, she was the sort of girl one married. And even if he had any wish to marry, which he most assuredly did not, he could hardly think of marrying Antonia. The heir to an earldom did not marry a penniless governess.

Still, as the viscount sat there reflecting, he realized that he had become very fond of Antonia. Had he found such a young lady in the London Marriage Mart, he would have definitely reconsidered his aversion to the wedded state.

A sharp high-pitched bark suddenly brought Warrington from his reverie. Looking over, he saw a small black dog approaching him. The creature seemed to appear from nowhere. It hurried forward and then stood there barking.

Warrington viewed the creature with disfavor. While he liked dogs well enough, he had never been partial to small, yapping lapdogs, which is what the animal appeared to be. Coal black and furry, it had a foxlike head, pointed ears, and a bushy tail that curled over its back.

"Go away," said his lordship, frowning at the dog. When the creature made no move to do so, the viscount grabbed his boot and threw it at the beast. "Be off with you!"

The dog dodged the boot, which had been thrown in a half-hearted manner. Then to Warrington's surprise, the animal lunged at the boot, picked it up and ran off.

"Why, you contemptible cur," shouted the viscount, jumping to his feet. "Bring that back!"

Ignoring him, the dog rushed down the road in the direction Warrington had come, carrying its prize firmly in its mouth. The viscount shouted a string of oaths, but the little black dog only ran faster.

As Antonia walked with Jem on the road toward Trudlow, they chatted about a wide variety of subjects. Jem's cheerfulness seemed to make Antonia feel better. As he talked about ideas he had for making his way in the world, Antonia wished that she had the means for helping him find a job or trade.

Of course, as she told herself ruefully, she must concern herself with finding her own way of supporting herself. But at least she had a little money and her education. Certainly she was far luckier than poor Jem, who had nothing but the clothes on his back and his willingness to work.

When Jem began to talk about the idea of going to sea, Antonia mentioned that her father had been a naval captain. This greatly interested Jem, who wanted to know everything about the late Captain Richards and the ships on which he sailed.

Antonia was talking about her father's last command when she was interrupted by the appearance of a small black dog running toward them carrying something rather large in its mouth.

"Oh, look, miss!" cried Jem. "A dog!"

Rushing up to them, the animal stopped and deposited the object, which Antonia could now see was a boot, at their feet. Then the dog stood looking up at them, wagging its tail.

"What a handsome fellow you are," said Jem, putting down Antonia's valise and then squatting down to pet the dog. "And whose boot do you have there?"

The dog wagged its tale furiously and jumped up on Jem, joyously licking his face. Jem laughed delightedly.

"I wonder where his owner is," said Antonia, staring down the road. Suddenly a man came into view from where the road curved. "Oh, there is someone ahead," she said, shielding her eyes from the sun's glare with her hand. "I believe he is missing a boot."

Jem looked down the road. Catching sight of the man walking slowly and awkwardly toward them, his face suddenly lit up. " 'Tis Mr. Bradford!"

Antonia stared at the man in surprise. "Why, I believe you are right, Jem. It is he."

Snatching up the boot, Jem started running toward the viscount. "Mr. Bradford! Mr. Bradford!" he shouted. The dog began to bark and went racing after the boy.

"Well, I'm damned," said Warrington as he recognized Jem running toward him. He stared beyond the boy to the woman standing there on the road. It was Antonia!

"Oh, Mr. Bradford! What good luck to find you!" cried Jem, stopping before the viscount and grinning broadly. "I hoped I'd find you. I know Miss Richards will be pleased to see you."

Taking the boot from Jem, the viscount glared at the small black dog, which was now wagging its tail at Warrington. "The accurst mongrel stole my boot. I've been chasing him for half a mile. Don't tell me he is your dog."

"Oh, no, sir. I've never laid eyes on him before. But he's a fine, clever little rascal, ain't he, sir?"

"Fine, clever?" said the viscount, putting on his boot. "I have other adjectives that would suit better."

Antonia picked up the valise and was starting forward toward the man and boy. Seeing this, Jem turned to run back to her. "Do let me carry that, miss," he said, taking it from her.

Warrington followed the boy. When he reached Antonia, he smiled. "Miss Richards, I didn't expect to see you."

"Nor I you, Jack," said Antonia trying to appear nonchalant, even though his presence was exerting its usual disconcerting effect upon her.

"But what are you doing here on the road?"

"Lady Mansfield packed me off to Cawley this morning. She no longer required my services."

"And I run off as well," said Jem proudly.

"And you're going to Trudlow?"

Antonia nodded.

"Then we can all go together," said Warrington. "Come, lad, I'll take the bag."

"But how did the dog get your boot, Mr. Bradford?" said Jem, as they started to walk.

"The little blackguard stole it from me. I was resting. I'd taken it off because my foot hurt."

"Oh, that is funny," said Jem.

"I didn't find it in the least amusing," said the viscount, scowling at the dog and shaking his fist at it. "Now, away with you or you'll feel my boot!"

"Jack!" cried Antonia. "It's only a little dog and he didn't mean any harm."

"Oh, I'm sure he was only playing a little trick on you, Mr. Bradford," said Jem, smiling at the dog.

"Well, I could cheerfully wring his neck," said the viscount.

Undaunted by this remark, the dog followed them, keeping close to Jem's heels.

"I think he's very sweet," said Antonia, glancing back at the dog.

"Sweet, is he?" muttered the viscount, but when Antonia looked at him with raised eyebrows, he couldn't help but smile.

"Do you like dogs, Mr. Bradford?" said Jem.

"In general, I'm quite fond of dogs," said his lordship, "but I have a distinct loathing for this one."

"How could anyone dislike such a lovely little dog?" said Antonia.

"I like him," said Jem. "I wish he was my dog."

"He very likely is owned by some poor unfortunate soul living nearby," said the viscount. "Let us hope he chooses to go home." He growled at the dog. "Go home!"

But the little dog took no notice and continued to follow after them. "I daresay he will leave us if we ignore him," said Antonia.

"I shall be more than happy to do so," said Warrington. "And you are to ignore him as well, Jem."

Jem nodded reluctantly, but he kept stealing a glance at the dog from time to time. Finally, he reached down to pet the dog again and Warrington and Antonia walked ahead.

"So what will you do now, Miss Richards?" asked Warrington.

"I'll take the coach at Trudlow. I'm not sure where I shall go."

"But haven't you any relations or friends with whom you might stay?"

"My mother's family is in Italy," said Antonia. "I have no one in England. But I shall find another position as a governess." She looked over at him. "It was very generous of you to give me some of the money Sir Harold gave you, but it is wrong of me to accept it. After all, it isn't as though you are a wealthy man. When we reach Trudlow, I shall return it to you."

"You'll do nothing of the kind," said his lordship. "It was little enough and it seems you are in need of it. No, I insist you keep it. It is useless to argue with me, miss."

"Oh, very well," she said, giving up. "It was very kind and I do need it. But I shall pay you back one day."

"It was a gift, not a loan," said the viscount. "And I'll not hear another word about it." He looked back at Jem, who was playing with the dog.

"Jem, I told you to ignore the miserable creature. I must insist you do as I say."

"Yes, sir," said Jem, hurrying to join them, with the dog following him.

"Look, there's a stream," said Warrington. "I'm dashed thirsty. Let's stop for a drink."

Antonia, who was also getting very thirsty, was very happy to do so. They left the road and walked a short distance to a small brook. It was a pleasant bucolic scene with willow trees and shining water.

The three travelers knelt down to take handfuls of water to drink from the brook. The black dog leaned down and began to lap up the cool liquid.

"Why don't we rest a bit?" said Warrington. "My feet hurt like the very devil." Sitting down, he pulled off a boot. "And don't you dare touch my boot again, you misbegotten little scoundrel," he said, addressing the dog, which sat regarding him with a quizzical look. The viscount took off his other boot and put his feet in the water. "That feels much better."

Following his friend's example, Jem sat down and removed his shoes. He then rose and began to wade in the water. The dog jumped in beside him and began to splash about.

"Why the wretched cur!" said Warrington, and Antonia laughed at his expression. He grinned. "Wading is an excellent idea." He rose to his feet and began to walk about in the stream. "Ah, that feels good. I haven't done this since I was a boy. Come on, miss, why don't you come in, too?"

Antonia shook her head. "I really don't think . . ."

"Oh, it is very nice, miss," said Jem. "Do come in."

Antonia hesitated a moment and then began to take off her shoes. "If you gentlemen would turn your backs."

The viscount and Jem obligingly turned while she took off her stockings. Standing up, she stepped into the water, lifting her skirt to keep it from getting wet.

Warrington looked over at her and was gratified by the display of the lady's shapely calves. "Doesn't that feel wonderful, miss?" he said.

"Oh, yes," said Antonia as she walked through the cold water. She smiled as she watched Jem run through the water with the dog chasing him. "I am glad to see Jem enjoying himself."

The viscount nodded. A memory from his childhood came to

him and he thought of himself wading in the fishing stream at his father's estate. "I remember when I was very young, I had a rat terrier. Boodles and I had many a good run in the stream. I also remember how my nanny would scold me for getting wet and muddy."

"Your nanny?" said Antonia. "So now I am hearing something of your mysterious past, Jack Bradford. You had a nanny."

"I confess I am at present less prosperous than I once was," said his lordship.

"It seems we've both come down in the world," said Antonia with a rueful smile.

"Perhaps so," said the viscount, gazing into her blue eyes, "but I don't know when I've had a happier moment than being here with you."

This remark caused her to look down. "Don't speak nonsense, Jack."

His lordship was about to protest that it wasn't nonsense, but Jem came hurrying back to them, laughing at the antics of the little black dog which, had begun to jump up at him and bark excitedly. Antonia was glad of the diversion and she retreated from the stream to sit down beneath the trees and allow her feet to dry.

Jem and the viscount came out a short time later and the black dog shook itself violently, causing Warrington to shout "Blast you!" as droplets of water fell all over him.

"He is a funny little dog," said Jem, sitting down beside Antonia. The dog hurried to his side and wedged against him.

"It seems he has taken a fancy to you," said Antonia.

"He seems rather thin, don't you think?" said Jem, patting the dog's sides. "And he doesn't have a collar. Perhaps no one owns him. I wish I could keep him. I'd name him Baldric. 'Tis a name I remember from a story Mrs. Clay told me about knights and dragons."

"Baldric suits him very well," said Antonia.

Suddenly there was the sound of hoofbeats and they looked toward the road. The viscount started when the horse and rider came into view. "Get down," he said to the others in a low voice. "Don't let him see you."

Antonia and Jem both gave him an odd stare, but bent down and observed the man gallop by on a fine bay mare. Turning to Warrington, Antonia was surprised to see an expression of anger on his handsome face. "What is it?" she asked.

"That was my horse and one of the villains who stole her."

Antonia looked back at the road. The horseman was now some distance away. "*That* was your horse?" she asked, raising her dark eyebrows.

"What a beauty!" exclaimed Jem.

"Yes," continued Antonia, eyeing the viscount curiously, "that wasn't the sort of animal that a poor man would own."

Warrington smiled. "I admit the animal is rather fine for the likes of me, but, you see, I won him in a card game."

Antonia eyed him closely. "You won the horse gambling?"

"Yes, I was having the devil's own luck that evening." Noting her frown, he added, "I know you disapprove of gambling, Miss Richards."

"I do," said Antonia. "There is no quicker route to ruin."

"You sound like my father," said Warrington.

"Your father must be a sensible man."

"He is credited as such."

Jem had listened to this conversation impatiently, but he finally broke in. "If only you could get your horse back from that robber," he said.

"I've every intention of doing so," said the viscount, a determined look on his face.

"We must go back to the village and find the constable," suggested Antonia.

"And let the fellow get away?" said Warrington. "No, I'm going after him. He's going toward Trudlow and his tracks will be easy to follow."

"You can't be serious," said Antonia.

"I am quite serious," said the viscount resolutely.

Antonia appeared worried. "But it is too dangerous. And how would you catch up with a man on horseback?"

"There is a chance he isn't going far." Warrington hurried to put his boots on. "I'd best hurry."

"We'll come with you," said Antonia, taking up her stockings, and putting them on with little regard for modesty.

"Yes, we will," said Jem. "I'll help you get your horse."

"I don't think that would be wise," said Warrington.

"No, it isn't wise," she admitted. "But it's only a little less fool-hardy than you going after these robbers by yourself. And he was going toward Trudlow, so we may as well come with you."

"Very well. Come on, then." He picked up the valise. "We must hurry." Making their way back to the road, Warrington, Antonia, and Jem started off after the robber with the little black dog following behind them.

15

Just as Warrington thought, his horse's tracks weren't hard to follow on a road that apparently had few other travelers. They had scarcely gone a mile when the tracks veered off onto a narrow path leading away from the roadway. "He turned off the road here. I shall follow him. I want you both to go on to Trudlow."

"No, you cannot go alone," said Jem.

The viscount's face took on a serious expression. "I will brook no argument from either of you. There is danger here and it is best I go alone. You go on to Trudlow and find the constable. Now, I insist you do as I say."

"But isn't it just as dangerous for us to go on to Trudlow?" said Antonia. "There was more than one footpad who assaulted you. We may meet up with him on the road."

Warrington hesitated. He had to admit that there was logic in what she said.

"And we might be able to assist you."

"Oh, very well," said Warrington, "but you must do exactly as I say. Is that understood?"

"Aye, sir," said Jem.

"Find something to tie that dog. I won't have him barking. We must be very quiet. And leave the mandolin, Miss Richards." He put down the valise under a tree. Jem reached into his pocket and found a length of twine. Tying it around the dog's neck, he secured the suddenly very unhappy animal to a tree.

They then proceeded down the path. They did not go far when the viscount suddenly put out his hand to stop them. "I see a building ahead," he said in a hushed tone. Antonia and Jem looked up the path and saw a dilapidated thatched-roof cottage which was almost invisible in the tall weeds growing about it. Warrington's bay horse was tied to a tree nearby.

"There's the cutthroats' hideout," whispered Jem. "I'll wager it would be Scar or Ginger Tom."

"Let us hope it is only one of them," said his lordship. "Now we must be very quiet. You both stay here and I'll go have a look in the cottage."

Antonia began to protest that it was too dangerous, but seeing Warrington's stern expression, she knew he was determined to go. "Do be careful, Jack."

Warrington nodded before proceeding cautiously ahead. The viscount gestured for quiet and then made his way slowly and quietly through the wooded area to the back of the house. Once there, he peered into the window to see a man sitting at a table, drinking. He recognized "Scar," the shorter of the two robbers. After draining his glass, Scar filled it again from a bottle. Downing that one quickly, he began to sing a few bars of a song as he poured still another glass.

Remembering how the man had taken his clothes and beaten him while he was helpless, Warrington's face grew grim. Thank God, he thought, there was no sign of his giant companion. The viscount was also encouraged by how rapidly Scar was emptying the bottle. With luck, the fellow's wits soon would be addled by drink.

Warrington knitted his brows in concentration, wondering what was the best course of action. The thought that Scar might be awaiting his accomplice gave the viscount a sense of urgency. He must do something before anyone else appeared, he concluded.

Leaving the window, Warrington crept along the back of the cottage to the side of it. Finding an open window, the viscount peered in to find an untidy bedroom. Glancing about, he saw that the highwaymen had stashed their booty on the floor of the slovenly room.

There were several pairs of brass candlesticks, a silver serving tray, and a number of bottles and gunnysacks. Then Warrington's eyes alighted on a brace of pistols on a small table in the corner.

As silently as possible, the viscount climbed through the window. He could hear the robber singing in a loud, slurred voice.

Going quickly to the table, he picked up one of the pistols. Checking it, he found that it was primed and ready.

Warrington started slowly across the room, stopping abruptly as a floorboard creaked. Scar continued to sing, blissfully unaware that he had an intruder. The viscount proceeded to the door of the room. Looking out, he could see the robber. His back was to him and the man was uncorking another bottle.

The viscount walked into the room. "Put your hands up!" he shouted.

The man started violently, jumping to his feet, and dropping the bottle. Turning, he gaped at Warrington. "What the devil!"

"Put your hands up or I'll kill you."

The highwayman reluctantly complied. He stared at the viscount in bewilderment. "Who are you?"

"Don't you recognize me? Then I shall refresh your memory. That's my horse you've been riding. And I believe that's my coat you're wearing. By God, I'm glad my tailor can't see what you've done to it."

The man scowled. "Damn your eyes, I thought you was dead."

"Sorry to disoblige you," said Warrington in a sardonic tone. "Now start walking out of the house. And don't attempt anything foolish. I assure you I am quite capable of using this pistol."

Scar hesitated for a moment. Then, when Warrington brandished the gun at him, he reluctantly moved toward the door, his hands raised above his shoulders.

The viscount followed him outside. But scarcely had both men cleared the doorway, when the robber turned suddenly and lunged at Warrington. The viscount, taken by surprise, struggled with Scar and the pistol went off with a loud report.

Scar knocked Warrington to the ground. Pinning him there, he wrapped his hands around the viscount's throat and began to strangle him.

Suddenly, there was a loud, shrill barking and Scar let out a shout of pain. The small black dog had come out of nowhere and had jumped at the robber, biting his ear. Crying out in pain, Scar swatted at the dog, but the animal jumped agilely out of his reach. Warrington then shoved him off himself and scrambled to his feet.

Jem, who had followed closely behind the dog, was armed with a stout stick. Scar, who was glaring from the dog to Warrington, didn't see the boy come up behind him. Summoning all the strength he could muster, Jem hit Scar squarely on the back. Scar staggered with the blow and Baldric then lunged at him again, sinking his teeth into his leg.

Scar yelped and shook off the dog. He then turned toward Jem, but Warrington was on him in a moment, rushing against him like a battering ram.

Scar fell heavily to the ground. As he started to rise, Antonia, who had been observing the struggle, hit him on the head with the butt of the pistol she had retrieved from the ground. He fell back and lay motionless.

Warrington looked up at Antonia. "Good God, madam, that was a mighty blow."

"Did I kill him?" said Antonia, a horror-stricken look on her face.

The viscount glanced down at Scar. "I fear not. He's breathing. And look, I'll wager this is my watch." Warrington took up the chain that was dangling from the unconscious man's pocket and pulled out the watch. Seeing the familiar coat of arms engraved on the back, he was relieved. "It is my watch. Thank God. I was very upset at losing it. Now if only I could find my money. Jem, I saw some rope in the cottage. In the bedroom. Quick, lad, fetch it."

Jem hurried into the house and returned with a length of stout cord. Warrington pushed the robber's inert form onto his stomach and began to tie his hands behind his back. He then tied his ankles together. "He'll not escape from that, I'll be bound," said his lordship, pulling the knots tight.

"He might have killed you," said Antonia.

"He certainly tried," said his lordship trying to make light of the matter. "Thank God for you both and that little cur." He looked down at Baldric, who was wagging his bushy tail.

"He broke loose," said Jem, reaching down and picking up the dog. "What a brave fellow he is."

"I daresay you must change your opinion of Baldric now, Jack," said Antonia with a smile.

The viscount grinned. "That I have."

There was a moan from Scar, who although still unconscious, was showing more signs of life. "What will we do now?" said Antonia, eyeing the man with a worried look.

"We'll leave him here and report what happened to the authorities in Trudlow," said the viscount. "We must be off. There is a chance that his accomplice might appear. There was another pistol inside and some of his loot. Perhaps I might find my money. Jem, you stay here with the dog and watch him. Don't go too near and call out if he stirs."

Jem nodded and took up his stick. The viscount and Antonia went into the house and began to look through the things stashed in the bedroom. They searched everywhere, but found no money. "Well, we'd best not linger here any longer," said Warrington.

Antonia nodded and they left the cottage to join Jem and his little black dog.

It was something of a relief to Antonia when they arrived back at the road. But when she went to retrieve her valise from under the tree where Warrington had put it, she was horrified to discover it was gone. Her mandolin, however, was there where she had left it.

Warrington, who could hardly believe that the bag was gone, began a thorough search assisted by Jem, but there was no trace of it. Antonia was plunged into despair, for everything she owned had been in the valise, including the money the viscount had given her. It took considerable self-control to keep from bursting into tears.

"Someone must have stolen it," said Jem glumly. "They must have seen it from the road."

"Damn and blast," muttered his lordship. "It is my fault, Miss Richards. I should have hidden it behind the bushes. What a dismal country this is when one can't put down something for a minute without it being taken. Thank God, you have your mandolin."

"Yes, I am glad about that," said Antonia, trying to be brave. "But I have no money for the stagecoach now. I'd hidden it in the valise."

"That is bad luck, Miss Richards," said Warrington, "but don't forget I have a bit of money. And my horse and saddle. And my watch. I'm far more prosperous a fellow than I was an hour ago. So you mustn't worry. We'll all do well enough. But we must go on to Trudlow. The authorities must be notified about our friend back there."

Antonia sighed, but realizing nothing more could be done,

agreed that they should begin their journey. Warrington suggested that Antonia ride the horse, but she refused, and they all set off on foot, with Warrington leading the horse behind him.

" 'Tis a lovely mare," said Jem, glancing back admiringly at the viscount's horse. "Sir Harold doesn't have a finer horse in his stables, save for Caesar, of course."

"Yes, Daphne is a right one," said Warrington, patting the horse's neck affectionately.

They had walked for a mile when a party of soldiers appeared before them. Waving for them to stop, the viscount informed the officer where the infamous highwayman known as Scar could be found. Eager to see if this information was true, the soldiers galloped off down the road in hopes of apprehending the area's most notorious criminal.

Warrington watched them ride off with considerable satisfaction. He noted that Antonia was still dispirited over the loss of her possessions. "Are you tired, Miss Richards?" he said. "Perhaps you'd like to rest. The sun grows very hot."

Antonia nodded. She was feeling tired and hungry as well.

Jem pointed toward a grove of trees at the side of the road. "Look, Mr. Bradford, there's smoke over there. And I think I can see some wagons." He paused, straining his eyes. "I'll wager they're gypsies!" he said excitedly.

Warrington and Antonia both glanced toward the spot. "Perhaps we could get something to eat from them," suggested the viscount. "You must be hungry. I confess I'm famished. And I'll wager Jem is very hungry as well."

"Aye," said Jem. He looked down at Baldric, who was walking at his side. "You'd like a bit of food, wouldn't you, boy?"

The black dog looked up inquiringly.

"Well, there is no harm in seeing if any food is to be had," said his lordship and they left the road to walk toward the wagons.

As they grew closer, they saw the encampment more clearly. There amidst a grove of trees were three brightly painted wagons and six large white-and-gray horses tethered to a line. Off to one side of the wagons, a man balanced another man on his shoulders, while a flamboyantly dressed woman danced beside them. A short, bald man stood some distance away, juggling balls high up into the air. Standing over a large kettle at a nearby campfire, was a gray-haired woman, apparently oblivious to the commotion about her.

Warrington noted the words written on one of the wagons. " 'Pickering's Amazing Circus,' " he read out loud.

"Is it?" cried Jem. "Why 'tis the circus that was at the market fair!" Baldric, sensing the boy's excitement, began to bark and run back and forth.

The dog's shrill barking got the attention of the people at the campsite. The man jumped down off the other man's shoulders, the woman quit dancing, and the juggler expertly caught up all of the bright red balls in his hands. They then proceeded to stare at the noisy black dog and his companions.

The woman at the campfire, who was quite short and stout, called out, and an elderly man emerged from one of the wagons. A tall, imposing-looking gentleman with a thick thatch of white hair and a patch over one eye, he grumbled a few words to the woman and then he looked over at them.

Warrington and Antonia began to walk toward the camp. Jem, after scooping up Baldric in his arms, eagerly scurried after them. "Good day to you," said the viscount, nodding at the elderly couple near the campfire.

The white-haired man eyed them for a brief moment. His gaze seemed to linger appreciatively on Antonia, and then he made a flourishing bow. "Good day," he said in a deep, melodious voice. "I'm Thadeus B. Pickering of Pickering's Circus." He motioned toward the elderly woman. "And that is Mrs. Pickering."

"How do you do?" said Mrs. Pickering, a rosy-cheeked, amiable-looking woman.

Warrington nodded politely and tipped his hat. "I'm Jack Bradford. And this is Miss Antonia Richards and Jem Perkins."

"I am very pleased to meet you all," said Pickering with a broad smile. "Perhaps you will join us for a bit of luncheon. You have no objection to having guests, do you, my dear?"

"Why, no indeed," said Mrs. Pickering. "We have plenty enough for all."

"Thank you very much," said Warrington. "We are pleased to accept your invitation. And I should be happy to pay you for some food."

Pickering seemed insulted. "Pay for your food? By God, man,

haven't you heard of the hospitality of the road? You are our guests!" He turned to his wife. "Mrs. Pickering, do take care or you will burn the stew again."

"Yes, of course," said his wife, hurrying off to see to her cooking.

"You are very kind," said Antonia. "We are very hungry. We have been walking a long way."

"Then you are fellow travelers," said Pickering. "Do you journey far?"

"To Trudlow," said his lordship.

"Well, that is scarce two miles distant," said Pickering. "We will not be going there. We'll take the road to Litchfield, for we have an engagement there."

"You were at the Cawley market fair," said Jem, who was emboldened to enter the conversation. "The circus was wonderful!"

"Ah, how good it is to hear the acclaim of the public. We were a great success at Cawley."

"I liked the trick rider," said Jem eagerly. "He was very good."

Pickering frowned at this remark. He cast his eye on Warrington's mare. "She's a fine one, sir. I know horses and I'd be surprised if the blood of Snowfire himself don't flow through her veins."

"You have a sharp eye, sir," said Warrington. "She's a granddaughter of Snowfire."

The circus man appeared pleased with himself. He patted the horse. "Yes, a damned fine specimen."

By this time the other people who had been near the wagons came forward and stood regarding the newcomers curiously. "I must introduce you to the rest of the company," said the circus owner. "We have guests, my friends. I must present Mr. Bradford, Miss Richards, Master Perkins and . . ." He looked questioningly at Jem's dog.

"Baldric, sir," said the boy.

"Ah, Baldric," repeated Pickering. "Allow me to introduce the members of Pickering's Amazing Circus." He pointed toward the dancing woman, who was attired in an exotic dress of pink gauze, a veil covering her face. "This is Princess Fatima, our dancer from faraway Araby. Of course, that is her stage name."

A voluptuous lady with red hair and green eyes, the dancer pulled away her veil to reveal a pretty, but decidedly unexotic face.

When she spoke, she took away some of her mystery by speaking with a Cockney accent. " 'Ow d'you do?" she said, casting a flirtatious glance at Warrington. "My name is really Tilly Blodgett. *Miss* Tilly Blodgett."

Antonia, who couldn't fail to note the bold way the woman was looking at Jack Bradford, eyed her with disapproval.

Pickering turned to the two men who were attired in purple tights. "And these are our acrobats, the Astounding Flying Flynns. This is Frederick Flynn, and this is his brother, Michael."

The two men bowed low, and then Michael Flynn gazed over at Antonia with considerable interest. Fair-haired with an athletic physique, Michael Flynn was taller and considerably more handsome than his elder brother. Popular with the ladies, the acrobat smiled his most charming smile at Antonia.

"And finally," said Pickering, pointing to the short, balding man, "this is Jocko MacBride, the juggler."

Jocko grinned and spoke in a broad Scots accent. "Good day tae ye," he said. He saw that Jem was looking at him with an awestruck expression. "Would ye like tae see me toss the balls, lad?" The boy nodded eagerly and Jocko began to throw the balls into the air, keeping them aloft with practiced skill.

The little dog, too, seemed transfixed, its small black eyes riveted on the balls. The juggler, grabbing up the balls, threw the last one to Baldric, who caught it in his mouth. The dog then jumped up on his hind legs and walked about with the ball in his mouth. Everyone laughed and clapped.

Jocko bent down and pet Baldric. "Why ye're a fine wee lad," he said, "and if I'm nae mistaken, a born circus performer." Jocko took his ball from Baldric and rubbed the little dog behind his pointy ears.

Pickering was regarding the animal with a speculative look in his eye. However, he suddenly sniffed the air with his rather prominent nose and frowned. "Good God," he muttered, turning back toward the campfire, "the woman *is* burning the stew again." Looking at Warrington and Antonia, he said, "Come, we must partake of my wife's dinner before she has it in flames."

The viscount and Antonia exchanged an amused glance, but followed the circus owner to the campfire. They all sat on the ground as Mrs. Pickering dished out generous portions of the stew from the large black kettle over the fire. Warrington frowned slightly when Flynn quickly took a place next to Antonia. He himself was soon set upon by Tilly, who took his arm and urged him to sit by her.

The viscount, Antonia, and Jem all ate with considerable relish. Mrs. Pickering also supplied Baldric with a bowl of food and the little dog gobbled it up greedily.

The circus performers were a boisterous group and they spent much of the meal joking and telling stories. Antonia seemed to forget about the loss of her valise. She soon found herself enjoying the meal and the company very much. Flynn was especially charming and he had her laughing at his amusing tales of the circus.

Warrington noticed the attention that the acrobat was paying to Antonia, and he was annoyed to see that she seemed to be so impressed with him. Tilly, slightly frustrated at the viscount's lack of interest in her, wouldn't give up, but continued to flirt and bat her long, dark eyelashes coquettishly at him.

"I do wish I'd seen your performance at the Cawley market fair," said Antonia.

"It was grand!" said Jem. "They were all splendid. But where is the man who rode the horse? The one who did the tricks? I'd never seen the like of it. Why, 'twas amazing how he could ride."

Jem's comment cast a pall on the group, and all grew silent. Wondering what he had said wrong, Jem regarded Pickering with a puzzled look.

"While I have no wish to ruin our meal, it seems I must explain," said Pickering. "Our troupe has just experienced a crushing blow due to the perfidy of two of its members. Former members, I must say.

"I had looked upon them as family. Indeed, no father could have been more considerate of them. And what did they do? The damnable ingrates! They deserted us! Sneaked off in the dead of night like guilty thieves without a word to me! After all that I've done for them!"

"Now, Mr. Pickering," said his wife, shaking her head, "it does no good for you to rant on about it."

"Hold your tongue, woman," said Pickering. "The tale must be told." He turned back to the viscount. "Not only did the rascals run off, they took Samson!"

"Samson is a horse," explained Mrs. Pickering.

"A damned magnificent creature," said the circus owner. "And that accursed Wilkins took him!"

"Now, my dear," said his wife, "do not act as if he stole the creature. Samson was Wilkins's horse."

Pickering's face reddened. "By God, I don't care whose horse he was!" he exploded. "The trick riding was our drawing card and now we don't have a rider or a horse! We're nothing without Wilkins and Samson." The other performers frowned and regarded Pickering somewhat resentfully at this remark.

"And why did he leave us?" continued Pickering. "It was the fault of that accursed Daisy Davis."

"She was a singer," added Mrs. Pickering, "but not a very good one."

"I know that she made him do it," said Pickering.

"It was very romantic," said Tilly, gazing at Warrington. "They fell in love and ran off together."

"That is enough of that nonsense, my girl," grumbled Pickering. "I'll thank you not to mention her name again to me. No, I'm not sorry to have her gone. She was a dreadful singer. But Wilkins and Samson! They were what the crowds came to see!"

"Mr. Pickering was a trick rider himself," said Mrs. Pickering. "One of the finest in England. That's what he was when I met him."

The circus owner put a hand through his thick white hair. "That's all in the past, woman," he said irritably. "Where will I find a man to replace Wilkins? No, a rider like him won't be found easily."

Jem, who'd been listening to this conversation with great attention, glanced over at Warrington and Antonia. "Mr. Bradford is a fine rider. He rode Caesar in the race at the fair."

Pickering regarded the viscount with new interest. "Why, I saw the race. That was a magnificent beast." He paused. "Have you done any trick riding, Mr. Bradford?"

A laugh escaped the viscount. "No, indeed."

"But you could," said Jem eagerly. "No one is better with horses. I bet you could learn, sir."

Warrington smiled at Pickering. "I hope you will tell the boy what a ridiculous idea that is, Mr. Pickering. You know how difficult it is to learn such skills."

To the viscount's surprise, the circus owner wasn't so eager to dismiss Jem's remark as absurd. "While it is true that trick riding is difficult, if a man has the knack for it, it can be learned. And the horse is equally important. That mare of yours. I don't doubt she'd do very well. The best horse I ever had was a bay mare very like her.

"Yes, maybe you would consider joining us. We need a rider and I can teach you."

"Really, that is good of you to offer, but it is quite impossible," said the viscount.

Pickering didn't seem to want to accept this answer. "We can have a try. I can teach you a few of the simplest things."

The idea of the Viscount Warrington becoming a trick rider in a circus seemed so totally ridiculous that Warrington couldn't help but smile.

The circus owner turned his attention to Antonia. "I don't suppose that you sing, Miss Richards?"

Antonia lowered her eyes modestly. "Actually I do, Mr. Pickering."

"She has the loveliest voice, sir," said Jem, "and she plays the mandolin. 'Tis an Italian instrument."

"Indeed?" said Pickering. "You sing and play? Are you looking for work, Miss Richards?"

"Oh, I hadn't thought of performing in a circus," said Antonia.

"Then you are looking for work!"

"Perhaps you might want to 'ear 'er first, governor," said Tilly, "before taking 'er on."

While this comment caused Antonia to regard the dancer a bit resentfully, Jem seemed pleased at the idea. "Oh, do sing for them, Miss Richards. I'll get the mandolin." He jumped up and fetched the instrument, which was tied to Warrington's mare's saddle. He handed her the mandolin. "Do sing. Please."

"Very well," said Antonia, taking the instrument. "It is probably dreadfully out of tune." She began to test the strings and make the necessary adjustments.

Tilly rolled her eyes. "I do 'ope it won't take all day," she said. "We 'ave to break camp and be on our way sometime today."

"Quiet," said Pickering sternly. "Miss Richards may take all the time she needs."

"Oh, I'm ready now," said Antonia, strumming the mandolin and seeming pleased at the sound. She started singing an Italian ballad. As her melodious soprano filled the camp, the listeners sat transfixed. Even Tilly stared at her with admiration.

When she had finished her song, everyone applauded. Warrington, who had no idea that she was so talented, regarded her in some surprise.

"That was wonderful!" cried Pickering. "You will do very well indeed, Miss Richards. You must join us."

"Oh, I don't know. I'd never thought of performing."

"But you must, my dear," exclaimed Mrs. Pickering. "One must not hide a talent such as yours."

"Miss Richards has no experience," said Warrington. "She has worked as a governess."

"A governess?" said Mrs. Pickering. "Surely no one could prefer that to performing. And you'd earn far more."

"I would?" said Antonia.

"Oh, yes, indeed," said Pickering.

Antonia looked thoughtful. She did need a job very badly and the idea of singing for her living was very appealing. "Why, yes, perhaps it would be a good idea."

"Then you will do it?" said Pickering.

"I would if you could find a place for Jem as well."

"Oh, I should like to work in the circus, Mr. Pickering," said Jem eagerly. "I can take care of horses and do all sorts of jobs. And I could teach Baldric tricks. Mr. Jocko said he is a born performer."

"Now that is an idea," said Pickering. "Yes, by heaven, it is a dashed good idea. Jocko will help you. He knows a thing or two about dogs."

"Aye, that I do," said the juggler, nodding.

"Well, Mr. Bradford," said the circus owner, "Miss Richards and the boy are going to join us. It is only for you to say yes."

Warrington looked over at Antonia, who was regarding him with interest, a slight smile on her lovely face.

"Very well. I shall join, but I cannot guarantee that you will make a trick rider out of me."

A broad grin crossed Pickering's countenance. "By God, it must be Providence. I lose a horse rider and a singer and now, look, they appear before me! And a bright lad and a performing dog in the bargain!"

Warrington grinned. The idea of being a trick rider in a circus was decidedly absurd. Yet he did have two weeks before his wager was finished. He couldn't return to town until then and he had no other plans. And besides, reflected Warrington, he didn't want to leave Antonia.

The viscount was also drawn to the idea of learning a few tricks from Pickering. He was a skilled horseman and as a youngster he'd occasionally alarmed his riding master with reckless behavior. As he sat there, eating his stew, Warrington thought of his father. He smiled again as he imagined how the earl would react if he knew how his son had been spending his time since they'd last met.

16

Antonia had little time to reflect on her decision about becoming part of Pickering's Amazing Circus, for they had scarcely finished their meal when Pickering announced that they must make haste and break camp. There was a bustle of activity as the dishes were cleared away and the wagons made ready.

Warrington found himself hitching one of the teams of horses to a wagon, while Antonia helped Mrs. Pickering and Tilly rinse off the plates and utensils in the nearby stream. Soon the three wagons were on their way, with Antonia riding in the last wagon, which was driven by Jocko. As she sat there beside "Princess Fatima," she found herself thinking that her life had certainly taken an interesting turn.

Mounted on his bay mare, Warrington rode alongside them until Pickering shouted for him and he rode ahead to the Pickerings' wagon, which was leading the party. "What a 'andsome man, 'e is," said Tilly, turning to Antonia. "And charming. You're a lucky girl to 'ave 'im. 'Ow long you and 'im been . . . you know?"

"Miss Blodgett," said Antonia, reddening slightly, "you are mistaken to think that Jack and I . . . that Mr. Bradford and I are . . ."

"Then you're not lovers?"

"Certainly not," said Antonia, shocked at the question.

"Well, you *are* traveling about with 'im."

"Jem and I only happened to meet him on the road this morning."

"I see," said Tilly, who seemed pleased to hear it. "Then you don't fancy 'im?"

"Really, Miss Blodgett . . ."

"Now I can't 'ave you calling me that. Tilly will do. And what'll I call you? What's your Christian name?"

Although Antonia felt this question impertinent, she answered civilly. "Antonia."

"Antonia? Why, that's a grand sort of name. I think I'll call you Tony. No point in standing on ceremony, two girls like us."

"No, indeed," said Antonia. While she had no wish to be addressed in such a manner by a person she had only just met, she felt it best to tolerate the unwelcome familiarity. After all, Mrs. Pickering had informed her that she would be sharing the dancer's sleeping quarters. It was best to be tolerant. Not wishing to discuss Warrington any further, she changed the subject. "Have you been with the Pickerings long?"

"Oh, yes. Nearly three years now."

"You must have had some interesting experiences."

"Why, yes, my dear, I 'ave," said Tilly who then launched into a number of anecdotes about her life as a dancer.

It was beginning to grow dark when the wagons pulled off the road into a meadow to make camp for the night. Mrs. Pickering set about making supper, assisted by Tilly. When Antonia and Jem offered to help, they were shooed away. Eager to make himself useful, Jem went off, whistling, to see if Warrington needed help grooming his horse.

The boy could scarcely believe his good fortune. To find himself a member of such a congenial and exciting company was simply amazing. And what was even more wonderful was the fact that Miss Richards and Jack Bradford were there as well, not to mention his new little friend Baldric.

Seeing how obviously happy Jem was with their situation made Antonia feel very well pleased. She, too, felt very lucky. A few hours ago, she had been nearly in despair to find her money and meager possessions gone. Now, she had a job and a place to stay and food to eat.

As the sun grew lower in the sky, Antonia stood apart from the group, staring out at the pastureland that surrounded them. The air was now cool and pleasant after the heat of the afternoon. She thought about the day's adventures and how quickly her life had changed so completely.

After a while Warrington joined her. "Well, Miss Richards, did you ever think that you'd be singing in a circus?"

"Never in a million years."

"Didn't you tell me that you wished for a more adventurous life?"

"Yes, and it seems I'm to get my wish," she said. "And you? I doubt that you have ever imagined yourself a trick rider."

He laughed and shook his head. "Certainly not!"

"But do you really think it's wise? I don't care what Mr. Pickering says, it sounds very dangerous."

His eyes met hers. "Are you so concerned about me?"

Antonia blushed and looked away. "I just don't want you to break your foolish neck, Jack Bradford."

He reached out and took her hand. "I promise I'll stay in one piece." Still gazing down into her eyes, he took a step toward her. Antonia felt her heart racing as his lips came close to hers.

"Mr. Bradford!" came a cry and they both jumped apart. Jem was hurrying up to them, Baldric at his heels.

Although Warrington felt the boy's arrival exceedingly ill-timed, he smiled indulgently at him. "What is it, Jem?" he asked.

"I finished grooming Daphne. She looks in fine fettle now." The boy smiled up at them. " 'Tis a great stroke of luck, getting work in the circus," he said, sighing happily. "Isn't it the grandest thing that could happen to anyone?"

The viscount looked over at Antonia. "Just about the grandest thing," he said. "What a day we three have had."

"We four," Jem corrected him, looking down at Baldric. The small dog wagged its tail furiously and they all laughed. " 'Tis the best day of my life," continued Jem, "but I do wish you hadn't lost your things, miss."

"Well, I must be grateful that we have a place to stay and food to eat," said Antonia.

The boy took hold of the viscount's sleeve. " 'Tis time for supper. Mrs. Pickering says we are to come."

Warrington took out his watch and glanced down at it. "Yes, it grows late and I'm dashed hungry."

" 'Twas lucky you got your watch back, sir," said Jem. " 'Tis a fine one by the look of it. Might I see it?"

"Yes, of course, lad," said the viscount, handing it to him.

Turning the watch over in his hand, Jem noticed that there was an engraving of a family crest on the back. "Look, Miss Richards," said the boy, giving the watch to Antonia. "This is pretty. 'Tis a deer, I think."

"What is this engraving, Jack?" said Antonia, studying it carefully. "It looks like a coat of arms." There was a shield and inside it was a stag standing on its hind legs with three diamonds in a row above it.

"It is a coat of arms," said Warrington.

"Yours?" said Antonia, eyeing him with amusement.

"It is the coat of arms of the gentleman who gave me the watch. It was a long time ago."

Antonia waited for further explanation, but the viscount said no more and she sensed that it was a topic he did not wish to discuss.

Taking the watch from her hand, he put it in his pocket. "We must go to supper before we vex Mrs. Pickering," he said.

They joined the others for a supper of cold mutton and boiled potatoes. After the hearty repast, the group gathered around the fire to talk for a while before going to their beds.

Warrington was so tired that he didn't care that his bed was a narrow, hard pallet inside the wagon. He and the Flynn brothers and Jocko had to share the accommodations, which were cramped at best. To make matters worse, both Michael Flynn and Jocko snored loudly. Yet by now the viscount was accustomed to less than comfortable quarters. He lay on his narrow bed and went quickly to sleep.

Antonia, however, found herself lying awake. She and Tilly shared the smallest of the wagons. Attired in Mrs. Pickering's spare nightgown, she occupied the bed of the departed singer Daisy and it was lumpy and uncomfortable. While her new roommate fell immediately into a sound slumber, Antonia lay there thinking about Warrington.

She hadn't expected to meet up with him. It seemed fate had thrown them together again. She thought of how they had stood together and how he had taken her hand. She imagined herself in his arms, his lips upon hers, and it was a long time before she fell asleep.

In the morning, Antonia rose early. Tilly, who was a very sound sleeper, did not stir as Antonia dressed and climbed out of the wagon. Mrs. Pickering, who was stoking the fire, greeted Antonia cheerfully. "Good morning, dear."

"Good morning, Mrs. Pickering. It seems we are the only early risers."

"Oh, my husband and the lad are about. They went for a walk with the dog. Mr. Pickering always likes to take a walk before breakfast. But where is Tilly?"

"Sleeping soundly."

"That girl is a slugabed, to be sure," said the older woman. "You must come to my wagon. I have some clothes you might have. 'Twas a pity you lost your things."

Antonia followed Mrs. Pickering into the wagon, and as she entered, she realized that she had never before seen such a small space crammed with so many things. Crowded inside were a couple of beds, a rocking chair and a small table, with a small window allowing some light in. Every space was packed with some box or object. Clothes were piled in untidy heaps and Antonia wondered how Mrs. Pickering could find anything.

Mrs. Pickering rummaged about for a short time before presenting Antonia with a green cotton garment. "You may have this dress."

"That is very good of you."

The older woman nodded and began looking through another pile of clothes. "I know we have the perfect costume for you. I thought of it last night."

"A costume?" repeated Antonia in surprise.

"Why, of course," said Mrs. Pickering, nodding. "Ah, here it is. Yes, this will do very nicely." Mrs. Pickering pulled out a dress and shook it out. "It will need some alterations, of course."

Antonia looked at the dress that the circus owner's wife was holding up to her. It was a flamboyant creation of scarlet satin, with a low bodice and a skirt decorated with black satin roses. "Oh, I don't think . . ." began Antonia doubtfully.

"It will be lovely on you, my dear, with that dark hair of yours. Come, take off your dress and we'll try it."

Antonia hesitated a moment, but then began to undress. It was rather difficult changing in such a crowded space, but with Mrs. Pickering's assistance, Antonia was soon attired in the red gown.

Antonia looked down at the dress's daring decolletage. "The neck-line is too low," she said.

"Nonsense," said Mrs. Pickering, eyeing the gown approvingly, "a girl as fortunate as you should show off her charms. Now, I shall have to take it in a bit, but otherwise, it seems as if it was made for you." After studying the dress for a moment longer, she helped Antonia take it off.

When Antonia was back in her own clothes, they left the wagon and Mrs. Pickering invited her to sit down on one of two stools that had been placed near the fire. "I'm so glad that you are to join us, my dear. Mr. Pickering has been in such a lather over Ben and Daisy running off like they did."

Antonia smiled. "We are grateful to find employment, Mrs. Pickering."

The old woman nodded. "Times have been hard hereabouts. And you were a governess?"

"Yes, at Larchmont, an estate near Cawley."

"Well, this will make a change for you."

"Indeed," said Antonia, "a welcome change. I am glad to be gone from there. I shall be very happy to never see my employer again or her stepson."

"Her stepson?"

Antonia nodded. "He was loathsome."

The older woman fixed a knowing look on Antonia. "Is that how it was? A young gentleman making unwelcome advances? I know what that is like." She paused to grin. "Aye, I was young once.

"When I was dancing in the circus there were all manner of men making improper advances to me. And the gentry were the worst. When I first married Mr. Pickering, he told a good many men to keep their distance.

"But the circus is a good life, my dear. It can be hard, but we've always had enough to eat. No, I've never regretted my life in the circus. And you've a great talent. You'll do very well."

At that moment Mr. Pickering and Jem appeared, with Baldric following them. Finding only his wife and Antonia were up, he went to the other wagons and banged on them with his walking stick. "Get up, you lazy beggars!" he shouted.

A short time later, the other members of the company came up, looking something less than happy at greeting the new day. After a breakfast of tea and bread, Pickering announced to Warrington that it was time for his first lesson.

"First, let me see what sort of rider you are," said the circus owner. "Get your horse."

Glancing over at Antonia and giving her a quick smile, Warrington obediently went to saddle Daphne. Then, leading the mare, he followed Pickering to a meadow.

Climbing into the saddle, the viscount began to put the mare through her paces, while Pickering stood there watching him, with his arms folded across his chest.

Daphne was a well-schooled animal and one of the viscount's favorite mounts. Warrington eased her into a trot and then cantered across the meadow. Urging her to increase her pace, Warrington had the mare over a stone fence, a brook, and then a high hedgerow.

Then he brought her back to Pickering. "She's a splendid creature," he said, eyeing the horse appreciatively. "And you're a tolerable rider, it seems."

The viscount raised an indignant eyebrow. "Tolerable?"

"I've seen worse in my time," he said. "I think I can make something of you. Yes, I'm sure of it. But you must work very hard and you must always concentrate on what you're doing. That's what Astley told me."

The viscount regarded him with considerable interest. "Astley?" He was quite familiar with the name of the famous trick rider and circus impresario.

"That's right," said Pickering proudly. "I used to ride for Astley at his Amphitheater when I was a young fellow like you. So you see, Bradford, I was taught by the master."

Warrington was quite impressed by this information. He smiled. "I remember going to Astley's Amphitheater when I was a boy. When I saw the trick riders, I thought they were marvelous. I might have seen you."

"I daresay you did," returned Pickering. "But we must get down to work. We'll try a few simple tricks first. We must have you ready within three days' time so you can perform at Shrewsbury."

"Three days' time!" cried his lordship, quite astonished.

"We are to appear in Shrewsbury on Friday. We'll do a simple program. Nothing too difficult."

"I cannot see how I can be ready in such a short time," said Warrington.

"You must be ready," said Pickering, "and, therefore, I suggest we waste no more time."

Warrington shrugged. The man must be mad, he thought, but he decided not to argue. "Very well."

They began to work. Pickering explained each trick and the viscount listened carefully. By noon, Warrington had mastered several stunts and Pickering was quite pleased at his pupil's progress. "Excellent," he said. "Try fetching the pennant once more and then you must rest your horse."

Warrington nodded. Riding off some distance, he turned his horse and started back toward a small pennant on a stick that Pickering had placed in the ground. He urged the mare into a gallop, but just as he neared the handkerchief and was ready to reach down from his saddle to pick it up, he caught sight of Antonia walking toward the meadow on the arm of Michael Flynn. The viscount frowned, lost his concentration, and thundered past the pennant.

"Damnation," muttered Pickering. Seeing Antonia and Flynn, the circus owner recognized the source of the viscount's distraction. "You mustn't let anything distract you."

"I know," said Warrington, staring at Antonia.

"Blast it all, Bradford," said Pickering. "You must keep your mind on your work."

When Antonia and Flynn arrived beside Pickering, the acrobat smiled up at Warrington. "Better luck next time, Bradford," said Flynn. He looked over at Pickering. "You cannot think he'll be ready for Shrewsbury?" said Flynn.

"He will indeed," snapped Pickering. "Now away with you. We have too much work to do. And why aren't you at work? You are in need of practice."

Flynn eyed his employer with a look that implied the remark should not be dignified with a reply. "Come, Miss Richards, let us return."

Warrington watched them go, an unhappy expression on his face.

17

When Warrington and Pickering returned to camp, the viscount spent some time seeing to his horse. Then he made his way over to Jem, who was working with Jocko in teaching Baldric some tricks. Warrington smiled as he watched the little black dog jump through a hoop.

Jem turned around on the viscount's approach. "Did you see that, Mr. Bradford?" he asked excitedly. "Baldric jumped it easy as you please."

"He's a verra clever wee dog," said the Scotsman.

"Yes," said Jem, reaching down to pet the dog affectionately. "Watch how he can dance."

Jem pulled a whistle from his pocket and started to play a simple tune. Baldric got up on his hind legs and began to walk around, moving his forelegs in time to the music.

Warrington laughed, and when Jem stopped playing, Jocko proclaimed Baldric a veritable wonder. "I've never seen a better dog for the circus," said the juggler. "Ye'll do verra well with him, laddie."

The viscount added his enthusiastic praise and Jem looked thrilled. Saying that it was time to have a rest, Jocko left them to go off and smoke his pipe.

"Where is Miss Richards?" asked Warrington.

"She's with Mrs. Pickering. She's helping her sew Princess Fatima's new costume."

The viscount seemed pleased to hear this. When everyone assembled for lunch, he was sure to take a seat beside Antonia. He wasn't able to talk to her very much, for his attention was commanded by Tilly, who sat at his other side. The dancer kept him well occupied with questions and stories.

In the afternoon Warrington was back at work with his riding. Antonia divided her time between practicing her mandolin and deciding which songs she should sing for her first performance. Everyone kept very busy and the day passed swiftly.

When night fell, the troupe joined together around the fire once again. Pickering and Jocko lit their pipes and sat contentedly staring at the flames.

Antonia was persuaded to sing and she kept them listening with rapt attention. When she was done, Pickering declared that he had never heard a better singer. "Yes, with Miss Richards and Bradford and young Jem and his dog, we'll have an even better show than before," he declared. "Why, it was damned lucky that Wilkins and Daisy left us. We are well rid of them.

"And while Bradford has far to go before he can compare to Wilkins, I don't doubt that he will soon surpass him. We will have new placards printed when we get to Shrewsbury."

"Do you think Jack Bradford is a dashing enough name for the placard?" said Michael Flynn. "It seems rather dull. Jack Bradford and Daphne doesn't sound in the least thrilling."

"And was 'Wilkins' so very exciting?" asked his lordship, eyeing Flynn with disfavor.

"Oh, he wasn't known by that," said Flynn. "He was 'The Great Count Orlando.'"

"Good God," said the viscount and Antonia laughed.

Jem spoke up. "At Larchmont, Mr. Bradford was sometimes called 'Gentleman Jack.'"

Pickering's face lit up. "Gentleman Jack? By God, it's right on the mark. 'Gentleman Jack' it will be."

"Gentleman Jack and 'is Magic Mare," suggested Tilly.

"Splendid, my girl," said Pickering. "That sounds very well indeed. Now, Miss Richards, do favor us with one more song before we retire."

Antonia rather reluctantly agreed and began to sing. When she was finished, the members of the troupe applauded enthusiastically. Then Pickering suggested they all retire. After all, he said, they must rise early and begin their labors.

Warrington, who had been rather frustrated that he hadn't had much opportunity to speak with Antonia, was disappointed that she went directly to her wagon. He stood outside his own wagon, none too eager to go inside.

Michael Flynn joined him. He took out a cigar. "Might I offer you one, Bradford?" he said. When Warrington declined, he went to the fire and, taking up a firebrand, lit his cigar. He then sauntered back to where the viscount was standing. "I wanted to ask you something, Bradford," said the acrobat, puffing on his cigar, "about you and Miss Richards?"

"I have no desire to discuss Miss Richards with you, Flynn," said his lordship, a trace of aristocratic hauteur in his voice.

"Come, come," said Flynn, "I only want to know whether you've a claim on the girl. She's a damned pretty little wench."

Warrington bristled. "You'll not speak of her in those terms. She is a respectable lady."

"Now don't get your back up, old lad," said Flynn.

"I suggest you keep your distance from Miss Richards," said the viscount, ill-humoredly.

"Oh, I shall do so," returned the acrobat, "but you cannot fault me for admiring the girl. What man wouldn't?"

Since the viscount had no wish to continue this conversation, he made no reply, but went into the wagon. Flynn stayed outside, smoking his cigar, and gazing meditatively at the wagon where Antonia and Tilly had retired to bed.

The next two days passed quickly for both Warrington and Antonia. The troupe remained encamped at the same location so that Pickering could instruct the viscount. Warrington worked tirelessly on his riding, and by the third day, he had mastered a routine that, although not spectacular by the standards of Astley's Amphitheater, would certainly do for local entertainments.

Antonia spent her time practicing her songs and assisting Mrs. Pickering and Tilly with costumes. Jem was busy as well, working with Jocko to teach Baldric enough tricks for the upcoming performance.

Very early on the morning of the third day, they packed up the wagons, broke camp and started for the town of Wenlock. Pickering had announced that they would have a short engagement there before proceeding on to Shrewsbury. Because the weather persisted in being dry and fine, they made very good progress and arrived at the small village of Wenlock in the early evening.

The next morning there was a sense of excitement among the circus troupe as they made preparations for the afternoon's show. Yet there was so much to do that Antonia had little time to be nervous about her upcoming debut as a performer.

Warrington, too, was well occupied with his own work, practicing his stunts one more time in the morning and then submitting to the final fitting of the costume that had been prepared for him. The viscount had insisted that he would not appear in the costume of a sheik of Araby as Tilly had suggested. Instead, "Gentleman Jack" was attired in a peacock blue waistcoat, white shirt, and buff-colored riding breeches.

As the afternoon performance time approached, the company made ready. Dressed in their purple tights, the Flynn brothers did a few stretches and flips to limber up, while Jocko tossed his balls in a final practice session.

Tilly and Antonia retired to their wagon to don their costumes. While Antonia still was none too pleased at how Tilly persisted in throwing herself at Warrington, she found it hard to dislike the dancer.

They helped each other with their costumes and hair, and each complimented the other on her appearance. Antonia, however, stared at her reflection doubtfully in the small mirror. "Perhaps I should put some lace in the neckline," she said, frowning at her decolletage.

"Lord in 'eaven, no," cried Tilly. "You'd disappoint the gents, my dear. Now, come, there's no time for fussing about. We must go. 'Tis nearly time."

The two young women climbed out of the wagon. Warrington, who had been talking with Jem and Jocko, turned to stare at them. Antonia stood attired in the scarlet gown, her dark hair festooned with ribbons of matching scarlet satin. The viscount was momentarily speechless. He'd never seen her look more beautiful. The flamboyant dress showed off Antonia's figure to full advantage, with the low-cut neckline providing an enticing display of her charms.

Noting that Warrington seemed focused on her companion,

Tilly stepped forward. She wore a daring new costume with a tight-fitting, low-cut bodice and filmy harem pants. "Don't we all look grand, gentlemen?" she said.

"Yes," said Warrington, smiling first at Tilly and then Antonia.

"You're both beautiful," said Jem, who appeared awed at the sight of the ladies.

Antonia, who felt rather self-conscious in her revealing dress, smiled graciously at the compliment. "You look wonderful, Jem," she said, "and Baldric looks very handsome."

The boy grinned. Like Jocko, he was attired in a multicolored harlequin costume, and Baldric had an Elizabethan ruff fastened around his neck.

Mrs. Pickering then appeared, causing Warrington to regard her in some surprise. The elderly woman was dressed in a mustard-yellow skirt and white blouse. A matching yellow kerchief was tied about her head and huge gold earrings dangled from her ears. Around her shoulders was a brightly colored paisley shawl with long fringe.

Noting the viscount's expression, Tilly laughed. "You've not seen Madame Lenska, the fortuneteller, before, 'ave you, Mr. Bradford? You must tell 'is fortune, madame, and Tony's. I've 'eard mine often enough. I'm to be rich and 'ave seven children."

"Why, what a good idea," said Mrs. Pickering. "We've a bit of time. Show me your palm, Miss Richards."

Antonia extended her hand. Taking it in hers, the elderly woman examined the lines of her palm. "Why, aren't you the lucky one? You'll be a great success in the circus."

"One don't 'ave to be a fortuneteller for that," said Tilly. "Tony's got the voice of a nightingale. Do tell 'er something we don't know."

Mrs. Pickering studied the palm again. "Why, you've a brilliant future and a long life. You'll marry a grand lord and be very happy."

"Aren't you the lucky one, Tony?" said Tilly with a merry grin.

Warrington, who had heard the prognostication, stared thoughtfully at Antonia. "And now you, Mr. Bradford," said Tilly. "Give Mrs. Pickering your 'and."

"And then I should like my fortune told," said Jem eagerly.

"Do the boy first, Mrs. Pickering," said Warrington. "I'm not so eager to know my future."

Jem held out his hand and was gratified when the circus owner's wife proclaimed that he would be rich and marry a sweet, lovely girl. Pickering appeared at this moment and commanded his employees to look sharp and cease their lollygagging about. They had a show to do, he reminded them, and it was nearly time for the performance to begin.

A large crowd had assembled and the audience seemed to be getting impatient for the circus to start. Four tough-looking men were particularly vocal in shouting for the show to begin.

Pickering gave the men a withering look and then he turned to Warrington. "As you're the last act, my boy, perhaps you might station yourself near those ruffians in case they cause trouble."

The viscount nodded and went to stand near the four rough men. Pickering, attired in black coat, a red waistcoat, white pantaloons, and a tall, black hat, made his way to the front of the crowd. After making a flourishing bow, he put a hand up to quiet the audience. "Ladies and gentlemen," he called out in his deep voice, "I'm Thadeus B. Pickering and I'm proud to bring you Pickering's Amazing Circus. Our company will delight and amaze you!"

"It'd better for sixpence!" cried one of the men near Warrington and the crowd laughed.

Pickering scowled, but then he continued. "Today we bring you a lady all the way from Araby! The lovely, exotic Princess Fatima!!"

The crowd clapped loudly as Tilly made her appearance. Jocko, who had an odd turban on his head, sat on a stool and began to play a near-eastern sounding melody on the recorder. Tilly began to dance. Tapping a tambourine, she moved her hips seductively, much to the delight of the tough-looking men, who whistled and shouted. When she finished her dance in a wild whirl, the audience applauded enthusiastically.

Pickering stepped out again and began to melodramatically recite a poem about a lass from Araby. Most of the crowd listened attentively to this, but the troublemaking men in back began to hoot and holler for the circus owner to stop. "Get on with the show!" yelled one burly fellow with red hair and freckles.

Raising his voice over the men, Pickering managed to finish and the crowd clapped. Frowning once more at the hecklers, he began his introduction of Jocko. The juggler came before them, expertly tossing up ball after ball and keeping them all aloft. A loud cheer came up from the crowd, but again, the men in back seemed dissatisfied. "Bring back the wench!" cried the burly redheaded man in a drunken voice and they all laughed.

When Jem appeared with Baldric, the men showed a little more interest in the little black dog's tricks. However, they were soon calling again for Princess Fatima's return. Warrington, irritated at the men's behavior, gave them disgusted looks, but they cheerfully ignored him.

Pickering, although he was used to such disagreeable elements in crowds, was growing exceedingly angry with the hecklers. He nonetheless retained his composure. "And now you will hear the most angelic singing outside of the heavens. May I present the beautiful songbird, Miss Antonia Richards."

Warrington smiled as Antonia appeared before the crowd with her mandolin. She looked radiant and very beautiful. She curtsied low and the drunken red-haired man grinned and shouted loudly, "By God, you're a pretty little thing!"

The viscount flashed a warning look at the man as Antonia began to strum her mandolin, and he was quiet. As she began to sing, there were approving murmurs among the onlookers. A respectful silence followed as Antonia's lovely voice enveloped them. When she finished the song, the audience erupted into deafening applause. Antonia sang three more songs, and each time the crowd loudly voiced its approval.

Pickering, looking exceedingly well-satisfied by the reaction to his new singer, bowed to Antonia. She curtsied to him and the crowd and then she walked off to the side.

The drunken man near Warrington shoved away several people in front of him and lumbered off toward Antonia, who had made her exit. The viscount, seeing him, hurried after him, but the red-haired man reached Antonia before Warrington could stop him. "You're the prettiest creature," he said, grabbing Antonia's arm. "I'll have a kiss, my girl."

She regarded him with a horrified expression. "Let go of me, sir," she said, attempting to pull her arm away.

Warrington was upon the man at once, giving him a mighty shove that sent him sprawling to the ground.

The drunken man seemed dumbfounded for a minute, but then he got up and lunged toward the viscount. "Jack!" cried Antonia. Warrington connected his fist with the man's jaw and the fellow went sprawling. He sat up and looked groggily around him for a moment. Then he fell back down.

The crowd's attention had shifted from the acrobatic Flynns to the fight occurring in the wings and they cheered loudly at the viscount's knockout blow. Several stepped forward to congratulate Warrington.

Michael Flynn was none too pleased to see the crowd's attention focused away from him. He and his brother continued on with their act, hoping that their daring maneuvers would soon reengage the audience. Once the red-haired man was sent on his way, the onlookers' interest in the Flynns was restored.

"The drunken idiot," muttered Warrington, taking Antonia by the arm and escorting her away from the crowd. "Are you all right, Tony?" The name "Tony" slipped out. He'd heard Tilly using it and had found it quite suitable for Antonia.

"Yes, of course," she said, smiling up at him. "Thank you."

"You were marvelous," he said.

"You are very kind. But you mustn't stay here. You'll soon be announced." She smiled at him again. "Your debut as a trick rider is upon you."

Warrington nodded. "I'd best get ready."

"Do be careful, Jack," said Antonia.

While the viscount had the urge to kiss her at that moment, he only nodded and went off toward his horse.

Pickering, who'd observed the viscount punching out the heckler, was very pleased to see the unruly spectator get his comeuppance. When the acrobats were finished with their act, he put up a hand. "Now, ladies and gentlemen, it is my special honor to present our next performer. Some of you have already witnessed the young man's skill with his fists." At this, several in the crowd gave a loud cheer. Pickering put up his hand again. "But now, my friends, you will see him as a daredevil on horseback. Ladies and gentlemen, may I introduce Gentleman Jack!"

The audience gave a mighty yell as Warrington rode into the

field before them. As he raced Daphne around in a ring, he proceeded to swing himself from one side of the horse to the other. The crowd gasped and then clapped as he nimbly jumped back into the saddle.

Antonia watched the viscount with considerable trepidation as he continued to perform various stunts. When he finally got to the most difficult maneuver, of standing up on the animal as it charged about in a circle, Antonia held her breath. However, much to her relief, he stayed on top of the horse, even managing to wave one arm above his head.

The crowd went wild at this daring display and Pickering looked out at the gathering with a satisfied expression. He was already calculating the money that such an act would bring in. Why with a trick rider like Gentleman Jack and Antonia's singing, Pickering was certain that they would no longer be limited to rural engagements.

The audience seemed thrilled by the afternoon's entertainments and milled about for some time, chattering to each other on Warrington's amazing feats and Antonia's exceptional voice. Jem and Baldric went into the crowd, continuing to delight them with the little dog's antics, while Mrs. Pickering made some additional revenue with her fortunetelling.

Finally, the last circus-goer had departed and the troupe was left alone. Fatima lavishly praised the viscount's riding, while Michael Flynn stayed next to Antonia, proclaiming that she had the loveliest voice in the kingdom.

Jem and Baldric hurried up to Antonia and the acrobat. "You were splendid, miss!" cried Jem and Baldric danced about and barked excitedly.

Antonia leaned down and gave him a hug. "Thank you, Jem. You and Baldric were wonderful." Flynn was a bit put out that Jem didn't mention his performance.

Warrington, finally freeing himself from Fatima, made his way to Antonia. He smiled at her. "So, Tony, how does it feel to be a sensation?"

She smiled back at him. "I could ask you that question. You were marvelous, Jack." Antonia paused and fixed a mischievous expression on him. "But I do hope you won't have to add fisticuffs to your act. I fear Mr. Pickering may think it a fine idea."

Warrington laughed and the two of them continued to talk about the day's exciting events. Flynn regarded them with interest. He had taken a distinct fancy to Antonia and, despite what he had told the viscount, he had never been a man to let the fact that a lady already had a lover or husband stand in his way.

Having great confidence in his ability to charm the female sex, he had no doubt that he could win Antonia away from Warrington. It was a pity that he had a rival, he thought, but that would make the game all the more interesting.

As Flynn watched Warrington, he decided it would be amusing to steal Antonia from the man. After all, he certainly didn't appreciate having the fellow getting all the acclaim. It was galling that a newcomer received so much attention. Yes, thought Flynn, it would be a distinct pleasure to gain Antonia's affections, and he resolved to do all he could to win her.

18

The next morning the circus company had to pick up and move on to Shrewsbury, some eighteen miles distant. After a hasty breakfast, Antonia was in the wagon, helping Tilly put away some of her clothes, when Mrs. Pickering appeared at the door.

"Tilly, my dear," said Mrs. Pickering, "I wondered if you might ride with me today. I was telling Mr. Pickering that you should have another new costume and I'd like to discuss the matter with you. I have had some very interesting ideas."

The young woman's face brightened. "Ooooo, another new costume?"

Mrs. Pickering nodded. "I thought we could go to a linen drapers while we're in Shrewsbury."

"Oh, yes!" cried Tilly, quickly stashing the last of her clothes in her trunk and shutting the lid with a bang. With scarcely a look at Antonia, she climbed down out of the wagon and began to talk excitedly about her ideas for a new costume. "I think I'd fancy a pink gauze," she was saying as she and Mrs. Pickering walked away, "and a gold tiara!" The old woman cast a backward smile at Antonia, and then she turned her attention to the dancer.

Picking up a filmy shawl that Tilly had left on the floor, Antonia stood in front of the dancer's small dressing table. Draping the material over her mouth like a veil, she stared into the mirror, trying to effect a look of mystery.

"Are you thinking of taking up dancing?" came a voice behind her and she jumped. Quickly putting down the shawl, she turned to find Warrington staring in at her, a broad smile on his face.

Antonia colored slightly. "I think one dancer is enough for Pickering's Amazing Circus," she said.

The viscount shook his head. "A pity," he said, his blue eyes twinkling. "I should've liked to have seen you as a dancing lady from Araby."

Antonia ignored this, noting that he had his horse behind him. "Are you riding Daphne today?" she asked.

"No, I'm going to tie her to your wagon since I'm to be your driver."

"What?" asked Antonia, with a surprised look. "I thought Jocko was . . ."

"Poor Jocko's feeling a bit under the weather," explained the viscount in a sympathetic tone.

"Oh, dear," said Antonia, looking rather worried. She had become fond of the Scotsman and was very disturbed to hear that he ill was.

"It's nothing serious," said Warrington, who knew that the only thing ailing Jocko was the fact that he had imbibed a good deal of gin the night before. "He'll be well soon, I assure you. I volunteered to drive you and Tilly."

"I fear you'll be disappointed. Tilly is riding with Mrs. Pickering."

Warrington put on a look of mock disappointment. "Is she?" He paused, and then he grinned up at her. "Well, I suppose I'll just have to make the best of it." After tying Daphne to the back of the wagon and hitching the wagon to one of the circus's large white horses, he returned to Antonia. "Come, Tony," he said, assisting her out of the back of the wagon and then up into the seat in front.

As he started to climb up, Jem appeared. As usual, Baldric was racing along at the boy's side.

"Mr. Bradford! Miss!" cried Jem. "Mr. Pickering said I was to ride with you!"

Since Warrington had been so pleased at having some time alone with Antonia, he was more than a little disappointed to see Jem. Yet, he nodded. "Then up you go, lad," he said, helping the boy into the wagon. The viscount grabbed Baldric and handed him to Jem. He then climbed up himself.

The seat didn't provide much room for three people and a dog, and Antonia found herself pressed against Warrington. Disturbed by the sensations his closeness was provoking within her, she hoped that she wasn't blushing.

As the viscount took up the reins and directed the horse onto the road, Antonia was glad when Jem began to chatter gaily about their visit to Shrewsbury. "It should be a bang-up fair, don't you think, miss?" he asked, fixing his lopsided grin on her.

"I'm certain it will be," she replied.

"And Shrewsbury is so much bigger than Wenlock," he said. "Baldric and I did quite well there. Two gentlemen gave me a shilling, and a lady and a gentleman sixpence. And Mr. Pickering said we could keep any money we made."

"That's splendid, Jem," said Warrington. "No one tossed me any coins. Did they give you any, Miss Richards?"

"Someone did throw me a rose," said Antonia, pleased to remember her triumph.

" 'Tis better to have a coin," said Jem, patting Baldric.

"Not to a lady," said Antonia, with a smile.

Jem reached into his pockets and proudly put out his hands. There were a several shiny coins resting in his palms. " 'Tis three shillings."

Warrington looked over at Antonia. "It appears our young friend is already on his way to making his fortune."

"It certainly does. You've done very well for yourself, Jem."

The boy smiled at her, and then he leaned back in the seat and sighed happily. "I do love the circus, don't you, miss?"

Antonia glanced at Warrington and found that he was regarding her with a mischievous expression.

"I daresay, she likes it better than being governess to the young misses at Larchmont," Warrington said.

Jem nodded vigorously. "Aye, 'tis much better not being in service. Why, a fellow feels more like his own man, don't you think, Mr. Bradford?"

Warrington smiled at the boy. "You're right there, my lad."

The boy patted Baldric on the head and turned a philosophical gaze out at the passing scenery. "A fellow ain't nothing being in service to gentry like Sir Harold and Mr. Geoffrey. Why, they scarcely know a body exists, excepting when you make a mistake and give you the end of their boot."

Warrington regarded the boy with a reflective look. The viscount had suddenly thought of his own servants. He had to admit that he'd been damned indifferent toward the men and women who'd kept his household running so efficiently. In fact, he realized, he knew practically nothing about any of his servants, even Bishop, his butler.

Frowning, the viscount remembered how he'd always thought his father showed too much concern over the welfare of his servants. He paid them ridiculously high wages and made a fuss over their anniversaries of service to him. Warrington's frown deepened. Society's rule was that one shouldn't be too familiar with domestics and, unlike his father, he had followed that law to the letter. He doubted that he would ever view servants in the same light again.

Antonia was also pensive, thinking about her brief employment at Larchmont. Remembering Geoffrey and his infamous conduct toward her, she shook her head. She was very grateful to be away from there. Turning to Jem, she suddenly smiled. "I do love the circus, Jem," she said.

The boy nodded again and petted the little black dog. "Aye, and so does Baldric. Don't you, boy?" he asked. Baldric turned around and grinned at them all, revealing his white teeth.

Jem then began to ask Warrington various questions about trick riding and the viscount was glad to be distracted from his unpleasant thoughts concerning his indifference as an employer. Soon, he was in much better spirits as he discussed riding.

After exhausting that topic, Jem began to talk about Shrewsbury. Never having been there, or to any city of any size, the boy was quite excited at the prospect. He continued to babble on about what a splendid time they would have.

Finally, when the boy ran out of subjects for discussion, he asked Antonia to sing. She agreed, with the stipulation that they accompany her. Jem sang along lustily, if somewhat off-key. However, Antonia discovered that Warrington had a fine baritone voice.

They were having such an enjoyable ride that the day went quickly. It seemed like no time at all before they reached their destination. Seeing the spires of the Shrewsbury cathedral and noting the bustle about him, Jem was quite thrilled as they drove into the city. He looked out at the scene around him with wide eyes.

The fair was in progress and brightly colored tents filled a large area on the outskirts of the town. A great number of people were milling back and forth. At one end of the fairgrounds, there was a

track with several sleek-looking racehorses prancing nearby.
"Look!" cried Jem excitedly. "It looks like there's going to be a
race!"

The viscount glanced over at the track and eyed the horses with
great interest. His sporting blood rose within him as he pulled up
the wagon to get a better look at the equine competitors. Warrington called out to a man who was walking past them leading a large
black stallion. "That's a fine animal," said the viscount.

The man stopped and looked up at them. "Thunderbolt is that all
right. And as fast as the wind. If you're wise, young man, you'll
lay your wager on him."

Warrington continued to cast a critical eye on the horse.
"When's the race?"

"At two o'clock," said the man. After exchanging a few more
words with the viscount, he led the horse away.

"Will you place a wager, sir?" asked Jem.

Antonia turned to fix an inquiring gaze on Warrington. He
smiled. "No, lad, not I. That should please you, Miss Richards."

Feigning indifference, she shrugged. "What you do does not
concern me, Jack Bradford."

Laughing again, the viscount urged the horse on, driving the
wagon to the spot where the other two circus wagons had stopped.
He jumped down from the vehicle, and was quickly followed by
Jem, who scrambled from the wagon seat just in time to catch
Baldric, who leaped into his arms. He put the dog down on the
ground and the creature dashed off. Jem ran after him.

"Oh, dear," said Antonia, "I hope Baldric doesn't get into any
trouble."

"I'd say that is inevitable for the little rascal," said the viscount.
He held out his hand and helped her down from the seat. When she
was on the ground before him, he kept hold of her hand. "I did
enjoy our ride, Tony," he said, gazing down into her eyes. He was
about to say something further when Michael Flynn gave a shout.

"Miss Richards!" cried the acrobat, striding over to them. Warrington inwardly cursed the fellow and released Antonia's hand.
Flynn stopped before them and fixed his most charming smile on
Antonia. "I hope you aren't too tired after your journey," he said
in a solicitous voice.

"Oh, no, not in the least, Mr. Flynn."

"Good," said the acrobat, "because I thought you might wish to have a look at Shrewsbury. We are very close to the cathedral. I should be happy to escort you."

"That is very kind of you," said Antonia. "I would enjoy seeing the cathedral." Flynn looked very pleased, until she added, "I'm sure Tilly would love to see it as well. I shall ask her."

"I'm deuced fascinated by cathedrals," said Warrington. "I'll go as well. Yes, we'll make a party of it."

"That is a good idea," said Antonia. "Perhaps we might go as soon as we are settled."

While this was hardly what Flynn had had in mind, he could only nod and return to help his brother unhitch the horses from their wagon.

A short time later, Michael Flynn joined Antonia and Tilly, who were ready for the excursion to the cathedral. The dancer had taken a great deal of care with her appearance. She wore a bright magenta dress and matching pelisse, and a bonnet decorated with ivory plumes.

Antonia wore a dress she had borrowed from Tilly. It was a high-waisted lavender creation, with long sleeves, and a low neckline trimmed with lace. She had also borrowed Mrs. Pickering's paisley shawl and straw bonnet.

"I doubt that Bradford truly wanted to come," said Flynn, offering an arm to each lady. "We should go without him."

Tilly, who had no desire to do so, looked over and was happy to see Warrington appear. He was accompanied by Jem, who had a broad grin on his face. "Here we are," said the viscount, raising his hat to the ladies. "I hope you weren't waiting long. We had to secure Baldric to a stout chain."

" 'Tis a pity that dogs may not visit cathedrals," said Jem. "Baldric would have liked to come."

"Well, we must be off," said Tilly, tucking her arm inside Warrington's. "This will be such great fun."

While the viscount would have preferred another partner, he had little choice but to escort Tilly. Flynn followed behind with Antonia, and with Jem on her other side.

They made their way along the narrow streets of the town toward the cathedral. Tilly chattered happily and pressed Warrington's arm.

Flynn, who devoutly wished that Jem had stayed with the Pickerings, nonetheless tried to make the most of it. After all, it was still very pleasant to walk the streets of Shrewsbury with such a lovely young woman on his arm. And although Antonia did not seem so very interested in him, she was in good spirits, smiling at his witticisms and being altogether agreeable.

They all found Shrewsbury Cathedral most impressive. Jem, who had never seen a cathedral before, was quite awed at the high vaulted ceiling and stone carvings. It was rather frustrating for Warrington that Tilly kept such a firm grip on him. He had little opportunity to speak to Antonia, and he wasn't at all happy to see that Flynn was so attentive to her.

On their way back to the camp, the group walked again along the narrow sidewalks. As before, Tilly walked with Warrington, with Antonia, Flynn, and Jem behind them. After walking a short distance, they were met by two well-dressed young gentlemen walking in the opposite direction.

The strangers wore tall beaver hats, well-tailored coats, and pantaloons with gleaming Hessian boots. When they came up to Warrington and his party, they stopped and stood as if waiting for something.

The viscount slowed his pace and finally stopped before the men, who stood blocking their way and eyeing them with the bored, haughty expressions Warrington so often met in London drawing rooms. "Do be so good as to allow us to pass," said the taller of the two men.

"You may go into the street to pass us," said Warrington, with a frown.

"Egad, no," said the taller man, "I might soil my boots. Now be a good fellow and go around us."

"A gentleman must give way to ladies," said Warrington. "Move yourself."

"Oh, I would give way to *ladies*," said the man, giving Tilly and Antonia scornful looks. "The likes of you must give ground to gentlemen."

"And you're a gentleman?" said Warrington, reddening with anger. "I'd thought you were just a damned, supercilious fool. Now you move out of our way or, by God, you'll wish you had."

The man raised his eyebrows. "How dare you speak to me like that! Do you know who I am?"

"By God, I don't care if you're the Prince Regent himself," said Warrington. "Now make way for us."

The tall man appeared indignant, but seeming to realize that Warrington was not in the mood to be trifled with, he and his companion moved into the street.

"That's gentry for you," said Tilly, looking back and casting a scornful look at the men. "You gave 'em a proper setdown, Jack."

"A victory for the common man," said Flynn, tipping his hat to Warrington.

Antonia smiled at the viscount and, with everyone now in a jubilant mood, they proceeded on their way.

19

When they returned to the wagons, they busied themselves with preparations for the afternoon performance. Warrington spent his time grooming Daphne and talking with Pickering, who was quite pleased with the crowds of people milling about the fair. He was sure that the circus would do very well and that it would be a profitable day.

After Pickering had taken his leave, the viscount looked over at Antonia. She was seated on a stool in front of her wagon, practicing a song, with her mandolin in her lap. He'd been watching her from time to time, hoping to have a chance to talk with her. Seeing his opportunity, he put down his curry combs and walked over to her. He stood waiting until she'd finished singing.

"That was a dashed pretty song."

"Thank you, Jack."

"Would you like to take a stroll, Miss Richards?"

"Oh, I don't know if there is time," said Antonia.

"Just a short walk. I had no chance to talk with you when we went to the cathedral. I had hoped that I would."

"Did you? I didn't know that you were aware of my existence, since you were so well occupied with Tilly."

"How could I not be occupied with her? She had a grip on my arm like a bulldog. Now let us take a small turn around the grounds."

"Very well, Jack," she said, rising from her stool and putting down her mandolin.

They started walking away from the wagons, toward the crowds and tents. "Pickering thinks there will be a large audience today."

"I do hope so," said Antonia. "Although I do get rather nervous at the idea of singing before so many people."

"You have no reason to be nervous. You sing like an angel."

She smiled at the compliment. "Thank you, Jack."

They walked on, looking at the people and the tents and animals. Suddenly Antonia caught sight of the two men whom they had met on their way back from the cathedral. "Look, Jack, there are those odious men."

Warrington looked over to see the two well-dressed gentlemen, who were now standing with two ladies, who were attired in very fashionable clothes. Antonia smiled up at the viscount. "I thought it splendid how you refused to be cowed by them."

"Cowed by them?" said Warrington with a laugh. "My dear Tony, surely you didn't expect me to be intimidated by an ill-mannered provincial popinjay?"

"No, I suppose not. You have a refreshing disregard for rank."

The viscount could not help but smile at this. He was about to reply, when there was a tug at his sleeve. Looking over, he saw Jem standing there. At his side was Baldric, who was on a leather leash. "Mrs. Pickering sent me, sir," he said. "Miss Richards is needed. She must help her with Tilly's veil. She wants you to hurry, miss. 'Tis urgent."

"I cannot imagine what could be urgent about Tilly's veil," said Antonia. "Very well. I shall go back." She looked over at Warrington. "There is no need for you to escort me. Do continue your walk. Jem can accompany you."

"Oh, I'd like that," said Jem, "and so would Baldric."

Although the viscount was disappointed at having his time with Antonia cut short, he watched her hurry off and then began to walk along with Jem.

" 'Tis a marvelous place, ain't it, sir?"

"The fair?"

"Aye," said Jem. "And Shrewsbury. I've never seen such a grand place."

"Yes, it is grand," said Warrington, suppressing a smile.

"Do you think we could see the horse race?" said Jem. "It will be starting soon."

"I'm always game for a horse race," said the viscount, and they set off for the race course.

When they arrived, the viscount eyed the horses with considerable interest. Spotting a handsome chestnut stallion, he studied it appraisingly. "There's a right one, Jem. The chestnut."

"He's a beauty," said Jem, "but I'll wager he couldn't hold a candle to Caesar."

"One can't expect to find the like of Caesar everywhere, lad," said his lordship. "But there are some good horses here. The chestnut is one."

A stout, gray-haired man, who was standing nearby, heard this remark. Identifying himself as the owner of the chestnut, he complimented Warrington on being an excellent judge of horseflesh. He then went on to discuss the horses's pedigree and racing history. Before he departed, he told the viscount that he could do far worse than placing a bet on his horse. The chestnut horse wasn't the favorite, that honor going to Thunderbolt, the black horse they had seen earlier.

"Do you think he'll win?" said Jem, after the chestnut stallion's owner had walked off.

"I shouldn't be surprised," replied Warrington, fixing a regretful look on the horse. The horse had the look of a winner about him and had the viscount not been bound by his promise not to wager, he wouldn't have hesitated to join the group of men who were placing their bets.

Warrington thought of the bargain he'd made with his father. He'd sworn he wouldn't gamble for a month and he would not. It occurred to the viscount that he had already gone a very long time without betting. Yet the odd thing was that he hadn't given much thought to it.

When he was in town, there was hardly a day that he didn't place a bet on something. If it wasn't a horse race, it was a bout of fisticuffs, a boat race, or a game of billiards. Oftentimes at his club, he'd placed wagers on all kinds of trivial and amusing things.

Now, however, he'd almost got out of the habit of wagering. Yet seeing the throng of men placing bets, Warrington felt the old familiar urge once again.

Lost in his thoughts, the viscount realized that Jem was tapping his arm. "Mr. Bradford," said the boy, "are you going to place a wager on the race?"

Warrington shook his head. "No, lad, I told you before I wouldn't."

"I was thinking of betting my money," said Jem, taking some coins from his pocket. "I've got ten shillings. 'Tis mine and Jocko's. He gave me some to wager, if you knew which horse to bet on."

"But where is Jocko?"

"Oh, he didn't want to see the race. He said he's very bad luck for races, and no horse he wants would win if he was there to see the race. Will you help me to place a bet, sir, on the chestnut to win?"

A smile appeared on the viscount's face. What harm was there in placing a small wager for Jem and Jocko? "Very well, lad, but we'd better hurry. There isn't much time left."

After placing the bet, they returned to watch the race. They didn't have to wait long for it to begin. The horses were quickly lined up, and in minutes they were off. The crowd yelled loudly as the horses raced past them. Jem could scarcely contain his excitement. Scooping up Baldric into his arms, he cheered loudly as the chestnut horse took the lead. Baldric also appeared thrilled by the race and gave several shrill barks.

The chestnut continued in the lead for a time, but then a black horse began coming up rapidly from behind. Jem's face fell as he watched the chestnut's lead crumble and the black horse striding neck and neck with him. When the black horse finished first by a head, Jem was devastated.

The viscount put a hand on the boy's shoulder. "Bad luck, lad," he said. "But it was very close."

"Jocko will be sorely disappointed," he said, putting Baldric down on the ground.

"A sportsman can't win every time, lad," said his lordship.

"I suppose not," said Jem gloomily. "We'd best be going back to the wagons, Mr. Bradford." Warrington nodded and they started walking back, the little black dog hurrying along with them.

When they arrived back at the camp, they met Antonia, who was dressed in her scarlet gown, ready for the afternoon's program.

"There you are," she said. "You haven't much time. You'd best get ready quickly." Then noting that Jem looked rather downcast, she added, "Is something the matter, Jem?"

Looking up at her, he sighed. " 'Tis only I put a wager on a horse, miss, and I lost all of my money and Jocko's. Ten shillings it was. I hate to tell Jocko."

"Oh, Jem," said Antonia, "haven't I told you it is foolish to gamble?"

"I know, miss," said Jem, hanging his head.

"Well, you'd best find Jocko and tell him."

"Yes, miss," said Jem, walking off with Baldric.

"Well, these things happen," said Warrington. "It was a pity, but the horse came in second. And it was very close."

Antonia frowned at the viscount. "What does that signify? The boy lost his money. He would have done just as well to toss it into the river. Did you know Jem was placing a wager?"

Warrington shrugged. "Yes, of course."

"And did you gamble as well?"

"No, I did not," said the viscount.

"But you didn't prevent Jem from doing so?"

"I don't see why you must fly into the boughs over the matter," said Warrington. "It was a stroke of bad luck."

"Bad luck indeed that Jem is to be influenced by a gamester," said Antonia angrily. "So you think it fine to encourage him in such evil folly?"

"Evil folly? Come, come, Miss Richards, you sound like a nonconformist preacher. The boy only lost a few shillings."

"He lost all the money he had," returned Antonia. "And what will it be the next time?"

The viscount frowned. "Dash it, Tony. I'm sorry you think me such a bad influence on the lad. Perhaps Jem should spend more time with Flynn. I suppose you think *him* a paragon."

"I don't see what Mr. Flynn has to do with anything."

The viscount regarded her with some frustration. "I think it best if we say nothing more about this. Excuse me, Miss Richards, I have work to do." He made a slight bow and then walked off, leaving Antonia to watch his departure with a frown.

20

Pickering was very pleased with the afternoon's performance. Everything went splendidly. There was a very large audience and no hecklers to deal with. The crowd appeared quite appreciative of all of the acts, applauding loudly and watching attentively.

Antonia received an enthusiastic ovation. The crowd cheered and called again and again for her to sing another song.

It was some time before she was able to break away so that the Flynn brothers could appear. The acrobats were also popular with the audience and many ladies in attendance were quite smitten with the good looks and charming smile of the fair-haired Michael Flynn.

The audience was especially fond of Jem and Baldric. Everyone roared with laughter at the antics of the little black dog, who danced about on his hind legs, jumped through hoops, and barked on command.

When Warrington rode out to do his daredevil stunts, the onlookers were delighted. The ladies all thought him very dashing and the gentlemen conceded that he was a fine rider indeed.

Antonia, who stood with the others watching the viscount's trick riding, held her breath several times as she feared that he might go tumbling off his mount. Yet it all went flawlessly.

At the conclusion of the show, the performers went out to take their bows and all were very gratified with the cheers and applause. As the audience started to depart, Pickering congratulated his troupe for their outstanding work.

Jem, who was in a euphoric mood, scurried off, saying that he and Baldric were going to perform among the crowds. The boy and the dog stopped in the midst of a number of people and the little black dog began to dance about. The crowd laughed and clapped, and a few of them tossed coins at Jem's feet. Picking up the money, the boy grinned, figuring that it would be no time at all before he replenished the funds he'd lost on the horse race.

"Come on, Baldric," he said, eyeing the dog with a gleeful expression, "let's try them over there." Baldric barked and the two of them ran through a milling mob of fair-goers. As he was moving through the crowd, he suddenly knocked into a man.

"I beg your pardon, sir," said Jem, looking up. To his surprise he saw the tall, young gentleman who had told them to get off the sidewalk.

The man glared down at Jem. Startled, the boy felt retreat was the most prudent course of action. He hurried off, vanishing into the crowd.

A pale, elegantly dressed, middle-aged lady, who accompanied the man, turned to him. "Why, Robert, that was the little urchin in the circus," she said. "What a coincidence that you were just telling me about how you met those circus performers this morning."

"Yes, Mama," said the gentleman. "I was very much surprised to recognize them. I might have known they were circus performers. They were so vulgar and insolent. I don't know why we must tolerate such ruffians in our town. And then to have the wretched boy nearly knock me down."

"He certainly ran off quickly," said his mother.

"Yes, like a guilty thief," he said. As soon as he had said these words, a thought occurred to him. "He might have been a pickpocket." He put his hand in his pocket and was glad to find his purse was there. Then he reached for his watch. "Good God!" he cried as he found his watch pocket empty. "My watch is gone! He was a thief!"

"Oh, dear!" cried the lady.

"Well, I shan't stand for this. Come, Mama, we must find the constable." The young gentleman took his mother's arm and escorted her away. It didn't take them long to find the police officer, who was a large red-faced man.

"What is the matter, Lord Sidgewick?" asked the constable, addressing the tall young gentleman.

"I was robbed," said Sidgewick.

"Robbed, my lord?"

"I was walking with my mother when a boy rushed into me. It was the brat from the circus."

"The lad with the little dog?" said the constable, surprised, for he had seen and very much enjoyed Jem's performance.

"Yes, that is the boy," said Lady Sidgewick. "You know what these circus performers are like, officer. They can't be trusted among decent folk."

"The minute the boy dashed away, I discovered that my watch was stolen!" said Sidgewick. "The little scamp pickpocketed it! I want him caught and punished."

"You can be sure that I will do all I can to restore your watch to you, my lord," said the constable. "I shall deal with the matter immediately."

Sidgewick nodded. "I expect you to bring him to justice, Dobbs."

The constable assured him that he would do his best and the young man and his mother seemed satisfied.

Jem, who had been rather unnerved by seeing the disagreeable young man, decided it was time to return to his friends. He had already collected several coins and he was eager to show Miss Richards how well they had done. Arriving at the wagons, he greeted Antonia warmly. They stood talking for a while, but were interrupted by the appearance of the red-faced constable, who was accompanied by a brawny young man.

"There you are," said the police officer, regarding the boy with a menacing expression. "You are to come with me."

"Whatever for?" said Antonia. "What is this about?"

The constable grasped Jem firmly by the arm. "This boy stole a watch from a gentleman."

"What!" cried Jem. "I didn't steal anything!"

Baldric, alarmed for his young master, lunged at the constable and would have bitten him if Warrington had not rushed to his rescue, grabbing the little dog and pulling him away. "What is going on?" demanded the viscount.

"I'm taking the lad into custody," said the constable. "He is accused of being a pickpocket, of stealing Lord Sidgewick's watch."

"That's utter nonsense," said the viscount. He looked at Jem. "Did you steal a watch?"

"I swear I didn't, sir!" cried Jem.

"There must be some mistake," said Antonia. "I'm sure Jem did nothing wrong."

"We will see about that," said the constable. "I'm going to search the boy. He may have the watch hidden on him."

Jem submitted to the search with an anguished expression. When the police officer found nothing but the coins Jem had just collected, he frowned. "It means nothing. The boy might have hidden it somewhere here. Or perhaps he gave it to one of you."

"We will search these wagons."

By this time Pickering had arrived and he began to protest. "Search our wagons? By God, you will not!"

"Then you have something to hide?" said the constable.

"No," sputtered Pickering.

"Mr. Dobbs," said the brawny young man who had accompanied the constable, "that man has a watch in his pocket." He pointed at Warrington.

The viscount's eyes widened in surprise. "This is my watch," he said.

"Give it here," said the constable.

Warrington regarded the man indignantly. Fearing that he would only make matters worse by losing his temper, Antonia caught his arm. "Show them the watch, Jack."

The viscount reluctantly handed it over and the constable frowned. "Where did the likes of you get a watch like this?"

"It was given to me on my sixteenth birthday."

"Indeed?" said the constable, noting that a coat of arms was engraved on the back of the watch. "We'll ask Lord Sidgewick if this be his watch.

"You'll both come with me. Right now."

"Very well," said the viscount. "You'll soon see that this isn't this Lord Sidgewick's watch."

"Yes, yes," said the constable, and he escorted Jem and Warrington away, with Antonia and Pickering following behind.

Lord Sidgewick and his mother had returned to their home, which was a short distance from the town. Young Baron Sidgewick and his mother lived in a grand country house of recent construction, which was surrounded by a spacious park.

After sitting in the drawing room for a time with his mother bemoaning the lawlessness of the era, Sidgewick retired to his room to rest before changing for dinner. When he entered his bedchamber, a shiny object on his dressing table caught his eye. It was his watch!

Sidgewick walked over and picked it up. "Damn me if I didn't take my watch today," he said aloud. "Thank God." The baron was very much relieved. He had paid a good deal of money for the watch and had been very unhappy at the idea of losing it.

Of course, his mother would think him addlepated when he told her. After staring thoughtfully at the watch for a moment, Sidgewick placed it in a drawer. He'd tell his mother about it later. He was in no mood to have himself made sport of, and his mother was the sort of woman who'd laugh and call him the greatest mutton head. Frowning at the thought, he closed the drawer.

Leaving his room, he walked slowly down the great curved stairway that led to the entry hall. He supposed that he must go back to Shrewsbury to tell the constable he'd found the watch. No, there was no getting around that.

Sidgewick was glad to find that his mother had gone out to take a look at her rose garden. He informed his butler that he had an errand in town. Then he left the house and had a groom saddle his horse.

When Sidgewick arrived in Shrewsbury, he went directly to the see the constable. He found Dobbs looking very pleased with himself.

"Lord Sidgewick," said the police officer, rising quickly to his feet, "I was just about to go inform your lordship that the miscreants have been secured. I have taken them into custody."

"Taken *them*?" said Sidgewick. "I though it was just the boy."

The constable shook his head. "He had an accomplice. I'll have Higgins fetch them." He went to the doorway of the office and called out for his assistant. "Bring the prisoners in here, Higgins."

"I don't think that will be necessary," said the baron, but Dobbs didn't seem to hear him.

"Excuse me, my lord," he said, vanishing for a short time.

He returned a moment later with his assistant, the brawny young man, and Warrington and Jem. Recognizing the viscount as the man he'd met on the street that morning, Sidgewick frowned. "You!" he said.

Warrington eyed him in surprise. So this was the man whose watch Jem had allegedly stolen.

"Have you seen this man before, my lord?" said the constable.

Sidgewick nodded. "Yes, he nearly pushed me off the sidewalk this very morning. He behaved in the most insolent and threatening manner."

"Did he?" said Dobbs. "Well, he was the one who had your lordship's watch."

"It's my watch," said Warrington. "Take a look at it. You'll see it isn't yours. And then tell this . . . man to release us. Jem never took your watch."

"Be quiet," snapped Dobbs, who then opened a desk drawer to take out the viscount's watch. He handed it to Sidgewick. "He claimed it was his watch, but it looks like the watch of a gentleman, not for the likes of a circus performer."

Sidgewick took the watch and turned it over in his hand.

Warrington regarded the tall young man expectantly. Sidgewick looked over at him, a thoughtful expression on his face. Then, turning to the constable, he nodded. "Yes, Dobbs, this is my watch."

Warrington gaped at him in astonishment. "What the devil?" he cried. "Take another look at it. You can see it isn't yours. There is a coat of arms engraved on the back."

"I am well aware what my watch looks like," snapped Sidgewick. "Do take these two culprits away, Dobbs."

"Wait a moment!" cried the viscount as the constable's assistant took him by the arm. "You must know that it isn't your watch." Warrington regarded him incredulously. "Why, of course, you do. You're lying because of this morning. By God, you are! You damned vindictive liar!"

"Watch your tongue or I'll clap you in irons," said Dobbs. "Higgins, take them back to their cell."

The brawny young man led the still-protesting Warrington out the door. "I am very sorry, my lord," said Dobbs.

"You can't control the behavior of every insolent ruffian," said Sidgewick, pocketing the watch. Then after complimenting the constable on his excellent work, the baron walked out, a happy smile on his face.

Warrington sat on the cot in his jail cell, with Jem sitting close beside him. "Now, lad, you mustn't worry," he said, placing a comforting arm around the boy's shoulders. "We won't be here long. You'll see."

"You don't think we'll be hanged, do you, sir?" said Jem, with a frightened look.

"Of course not," said his lordship.

"He must be an evil man," said Jem, leaning against the viscount.

"I daresay he is," said Warrington, frowning darkly. "And one day he'll regret what he did. I promise you that. And cheer up. We'll be out of here very quickly."

"I hope you're right, Mr. Bradford," said Jem dispiritedly. He paused a moment. "Perhaps they'll send us to Australia."

"Certainly not," said Warrington. "Don't worry about that."

"I wouldn't want to go," said Jem, tears forming in his eyes. "I want to stay here in the circus with you and Miss Richards. I was happy, sir. For the first time I was truly happy."

Warrington patted his shoulder. "You must trust me, lad. There is nothing to fear. Now why don't you lie down? You look tired."

Jem nodded and then lay down on the hard cot. Curling up, he soon fell asleep. The viscount looked down at him. It was surprising how fond he had become of the boy. It was monstrous that the poor lad was being subjected to this.

Folding his arms across his chest, Warrington grew thoughtful. He would have to reveal his identity. There was no choice.

Certainly the police would behave very differently if they knew that he was the Viscount Warrington, the only son and heir of the Earl of Gravenhurst and not a lowly circus performer. He frowned as he pondered the injustice of this.

A rueful smile came to the viscount's handsome countenance. He could imagine what his father would say when he heard that he had been thrown in jail, accused of stealing a watch. Indeed, the earl would be very much surprised to learn the truth of his son's strange odyssey. He could imagine the earl's expression if he heard that his son had survived by working as a groom and a trick rider in a circus.

Warrington's smile grew wider. His life had certainly been eventful since leaving London. Who would have thought that so much could have happened in so short a time?

Suddenly the door opened, bringing the viscount out of his reverie. "You have visitors," said Higgins and in walked Antonia and Tilly.

"You're allowed ten minutes," said the brawny young man.

"Why, you'll allow us a bit more, won't you, Mr. 'Iggins?" said Tilly, batting her eyelashes at him. "You seem like such a kind man. Kind as well as 'andsome."

"Well, perhaps a bit longer," said Higgins, who, despite his devotion to duty, wasn't immune to Tilly's charms.

"Thank you," said the dancer, smiling brightly at him.

"Oh, Jack," said Antonia.

"Tony," he said, getting up from the cot.

Jem, who had awakened at the noise, looked a bit groggy. But seeing the women, he grinned and hurried to his feet and rushed to embrace Antonia. "Miss Richards! I'm so glad you're here."

"And we've brought you some food, my dear," said Tilly, extending a basket she was carrying. "Mrs. Pickering has sent some meat and cheese and there are buns and bread."

Jem, who was very hungry, was delighted to hear this. "Oh, thank you, Miss Blodgett."

"Well, let us all sit down and try to discover what is to be done," said Antonia.

"That is a good idea," said Tilly, taking a seat on the cot. "But I 'ave no idea what we can do. They say this Lord Sidgewick said you 'ad his watch, Jack."

"But it is Jack's watch," said Antonia, "He showed it to me a few days ago. We talked about it and the crest on the back. I shall swear to that in court."

"But what's your word against a lord's?" said Tilly. "Very little, I daresay."

"That may be," said Antonia, "but why does he think your watch is his, Jack?"

"He doesn't," said Warrington. "I will tell you who this Lord

Sidgewick is. He's the man we met when we walked from the cathedral. The one who told us to get out of his way."

"God almighty!" exclaimed Tilly. "Why ain't that the most accurst bad luck? You made 'im an enemy, you did, Jack."

Warrington nodded. "I fear so."

"Oh, Jack," said Antonia, remembering the angry look Sidgewick had given them.

"But can you imagine him being willing to send an innocent man to prison?" said the viscount. "And a boy as well, a boy who did nothing to him."

"This is terrible," said Antonia. Then suddenly she brightened. "But there is someone else who knows about the watch. That is the gentleman who gave it to you, Jack. We must notify him at once so that he might come and say that he gave it to you."

"Well, I should prefer not to involve him," said Warrington.

"Don't act daft," said Tilly.

"Tilly is right," said Antonia. "I know you said that you and he were not on the best of terms any longer, but surely he would wish to help you."

Warrington hesitated, realizing that he was in a very awkward position. "I should like to speak with a lawyer. You must find one to represent us. If it is necessary to contact the gentleman, I shall have him do so."

"Mr. Pickering is looking for a lawyer," said Antonia. "He said he will spare no expense to find you a good one."

"I'm glad to hear it," said the viscount.

"But won't you tell me the name of the gentleman who gave you the watch so that we might send word to him?"

"I shall prefer to discuss that with the lawyer, Tony," said the viscount. "But I promise that, if it is necessary, I shall send word to him. And he will help. We have nothing to fear, I can assure you of that."

Antonia's blue eyes met his gray ones. He seemed confidant and she felt that she must trust him. Still, she was worried.

"How is Baldric?" asked Jem. "He is probably worried about me."

"He is very well," said Antonia. "Jocko is looking after him. And he does miss you."

"I miss him," said Jem glumly.

Antonia tried to cheer him up by saying that she was sure that everything would be straightened out in a very short time. They talked for a few more minutes until Higgins returned and ushered the ladies out.

As they walked through the narrow streets, Antonia was lost in her own thoughts.

"Jack didn't seem worried," said Tilly. "And if 'e didn't, perhaps we shouldn't be either."

"But one can't help but worry," replied Antonia. "It is a very serious charge."

"Well, there's naught to do, but go back to the camp," said Tilly. "Perhaps Mr. Pickering found a lawyer. We must see what he has to say."

Antonia nodded and the two of them continued on their way.

21

Antonia slept very little that night. She lay awake in the wagon, thinking about Jem and Warrington and how they were spending the night in jail. She knew that Jem must be very frightened, and she wished that there was something that she could do to help.

In the morning she and Tilly dressed and joined the others for breakfast. The troupe was in a gloomy mood, with everyone thinking of Jack and Jem.

Even Michael Flynn, who considered Warrington his rival, wasn't happy to think that one of his colleagues was imprisoned in the town. Pickering, while concerned for his comrades on a personal level, was also keenly aware that the absence of two of his performers would hurt the circus. They were to spend only one more day in Shrewsbury and then make their way north. If Pickering did not keep his scheduled engagements, it would be serious indeed.

To make matters worse, the lawyer that Pickering had hired the previous day was not very optimistic about defending his new clients. He had made it clear to Pickering that Lord Sidgewick was a wealthy and powerful man. The magistrate who would be hearing the case was Sidgewick's cousin and he was a man known for his harsh sentencing. When Pickering had relayed this information to the company the evening before, Antonia had been very upset.

After breakfast, she stood by the wagon she shared with Tilly, wondering what she should do. "Will you go to the shop with me, Tony?"

Antonia turned to see Tilly standing next to her. She was wearing a bonnet and had a shawl thrown about her shoulders. "What?" said Antonia.

"I could use a bit of ribbon," said Tilly. "And it would do us good to have a walk."

Antonia readily agreed. She went into the wagon to fetch her hat and shawl, and then the two young women started off. They spent a good deal of time in several shops, for Tilly dearly loved shopping and had the greatest difficulty in choosing the sort of ribbon that would best adorn the new bonnet she was making.

As they came out of one of the shops, Antonia caught sight of a tall gentleman in a beaver hat, walking briskly along the sidewalk on the other side of the street. "Look, Tilly!" she said. "That's he! Lord Sidgewick!"

"By God, 'tis the blackguard," said Tilly. "If I was a man, I'd plant 'im a facer. Indeed, I would."

They watched Sidgewick as he continued on. He carried a walking stick and wore a well-cut coat of olive superfine. "Perhaps I might try to reason with him," said Antonia.

"Reason with 'im?" said Tilly. "I don't fancy there's much chance of that."

"Still," said Antonia, "it wouldn't hurt to try. Come on, Tilly. Let's follow him."

The two women hurried after Sidgewick, who was walking with long strides. Turning down another street, he entered a glove maker's shop.

Antonia and Tilly arrived there quickly. They stood at the shop window, gazing in at Sidgewick, who was having a long conversation with the proprietor of the shop. "What will you say to 'im?" said Tilly.

"I don't know," said Antonia, watching Sidgewick. What could one say to such a man? She didn't have much time to decide, for Sidgewick concluded his business and started out of the shop.

When outside, he turned and started off in their direction. "Lord Sidgewick," said Antonia in a determined voice.

He stopped and regarded her curiously. Then he recognized Tilly. "You were with that man. The one who stole my watch. I have nothing to say to you."

"I believe you do, my lord," said Antonia. "If you do not listen to what I am going to say, you will have cause to regret it."

"What?" he said, very much annoyed. "Is that a threat?"

"Call it what you will," said Antonia bravely. "You know the watch Jack Bradford had isn't yours. Mr. Bradford had it before yours was stolen. I will swear in court that I saw it before. And others in the company saw him with it was well."

"Others in the company? You mean circus performers?" he said scornfully. "Yes, you are all credible witnesses."

"We're not liars," said Tilly, "like some gentlemen."

Sidgewick fixed a scornful look at the dancer and started to walk off, but Antonia hurried to block his path. "There is a crest engraved on the back of the watch. I daresay it isn't your coat of arms."

"Stand aside," said the baron testily, but Antonia made no move.

"That watch was given to Jack Bradford by a distinguished gentleman," she continued. "It is *his* coat of arms engraved on the back of it. You risk the wrath of this gentleman if you claim the watch is yours. We have sent word to him and he will be arriving shortly from London. He will identify the watch in court."

"What nonsense!" said Sidgewick, pushing past her and rushing off down the street.

With some frustration, Antonia watched him go. "I fear I did no good, Tilly."

"Oh, but you were splendid, Tony. Proper brave you are, speaking to 'im like that. And very clever saying what you did. But we'd best 'urry on. 'Tis getting late. Mr. Pickering will be looking for us."

Antonia nodded and they began walking back to the camp.

As Sidgewick walked along the narrow street lined with black and white Tudor–era buildings, he frowned to think of the young woman's audacity. She had been spouting nonsense. He knew that well enough. This Bradford person had probably stolen the watch or bought it from a thief.

Still, as he walked along, he thought of the coat of arms engraved on the watch. How would he explain it? Sidgewick frowned. He had never thought about appearing in court and showing the watch. If he were asked if the engraving was his coat of arms, he could hardly say it was. The Sidgewick coat of arms was well known in Shrewsbury.

The baron slowed his pace as he thought over the matter. Perhaps he should consult the vicar of St. Mary's Church. The Rev. Mr. Peabody had an obsessive interest in heraldry and was well-versed in coats of arms. Sidgewick usually avoided him, for he considered him an extraordinarily boring fellow. But it was very likely that the Rev. Mr. Peabody might know whose coat of arms was engraved on the back of the watch.

Stopping abruptly, Sidgewick turned and started walking in the opposite direction. When he arrived at the vicar's home, he was ushered inside by a maid. Mr. Peabody, surprised to hear that he had such an illustrious visitor, hurried to greet the baron.

When he found that Sidgewick had a question about coats of arms, he was even more pleased. Leading his guest to the library, the vicar took up a large reference book. "Can you describe the coat of arms, Lord Sidgewick?"

"There is a stag below and three diamonds in a row above it."

"Why, that sounds familiar," said the vicar, rubbing his chin thoughtfully as he paged through the book. After what seemed to Sidgewick a very long time, he found what he was looking for. "Is this it, my lord?"

The baron looked down at the page and nodded. "Yes, that's it. I'm sure of it."

"Why, that is the coat of arms of the Earl of Gravenhurst."

"Gravenhurst?"

"Surely, you've heard of him. He is one of the richest men in the kingdom, and he owns vast estates in Northumberland. He is considered a very hard, distant man with progressive views. If my memory serves, the first earl fought at Agincourt and—"

Sidgewick cut him off. "That is very interesting, Vicar. I do appreciate your information, but I must be going."

The vicar, who was just warming to his topic, was clearly disappointed. He showed the baron to the door and expressed the wish that he would call again very soon.

As Sidgewick walked away from the vicarage, he wondered what he should do. He sincerely doubted that the Earl of Gravenhurst had given his watch to a trick rider in a circus. It was most likely that the watch had been stolen. Yet, again one couldn't be sure. Regardless, he'd have to admit the watch wasn't his and it could be very embarrassing.

The baron pondered these matters as he made his way out of town and walked along the road to his house.

Warrington sat on the narrow cot, telling Jem stories about London. They had both spent a very uncomfortable night in the jail. The viscount had slept very little, since his bed was rock hard and there was the constant scurry of mice on the floor beneath his cot.

They had both awakened cold and hungry and had been fed a bowl of unpalatable porridge. In order to keep the boy's spirits up, Warrington had begun to tell him about London. Jem wanted to hear everything about the great city and the viscount was able to keep him well entertained.

Then when it was nearly noon, the door opened and Higgins ordered them out. "Mr. Dobbs wants to see you," he said.

They were led to the constable, who stood regarding them with a sour expression. "You're being released," he said.

"What?" said Warrington in considerable surprise.

Dobbs nodded. "You heard me. Lord Sidgewick was here. He said there was a mistake. He hadn't had a good look at the watch before. This morning he realized he'd erred. So here is your watch and you're free to go."

Warrington stared at the constable for a moment before taking the watch from his outstretched hand. Relief mixed with anger filled him in equal measure.

"I suggest you be off," said Dobbs curtly.

Jem clutched the viscount's hand. "We're free, Mr. Bradford. Come, let us leave here, sir!"

While his lordship would have liked to have vented his spleen upon the constable, he was dissuaded by Jem tugging at his hand. "I want to leave, Mr. Bradford. I want to see Miss Richards and Baldric."

Fixing an icy look at the constable, he turned and departed. Jem was ecstatically happy to be free. They walked quickly through the town. When Jem saw the familiar wagons, he started to run and cheer.

Antonia, who had been glumly assisting Mrs. Pickering to prepare the luncheon, looked up at the boy's cries of joy. Seeing Jem, she broke into a delighted grin. "Jem!"

The boy dashed into her arms and she gave him an exuberant

hug. Baldric, who was tied to one of the wagon wheels, began to bark wildly. Laughing delightedly, Jem left Antonia to greet the little black dog, who jumped up again and again, trying to reach his young master's face.

"And what about me?" said Warrington, coming forward to grin at Antonia. "Don't I get an embrace, miss?"

"Oh, Jack," said Antonia, allowing herself to be taken into his strong arms and pressing her face against his chest. "How did you get out?"

The viscount hugged her tightly. "Damned if I know, Tony. Our friend Sidgewick must have had a change of heart."

By now the rest of the circus troupe had gathered around them. Jocko slapped Warrington on the back and once Antonia had released him, Tilly stepped forward to kiss him firmly on the lips. "Praise God, you're back, Jack Bradford," she said. "And in need of a shave!"

Antonia was so happy at his return that she didn't even seem to mind Tilly's greeting. "But tell us what happened," she said.

"The constable informed us that there had been a mistake. He gave me my watch back and told us we could go. I felt like strangling him, but Jem prevented me."

"It would have been understandable had you done so, Bradford," said Pickering. In his years as a circus performer, he had had many unpleasant experiences with local constabularies and he viewed officers of the law with a jaundiced eye. He was very happy to have two of his troupe back. It was especially good to know that the services of the lawyer he had hired would not be needed.

Jem, who had become a pet among the company, found himself being lavished with attention after his ordeal. Jocko gave the boy a set of brightly colored balls, with the promise that he'd teach him the art of juggling. Tilly smothered the boy's face with kisses, telling him he was very brave, while the Flynn brothers lifted him up on their shoulders and hoisted him about the camp. Mrs. Pickering gave the boy a piece of lemon cake and even threw a tidbit to Baldric.

When they sat down to luncheon, everyone was eager to hear about their ordeal. When enough had been said about hard beds and mice and fears of being deported to Australia, Tilly spoke up.

"I do expect it was what Tony said to 'im what made Lord Sidgewick give your watch back."

Warrington turned to Antonia. "You talked to Sidgewick?"

"We saw 'im in the town," said Tilly, "and Tony said she would talk to 'im. You should 'ave seen 'er. She sounded like a grand lady. She told 'im 'is coat of arms wasn't on the watch and it 'ad been given you by some toff who'd be sore angry to find 'e'd lied about it. And that this 'igh-and-mighty gentleman was coming 'ere to identify the watch 'e give you."

"I doubt what I said had anything to do with it," said Antonia modestly.

"I daresay it had," said the viscount, smiling at her.

"Well, I don't like to cut short our celebration," said Pickering, "but we have a performance this afternoon and most of you need time to prepare."

The happy group broke up, with Warrington retreating to his wagon to make himself presentable. Jem went off with Jocko to put Baldric through his paces and Antonia went to her wagon. Taking up her mandolin, she sat on the front seat and began to play a joyful Italian melody.

Seeing her sitting there alone, Michael Flynn could scarcely believe his good fortune. He hopped up on the seat beside her. "That's a lovely tune, Miss Richards."

"It's an Italian song my mother taught me," she said, putting the mandolin down in her lap.

"Oh, please, don't stop," urged Flynn. "It's such a great pleasure to listen to you." He paused and gazed intently at her. "The only greater pleasure, my dear lady, is to feast my eyes upon you."

"Really, sir, I'm not accustomed to hearing such flummery."

He suddenly reached over and grabbed her hand. "It's not flummery! Indeed, I've never been more sincere in all my life. My darling Antonia, don't you know I'm mad for you?" He raised her hand to his lips and gave it an ardent kiss.

Antonia was at first too startled to react. Then, she quickly snatched her hand away. "Mr. Flynn . . ." she began, regarding him with a look of dismay.

"Call me Michael," said the acrobat, smiling his charming smile at her. "Say that you'll be mine."

"Really, sir," said Antonia severely, "you are being ridiculous."

The acrobat frowned. "There is another man. It's Bradford, isn't it?"

"Yes, it is."

Muttering an oath, the acrobat jumped down from the wagon. As he started off, there was a laugh behind him. Turning around, he saw Tilly. "Poor Michael," she said, "it ain't often a girl refuses you, is it?"

He eyed her resentfully. "And so you were eavesdropping on us?"

Tilly smiled and ran a hand through her unruly red hair. "It's not my fault that I just 'appened by when you were making a cake of yourself. What a shame, Michael, but a better man than you 'as won Tony's 'eart."

He frowned. "Better is he?"

"In my opinion," said the dancer, smiling at him.

Flynn made no reply, but stalked off, leaving Tilly very much amused. Walking to the front of the wagon, she found Antonia sitting there looking a bit disturbed.

The dancer climbed up on the wagon seat beside her. "I 'eard Michael and you. Oh, I couldn't 'elp it. 'E's not used to 'earing the word 'no' from a female." She smiled. "I know from experience. Of course, I'm not in the 'abit of saying 'no' much myself. But Michael was sore vexed. I could see that. 'E'll be 'ard to live with for a time, you can be sure of that."

Antonia frowned, not too pleased at the prospect of seeing Flynn each day. It would be very awkward, now that she had rejected his advances.

"Oh, 'e'll soon get over it," said Tilly. "'E'll find another girl to keep 'im 'appy. You can be sure of that. But 'tis time we were getting dressed."

Antonia nodded and the two young women retreated into the wagon to prepare for the afternoon's performance.

22

While the crowd wasn't as large as the previous day, it was enthusiastic. When it was time for Antonia to sing, Warrington flashed an encouraging smile at her as she took her seat and began playing her mandolin. By God, she was wonderful, thought the viscount, as she began to sing.

Standing watching her, Warrington was filled with unmistakable longing. He wanted her. Yes, he'd wanted her from the first time he laid eyes on her. But now his feelings were more complicated. He found himself wondering what his parents would say when he announced his choice of bride. He expected it would create a furor, but he didn't care.

Of course, first he'd have to convince Antonia to have him. He realized that, in her eyes, he wasn't much of a matrimonial prize. After all, she knew him as Jack Bradford, a penniless, aimless sort of fellow who now made his living as a trick rider in a circus.

Warrington's expression grew thoughtful. Whatever would she think when she learned the truth about him? And how was he to tell her? It was a very odd story, to be sure, and he mustn't forget that, by his agreement with his father, he wasn't to reveal his true identity until the month was over.

But the viscount had reason to believe that Antonia shared his feelings. He resolved to declare himself at first opportunity.

At the end of the performance, the troupe assembled at the wagons for sandwiches and tea. There was a good deal of cheerful talk. The only one who didn't seem merry was Michael Flynn. He sat there, staring at the company with an unhappy, resentful expression.

Warrington took no notice of the acrobat. He was intent upon

Antonia, who looked stunning in her red dress with her dark curls piled atop her head.

When the meal was over, the company broke up to rest before their evening performance. Jem, with Baldric at his heels, hurried to the viscount and suggested that they take a walk. "Perhaps you might ask Miss Richards if she'd accompany us," said Warrington.

Thinking this a splendid suggestion, Jem hurried to ask Antonia. Happy at the idea of having some exercise, Antonia allowed Jem to take her by the hand as they walked over to join the viscount.

As they started off, Baldric, who was eager for a run, raced ahead, and Jem ran after him.

"I must say you were splendid this afternoon, Miss Richards," said Warrington, offering his arm to her.

She tucked her arm under his. "Thank you, sir. And you were splendid as well." Pausing, she glanced up at him. "Jack, I'm not so sure you should continue the trick riding."

"But you said my performance was splendid."

"Oh, it isn't that you aren't good at it. Indeed, you are. It is truly amazing that you could learn so much in so short a time. You are a talented rider. That was clear at Larchmont." Antonia smiled. "It's odd, but it seems a very long time ago since we left there."

Warrington nodded. "We've had a good many adventures since then, haven't we, Tony?"

Antonia laughed. "I daresay too many."

"I doubt either of us ever imagined ourselves part of Pickering's Amazing Circus, but I don't know when I've enjoyed myself more."

"But I worry about you, Jack."

"Worry about me?" he replied, regarding her in surprise.

"Being a trick rider is dangerous."

"Why, my dear Tony, I believe you care about me."

She looked down in some embarrassment. "I know that Mr. Pickering intends for you to do a good many other dangerous tricks. You might fall and be killed."

Gazing down into her blue eyes, the viscount smiled. "And that would upset you?"

"Of course it would, you great simpleton."

Warrington seemed delighted by this remark. He responded by stopping abruptly and pulling her to him. Then before she could say another word, he covered her mouth with his own and kissed her passionately. Antonia responded with long-suppressed ardor, delighting him and enflaming him further. "Oh, Tony," he murmured and then kissed her again and again.

Jem, who had run ahead with Baldric, turned to see the two people he loved best in the world locked in an embrace. He stared for a moment and then broke into a grin.

Noting the strange behavior of the two humans, Baldric started barking furiously. Then the little black dog ran back to the ardent couple before his young master could stop him. He started jumping up on Warrington, all the while barking shrilly.

The noisy dog brought them both back to their senses. Warrington scowled at Baldric and muttered, "Damn!" while Antonia reddened at the realization of how she had completely lost her head.

"I'm sorry, Mr. Bradford," said Jem, hurrying to them and scooping up the wayward canine. "Bad dog, Baldric!"

"Yes, exceedingly bad dog," said the viscount, who devoutly wished that both Jem and Baldric might vanish.

Jem smiled at them both. "I couldn't help but see," he said. "I am glad. I'd hoped you'd get married. I thought of it from the start. Even when Mrs. Pickering said you'd marry a lord, miss, I was hoping that you'd choose Mr. Bradford. You will be married, won't you?"

"That depends upon Miss Richards," said Warrington, regarding her expectantly. "She must agree to have me."

"Oh, you must say yes," said Jem.

Antonia, who had by now started to think a bit more clearly, was rather alarmed at the intensity of her passions. Yet she hesitated only a moment. "Yes, I will marry you, Jack."

"Hurrah!" shouted Jem, dropping Baldric to the ground and beginning to hop about, much to the delight of his canine friend.

"I can scarcely wait to tell Jocko," said Jem. "I can tell them, can't I, sir?"

"Of course," said Warrington. "Then Miss Richards won't be able to change her mind."

"Oh, I shan't do that," said Antonia, taking his arm.

They started back to the wagons. "Tony," began the viscount, "there are some things I'll have to explain to you about myself."

She looked up at him curiously. "What is it, Jack?"

Warrington looked over at Jem, who was skipping along beside them, whistling merrily. "I shall tell you later tonight. After the performance when we're alone."

"It sounds mysterious."

He was spared the necessity of replying by the appearance of Mrs. Pickering and Tilly, who were walking toward them. Jem ran up to the women to deliver the good news. Tilly let out a whoop and rushed to them. She then planted congratulatory kisses, first on Antonia's cheek and then on Warrington's lips.

Mrs. Pickering was also very thrilled, declaring that they must have a fine wedding feast. When they arrived back at the wagons, Tilly and Jem rushed to inform Jocko, Mr. Pickering, and the Flynn brothers. All except Michael Flynn received the news with broad smiles, clapping Warrington on the back and kissing Antonia.

Flynn feigned indifference, though he was very much irritated by the news and the fuss that was being made about the happy couple. His animosity toward Warrington grew even stronger as he watched the viscount accept the hearty congratulations of his colleagues.

In the evening, a great number of people visited the fair and Mr. Pickering was delighted that their last performance in Shrewsbury was well attended. At the conclusion of the program, the troupe was in a celebratory mood.

Although Warrington had hoped to have the opportunity to speak privately with Antonia, he never had the chance. The company sat down to dinner, and then a good many toasts were given and a good many glasses of gin and rum dispensed.

Jocko fetched a hornpipe from the wagon and started to play a number of sprightly tunes. Most of the troupe began to dance, with Mrs. Pickering astounding Antonia with her agility.

Antonia, who was completely happy, realized that she had never enjoyed herself so much. She danced with Warrington, and then with Jem, Pickering, and Flynn's brother. Flynn himself stood apart, frowning at the merriment and drinking a good deal of spirits.

It was very late when everyone went to their beds. Tilly fell asleep immediately, but Antonia lay awake for a time before finally falling into an exhausted slumber.

23

Warrington woke early in the morning. His companions in the wagon were asleep, with Jocko and Michael Flynn snoring noisily. There was a strong smell of liquor and sweat in the wagon and the viscount was eager to get up and go out into the fresh air. After quickly throwing on his clothes, he grabbed his boots and went out of the wagon. Once outside, he put on his boots and pushed his disheveled brown hair from his brow.

The cool morning air felt good on his face as he walked across the camp area toward where the horses were tethered. As he did so, he paused to stare at the wagon where he knew Antonia was sleeping. If only he could be there with her, he thought, conjuring up the delightful picture of making love to her.

But soon it would be so, for they were to be married. The thought cheered his lordship. As he neared his mare, he found himself thinking how ironic it was that a short time ago the idea of marriage was repugnant to him. Of course, that was when he was to marry a woman chosen for him by his father.

Now the idea of becoming a husband seemed very appealing. And if his family and society disapproved of his choice, he told himself, they may jolly well be hanged.

"Good morning, Daphne, my girl," said the viscount, patting the horse's neck. The animal snorted. "We'll be going from here today," he said, talking to the animal in a soothing voice. He took out his watch and checked the time, discovering it was not yet six o'clock. Glancing back over at Antonia's wagon, he felt suddenly restless and decided to take the mare for a short ride.

After saddling the horse, he led her to his own wagon. No one in the troupe was yet stirring. Opening the door, he peered inside. "Jocko?" he said.

There was no answer. Climbing in, he shook the Scotsman by the shoulder. "Och, what is it?" he mumbled.

"I'm taking Daphne for a short ride."

"Aye," said Jocko. Warrington turned and left the wagon and Jocko fell promptly to sleep again.

Warrington started off, easing the mare from a walk into a trot. He hadn't gone far, when his mount threw a shoe. "Damn," said the viscount, dismounting and examining Daphne's hoof. "Well, we'll have to see the blacksmith, my girl. We're dashed lucky we're so close to the town."

Leading the horse, he walked into Shrewsbury. There was little activity on the quiet streets, but Warrington did find a blacksmith's shop where the smith had already started work. The farrier agreed to see to Daphne at once.

While he stood waiting, Warrington saw a newspaper lying on the floor. Picking it up, he discovered it was the *London Times*. He started to look through the newspaper, reading an article about the Prince Regent, and then one on a bill being considered in the House of Commons.

He saw items about society that mentioned a number of his acquaintances. To his surprise, he realized that he hadn't missed society at all. In fact, he'd scarcely given it a thought in the near month that he'd been gone.

A small item in the newspaper suddenly caught his eye. As he read through it, a grim expression appeared on his face. The brief paragraph reported that the Earl of Gravenhurst was seriously ill, and that his family was gathered at his bedside at his lordship's London residence. Warrington scanned through the story a few times, and then he looked at the date of the paper. Dismayed to find that the newspaper was a week old, he hastily threw it down.

He must return to town at once, he told himself. Good God, he didn't know if his father was alive or dead. Warrington paced across the yard, watching the blacksmith in some agitation. The man was working diligently, but it still seemed to be taking a long time.

While he stood impatiently waiting, a small, stout, middle-aged man stepped up beside him. "Why, aren't you the rider from the circus?"

Warrington nodded.

"I saw you yesterday afternoon. You were very good. That's a fine horse you have there. Yes, I enjoyed the circus. So did my wife and my daughters. I liked Princess Fatima very much. What a beauty. And the girl who sang like an angel, and the boy and the clever little dog."

The viscount said that it was very good of him to say so, but turned his attention back to the farrier, who was finishing his work.

"Your Mr. Pickering is having a visitor this morning," said the man, who seemed far too loquacious for Warrington's taste. "I saw the gentlemen on their way a short time ago. They were in Sir Osbert's carriage. Sir Osbert keeps a fine carriage. And the best horses in the county.

"They stopped to speak to me. Sir Osbert is such a considerate gentleman. He's taking his friend Mr. Crawford to see your Mr. Pickering."

"That is all very interesting," said Warrington, a trifle impatiently. The blacksmith was giving the shoe a final check and Daphne was almost ready.

"Mr. Crawford knows your Mr. Pickering. He was going to see him. Sir Osbert is a fine gentleman to take him in his carriage. I always say there is no finer gentleman in all the land than Sir Osbert Lumley."

Warrington, who was barely attending, stared at the man. "Did you say Sir Osbert Lumley?"

The stout little man nodded. "Oh, yes."

The viscount frowned. Of all the cursed bad luck, he said to himself. He was well acquainted with Sir Osbert Lumley. He had spent many a night playing hazard with him at White's. And surely it was unlikely that there would be two men with such a name.

"You said Sir Osbert was going to see Mr. Pickering?"

"Yes, he would be there now. Mr. Crawford was staying with him in the country, you see. They are distant cousins through a connection of Lady Lumley's."

Warrington pondered this information with a serious expression. If he went back to the wagons now to tell Antonia he must go to London, he would be recognized by Lumley. And how would he explain to Lumley what he was doing in Pickering's Amazing Circus?

The viscount knew that Sir Osbert was a notorious gossip. He would spread the tale all over town. No, he must not see Lumley under any circumstances.

Perhaps he could send a note. Yes, that would be better. "I will have to send a message to someone," he said, addressing the blacksmith. "Where could I find pen and paper?"

"Oh, I can help you, sir," said the talkative man. "My home is there across the street."

Warrington followed the man to his home, a small but well-appointed Tudor–era house. There he penned a brief note to Antonia, explaining the fact that an emergency called him to London and he would join her as soon as he could.

"I am called away to London on urgent business," he said, blotting the letter and folding it. "I must have this note delivered to a lady who is with Pickering's Circus. Miss Antonia Richards." The viscount wrote Antonia's name on the note.

"Oh, I can take the note myself," said the talkative man. "I would be more than happy to do so."

"That would be good of you, Mr. . . ."

"Mr. Hopkins," said the man, happy to supply his name.

"And I am Jack Bradford." The viscount extended his hand and Hopkins shook it eagerly. "I shall be obliged if you could deliver this into Miss Richards's hands."

"Oh, I shall be happy to do so," said Hopkins, knowing that Miss Richards was the lovely singer.

"And tell her I am sorry to depart so hastily, but I have no choice. Tell her I'll return as soon as I can."

Deciding that he had no more time to waste, Warrington took his leave of Hopkins. Going back to the blacksmith's shop, he paid the farrier and mounted his horse. "Pray God, I'm not too late," he muttered fervently as he started off on the road toward London.

24

Pickering was surprised to see a carriage pull up beside the circus wagons. When a short, wiry-looking gentleman with gray hair climbed out and greeted him with "Pickering, you old rascal!" Pickering let out a cry of astonishment.

"Damn me if it ain't Will Crawford!" Pickering shook his visitor's hand. "Why, how long has it been, Will? Seven, eight years at the very least?"

"Aye, that and more," said Crawford.

"But what the devil are you doing here?"

"I'm visiting my friend, Sir Osbert Lumley." Crawford nodded to his companion, who had also emerged from the carriage. "I must introduce you. I have the great privilege to present Sir Osbert Lumley, a very fine gentleman who is married to my cousin, Isabelle. Sir Osbert, this is Thadeus Pickering. Mr. Pickering and I once were colleagues at Astley's Amphitheater."

Sir Osbert, a ruddy-faced gentleman, nodded in a civil fashion.

"When I saw the signs about Pickering's Amazing Circus, I thought I must come and see my old friend," said Crawford. "By God, it's been a long time since the two of us rode in Astley's Amphitheater."

"Aye, Will, we were quite the young blades then, weren't we?" said Pickering, with a nostalgic gleam in his eye.

Crawford nodded. "We were, indeed."

"And you've done very well for yourself, Will," said Pickering, with a trace of envy in his tone. "I've read in the newspapers that your amphitheater in London packs in the crowds."

"Yes, I have had some success," said Crawford modestly, "but from what I've heard, your show was quite excellent. I regret that

I missed your performance, but from all accounts, it was very good indeed."

"Oh, yes," said Pickering, smiling at the praise, "I must say I have an exceptional company. I have a new singer, Miss Richards. She has a wonderful voice. And a new trick rider. Although a bit raw, he has the makings of a great one. I'm told the fellow has gone off on a ride. He'll be back soon and you can meet him. And of course the Flynn Brothers and Princess Fatima, our lovely dancer. And a very clever young lad and his little black dog. The audiences love them."

At that moment Mrs. Pickering came out of the wagon to see who the visitors were. Recognizing an old acquaintance, she greeted him enthusiastically. Then Mrs. Pickering called the others so that they could meet their old friend and Sir Osbert.

Pickering introduced Crawford as his former colleague who had now become a great man in London. Tilly, the Flynns, and Jocko had all heard of Crawford's Amphitheater, so they were suitably impressed to meet a man whom they knew to be a wealthy impresario.

After a long and pleasant visit, in which Pickering prevailed upon Antonia to sing a brief song, the Flynns to do a few flips and handstands, and Jem to show what tricks Baldric could do, Crawford pulled his old friend aside. "I must talk to you, Thadeus. I have had a thought, an idea of a mutually beneficial arrangement."

"What do you mean?"

"I want you to join my company. Yes, Pickering's Amazing Circus could join me in London."

"What!" exclaimed Pickering, eyeing him in considerable astonishment.

"Come, man, think of it! You'd be back in the thick of things, not playing to farmers out here in the provinces. I am in need of some new talent. And we would be working together again. It would be like the old days."

"You mean you'd want the entire troupe?"

Crawford nodded. "Aye, there's a place for all of them."

"I don't know," said Pickering, rather overwhelmed by the offer. "I must think on it. We were to be off today to other engagements."

"My dear fellow, you'd do far better in town than out in the provinces."

Pickering looked thoughtful. He had to admit that he'd been getting tired of traveling from one small rural town to the next. "What sort of offer are you willing to make?"

Pleased with this show of interest, Crawford began to talk of money and business arrangements.

After doing a short acrobatic demonstration for the visitors, Michael Flynn had retreated. He wasn't in a very good mood and he was still feeling the effects of the previous night's revelries. He was particularly displeased to see Antonia and remember how she'd rejected him. Now she was to marry Jack Bradford and all the company, save him, of course, seemed to think it so marvelous.

Flynn also hadn't appreciated being called upon to perform for the Pickerings' friend, and he had been eager to get away. Deciding that he needed a walk to clear his head, he started off toward the village. He hadn't gone too far when he came upon a stout man walking slowly toward him. Hopkins, the man Warrington had spoken with a short time before, was red in the face and seemed to be finding the walk uncomfortable.

"Excuse me," said Hopkins as Flynn came up to him, "aren't you with Pickering's Circus?"

"Yes," said Flynn, regarding the man with a look akin to suspicion.

"I thought I recognized you. You are one of the flying Flynns. Oh, I thought you quite wonderful!"

This seemed to soften Flynn up a good deal. "That is kind of you to say."

"Oh, yes, you were excellent. Well, I am very glad to see that you haven't left Shrewsbury yet. I have been entrusted with a message for Miss Richards." Taking a handkerchief from his pocket, he wiped his forehead with it. "It is rather a farther walk than I thought."

"You have a message for Miss Richards?" said Flynn. "Why don't you give it to me? I'll take it to her."

"Oh, I do think I should take it to her myself. I was told to do so, for it is very important."

"Told to do so? Who gave you this message?"

"The trick rider, Gentleman Jack. I met him a short while ago. He was at the blacksmith's having a new shoe put on that fine mare of his. What a pleasant, well-spoken man he is. He said he must go to London on urgent business and wished for me to give this note to Miss Richards."

"What?" cried Flynn. "He went to London?"

Hopkins nodded. "In a hurry, he was."

Well, this is damned odd, thought Flynn. Wait 'til Pickering hears of this.

"I was very happy to take this letter to Miss Richards for him," said Hopkins, holding up the note.

"That is very good of you," said Flynn, snatching the letter from the man's hand, "but there is no need to trouble you any more. I'm a friend of dear old Jack's, and I'll be happy to take the message to Miss Richards."

"But—" began Hopkins, but Flynn cut him off.

"Thank you, sir. I shall complete your errand."

Then turning around, Flynn started back. While Hopkins was a little disappointed at not getting to place the letter in the hands of the lovely singer, he was growing rather tired from his exertions. He shrugged, and then turned to walk back to the village.

As Flynn strode along, he thought it very curious that Warrington would have gone off to London without a word to any of them. Glancing back to see Hopkins walking slowly away, he unfolded the letter. He frowned as he read it, and then he folded it up again and put it into his pocket.

While Antonia stood with the others talking to Sir Osbert, she wondered where Warrington was. When she had awakened that morning, she'd thought of him and how he'd kissed her.

She'd wondered for a moment whether it had been a dream, but then had realized that it was true. They were going to be married! The idea had filled her with a sense of eager anticipation. In a short time she'd awaken to find Jack beside her!

When Warrington had not been with the others that morning, Antonia had been disappointed. Since Jocko had told her he'd gone for a ride, she had kept watching for him to return. Then a distraction had appeared in the form of Pickering's old friend and Sir Osbert. Yet, while she listened to Sir Osbert and Mrs. Pickering chat about a variety of subjects, she kept scanning the area around the wagons for Jack.

Michael Flynn, who had departed, now rejoined them.

A short time later, Pickering and Crawford returned to the group. "Ladies and gentleman," said the circus owner, "I have a rather surprising announcement to make. My dear friend, Mr. Crawford, wants Pickering's Amazing Circus to become part of his London Amphitheater. He wants the entire troupe to join him. He has made a most generous offer and I have agreed. We will go to London."

"What!" cried Mrs. Pickering in amazement.

Tilly clapped her hands. "London! Oh, I shall be glad to be 'ome. Why, 'tis wonderful news!"

Michael Flynn broke into a grin. Crawford's Amphitheater! He would finally leave these small rural audiences behind him.

"London!" cried Jem, picking up Baldric. "I've always wished I might see London." He looked around. "Mr. Bradford will be glad. But isn't he back from his ride yet?"

"I fear Bradford isn't coming back," said Michael Flynn, enjoying the reaction this news caused among his listeners. In particular, he noted Antonia's look of disbelief.

"Not coming back?" said Tilly. "What do you mean?"

Flynn hesitated. Since reading the note to Antonia from Warrington, he'd been thinking about what he should say. He had tossed the viscount's note into the fire on his return to the camp. "I suspect he hasn't just gone for a ride, but he's taken his horse and left."

"Left?" cried Pickering. "Left the troupe?"

"Yes," said Flynn. "Flown off."

The circus manager fixed an incredulous eye on the acrobat. "Flown off? Flown off? What the devil do you mean? And why didn't you say anything about this sooner?"

The acrobat shook his head regretfully. "I kept hoping he would return, and I hated to upset Miss Richards. But late last night, Bradford expressed some reservations about marriage and staying with the troupe. Of course, I didn't think anything of it. 'Tis common for a bachelor to have some second thoughts."

"Oh, that must be nonsense," said Tilly.

"I wish it were," said Flynn, attempting to look sincerely pained at the information he was imparting.

"Damn and blast!" cried Pickering. "Another rider bolted!"

"I can't believe it," said Antonia. "He wouldn't have left without a word to anyone."

"I'm sure that's right," said Jem. "Mr. Bradford wouldn't go off like that. Not without telling us."

"Well, I hope I'm wrong," said Flynn. "I imagine we must wait and see."

Antonia felt as if the wind had been knocked out of her. It couldn't be true, she told herself. Seeing Antonia's distress, Mrs. Pickering put a kindly hand on her shoulder. "Don't worry, my dear," she said, "I'm certain Mr. Bradford will be back."

Her husband grimaced at her words. "I'm glad you're so dashed sure about it, Mrs. Pickering," he grumbled. "By God, the fellow's ruined everything! Crawford wanted our entire company." He looked tragically over at his friend. "You will probably wish to reconsider our arrangement, Will."

Crawford shook his head. "No, indeed not. You will all come to London."

While this information pleased most of the company, the news about Warrington had cast a pall on the gathering. Jem took Antonia's hand and tried to assure her that, despite what Flynn had said, Jack Bradford would be back.

25

Warrington made the trip back to London in record time. Throughout his journey, his thoughts had centered on his father and Antonia. Afraid that he would be too late in arriving home, he had brooded that he would have no opportunity to mend his relationship with the earl.

It was late in the evening when the viscount arrived back in town. Feeling exhausted and grimy, he decided that he'd stop at his own house first before going on to his father's.

His butler, Bishop, was quite shocked to see his master appear at the door in his shabby, dust-covered clothes, with dark stubble upon his face. "My lord!" said the butler in a surprised tone. "I am very glad to see your lordship returned."

Warrington nodded at him as he strode into the entrance way. "What news is there of my father? Is he . . . ?"

"Lord Gravenhurst remains in precarious health, my lord."

Despite the butler's grave tone, the viscount was relieved. He had been very worried that he'd be too late to see him. "I came back as soon as I heard he was ill. I read it in the newspaper."

"Your lordship's family has been attempting to find you for more than a week, my lord."

"Damn," muttered Warrington. "I must go to him at once. I'll need a bath and a change of clothes, Bishop. Then I'll be off to Gravenhurst House. Have Jenkins get the phaeton ready."

"Very good, my lord," said Bishop.

The viscount made his way to his room. His valet quickly appeared to assist him. Although dismayed by Warrington's appearance, Finch's face bore no trace of emotion as he hurried to do his work. After a bath and shave and a new suit of clothes, the viscount once again appeared as a man of fashion.

While Finch brushed off the shoulders of his coat and adjusted the arrangement of his neckcloth, Warrington stared impatiently into the mirror. He'd forgotten what it was like to have the man fussing about him, concerned about what now seemed the most trivial details of dress.

Leaving the house, Warrington was soon perched at the reins of his phaeton. He drove quickly toward the Earl of Gravenhurst's residence.

When he arrived at the impressive gray-stone mansion, the viscount threw his reins to his footman and hurried up the walk to the front door. His father's butler, relieved to see the young gentleman had finally returned home, ushered Warrington into the drawing room.

Pacing restlessly in front of the windows, Warrington looked up expectantly as the door opened and his mother came into the room. The Countess of Gravenhurst was a tall, elegant lady of middle years, with streaks of gray in her brown hair. Seeing her son, she gave a cry and rushed to embrace him. "My dear boy," she said, "I thought you would never come!"

"I didn't know about Father," he said, holding her close. "How is he?"

"He's very ill, Warrington," she said, pulling away and regarding him with a frown. "It was very bad of you, Warrington, to fly off and not tell a soul where you were going. And then to only send me only one letter with a few lines scrawled on it. Between you and your father, I've been frantic."

"I'm sorry, Mama," said the viscount. "But I should like to see my father."

The countess nodded. "Of course, my dear," she said, pressing her lace handkerchief to her cheek to wipe away a tear. "He is very ill. Your sisters are with him. Come with me."

The viscount took her arm and the two of them went off to his father's room.

As he entered the room, his two sisters glanced toward him. Seeing who it was, they sprang up from their chairs and hurried over to him.

Like their mother, each sister gave him a hug and then scolded him for his absence. The youngest, Fanny, a pretty redhead of sixteen, shook her head at him. "Jack, where have you been?" she asked. "We've all been so worried."

He patted her cheek affectionately. "I'm sorry, Fan," he said. "I'll tell you all about it later." Warrington looked over at the canopied bed and then glanced back at his sisters. "How is Father?"

His other sister, Catherine, an attractive brown-haired lady of fashion, grew teary eyed. "Oh, Jack, not well at all."

Warrington took her hand and squeezed it. He then made his way over toward the bed.

Looking down at his father, the viscount was shocked by the change in that gentleman's appearance. The earl, who'd looked quite robust a few weeks before, now lay there, looking extremely pale and gaunt. Gravenhurst suddenly opened his eyes and stared up at his son.

"Father," said Warrington, gazing down at him, "I'm here."

The earl's dark eyes looked uncomprehending at first. Then they seemed to take on a glint of recognition. "Warrington?" he said in a whisper.

Smiling, the viscount reached out and pressed his father's hand. "Yes, Father. I've returned."

The earl began to mumble something, and then he closed his eyes again. The viscount took the chair next to the bed and watched his father with anxious eyes.

The wagons made their way along the road to London, with Tilly and Antonia riding with Jocko. The Scotsman was in a talkative mood, and he and Tilly chatted on about London and the excitement that awaited them in the great metropolis. They were getting close to London and, if all went well, they would be there before nightfall.

Antonia sat quietly as the wagon continued on. It had been six days since they had left Shrewsbury and started for London. Throughout that time, Antonia had been terribly depressed.

While Jocko told an amusing anecdote, Antonia scarcely listened. She thought of the day Flynn had told them that Warrington had left. At first she hadn't believed that he could desert her in such an infamous fashion. Yet, when Warrington had not returned that day, she'd begun to think that Flynn had been right.

The next morning, when Pickering had announced that they must leave Shrewsbury, Antonia had climbed into the wagon and had tried to bear up the best she could. As they had traveled the long miles toward London, Tilly had tried to cheer her up, but Antonia was devastated to think that Warrington had abandoned her.

Now, although nearly a week and many miles had gone by, the pain hadn't lessened. She'd been a great fool to fall in love with a man like him, she told herself. After all, his past was a mystery. She knew almost nothing about him.

As they drove past a crossroads, Tilly excitedly pointed to a signpost. "Look! London is but seven miles! I shall be very glad to get there. Lord, I'm sore from so much jostling about in this wagon. Won't you be glad to arrive, Tony?"

"Yes, of course," said Antonia listlessly.

"You must buck up, my girl," said Tilly. "I know you 'ave cause to be sad, but you must look on the bright side. After all, ain't it better that Jack would leave you now instead of later when you 'ad a passel of children to be looking after?"

"That is hardly going to cheer me up, Tilly," said Antonia with a frown.

"No, I suppose not," said Tilly. "Well, try not to dwell on it. Think instead of the larks we'll 'ave in town. We'll stroll about in Vauxhall Gardens and charm the nobs. Don't forget what Mrs. Pickering said. You're to marry a lord. I don't doubt you'll meet 'im in London."

"I don't think I'll ever marry," said Antonia.

"What nonsense," said Tilly. "You'll find a husband and so shall I."

"Och, Tilly," said Jocko, "if ye want a husband, ye need tae look nae farther than the lad sitting beside ye."

"Oh, Jock," said Tilly, shoving him playfully, "what a daft fellow you are. I need a man with money in his purse. No, you must find yourself a rich widow. There be plenty of them about in town."

"'Tis a fine idea, lass," said Jocko with a grin. "Aye, I'll keep my eyes peeled for rich widows."

They both laughed and Antonia found their jocularity hard to tolerate. She was glad when Jocko saw a goat and began to talk about a wayward billy goat he'd once tangled with in his boyhood.

It seemed a very long time until they entered the city. And it took even longer to pass through the increasingly crowded streets. As they made their way through town, Antonia perked up at the sights and sounds of the great city.

It had been many years since she had visited London. She'd been a girl of eleven when her parents had taken her there. Antonia remembered the thrill of seeing the bustling, noisy streets. As they rode along, Antonia forgot about Warrington for a time. There was so much to see. There were fashionable ladies and gentlemen riding in shiny new phaetons, and lumbering mail coaches driven by rakish coachmen wearing many-caped coats. There were streets lined with shops and vendors roaming about selling their wares.

Antonia watched as they passed grand buildings and tall churches and all manner of people, horses, and vehicles. Then suddenly she saw a tall man walking down the street. For a moment she thought it was Warrington. When they passed him and she saw there wasn't the slightest resemblance, she felt foolish.

He probably wasn't even in London, she told herself. And even if he were, one couldn't expect to meet up with him, especially on one's arrival in town. Antonia's gloom returned as they completed their journey, finally pulling up near Crawford's Amphitheater, a vast wooden structure that dominated the street.

The weary members of Pickering's troupe were glad to retire to a nearby boarding house. Crawford had made arrangements for them to stay there, and while the accommodations were modest, the rooms looked luxurious compared to the circus wagons.

Jem, who had ridden most of the way with the Pickerings, was glad to join Antonia in the dining room of the boarding house. Baldric followed close behind him, wagging his tail and appearing very pleased to find himself in a new and interesting location.

"You must watch that dog, my boy," said a large, gray-haired woman in a blue dress and white cap. "I won't have dogs destroying my house."

"Oh, no, ma'am," said Jem, addressing the woman, who was the proprietress of the establishment, a formidable woman named Mrs. Beamish. "Baldric is very well trained. He's to perform in the circus. Baldric, do a dance for the lady."

Baldric got up on his hind legs and began to twirl around, much to Mrs. Beamish's delight. Jem then commanded the dog to sit and lie down beside his chair, making Mrs. Beamish declare that she'd never seen a better-behaved animal and she was sure that Baldric would cause no trouble.

When dinner was served, everyone ate with relish. They were all very hungry and Mrs. Beamish's cottage pie and boiled mutton seemed altogether delectable.

Jem sat beside Antonia, devouring his food with the enthusiasm most growing boys bring to the dinner table. "And what do you think of London, Jem?" said Tilly.

"Oh, 'tis very grand," said Jem. "I've never seen so many people. Why, who would have thought there were so many?"

Antonia smiled. "London is a very large city, Jem."

"Indeed so, miss," said Jem, taking another forkful of food. "And 'tis very grand, ain't it?"

"There is no grander city in all the world," said Mrs. Pickering.

"Come, come, Mrs. Pickering," said Flynn. "What of Paris? What of Rome?"

"What of them?" said Mrs. Pickering. "They are foreign cities and while I haven't seen them, I should think they are a good deal inferior to London."

This seemed to settle the matter and the conversation turned to the troupe's prospects for making a great success in town. There was a great deal of optimism and high spirits among the group, with the exception of Antonia, who could not help but think about Warrington.

26

For four days after Warrington's arrival in London, the Earl of Gravenhurst had remained seriously ill. And although Lord Gravenhurst had recognized his son when the viscount had first arrived, he had soon lapsed into an unconscious, feverish state. The viscount had spent many hours at his father's bedside, praying for the earl to recover, but the earl's condition had not improved.

The countess and Warrington's two sister's had been so preoccupied with the earl's condition that they hadn't pressed him much about his whereabouts during the past month. The viscount had been glad of that, for he hadn't wanted to tell them the details of how he had spent his time. He could imagine how his mother and sisters would respond to the news that he'd labored as a groom and a circus performer.

Shortly after his arrival in London, Warrington had sent a servant to the next village on the circus's itinerary with a letter for Antonia. In the letter, he had explained more about his father's illness, and had said that he'd come as soon as possible.

On the morning of the fifth day, Warrington entered his father's bedroom. It was early and his mother and sisters, who had stayed up very late the night before at the earl's bedside, had not yet risen. "Good morning, Father," said the viscount, sitting down in the chair next to the bed.

Warrington hadn't expected a response, for the earl hadn't said a word in days. He lay there sleeping quietly.

"I do wish you could hear me, Father," said the viscount, pressing his father's hand. "I have so much to say to you. I learned so much during the time I was away. Indeed, I doubt I shall ever be the same."

Leaning back in the chair, he fixed his gaze upon the earl's face.

"You were right in thinking me a coxcomb and a wastrel." A slight smile crossed his lips. "I'd dearly love to tell you how I've spent the past month. I've had some interesting times. And I've fallen in love. I'm going to be married to a wonderful lady. So you must recover so that you can be at the wedding."

The earl continued to sleep, expressing no reaction to this announcement. Warrington continued. "Yes, you must recover, Father. I'm not ready to be the earl. Not for a very long time. And I want you to meet Antonia Richards. She's the girl I'm going to marry. I'm sure you'll be very fond of her.

"And she doesn't even know who I am. It will be deuced awkward telling her. But then Mrs. Pickering did say she'd marry a lord, so perhaps she won't be so surprised.

"Yes, I do have a good many things to tell you, sir. So you must get well." Warrington reached over and pressed his father's hand once more. Then he sat, watching the earl and waiting for his mother and sisters to arrive.

Several minutes passed and then, suddenly, Lord Gravenhurst's eyelids flickered and he opened his eyes and muttered an incoherent word.

The viscount, who was lost in thought, nearly jumped out of his chair. "Father!" he cried, leaning over and grasping the earl's hand. "Can you hear me? It is I, Warrington."

The earl looked over at his son. "Warrington?" he said in a weak voice.

"Yes, Father," said the viscount eagerly.

Gravenhurst eyed him for a moment with a rather confused look. Then he spoke in a weak but coherent voice. "I suppose you're going to tell me you've won the accurst wager."

The viscount's eyes widened and he regarded the earl with an astonished expression. Reaching over, he put his hand on the earl's forehead. "Your fever is gone! Thank God!" He stood up. "I must go tell Mama and my sisters!"

"No, wait a moment, Warrington," said the earl in a low voice. "I think you said something about a wedding."

The viscount grinned. "Yes, I shall tell you all about that."

"You didn't want to be married," said Lord Gravenhurst, his voice now growing stronger. "I'd hoped your time away would help, boy. I'd begun to regret that damned silly wager, sending you off like I did. I imagined you'd got yourself into all kinds of scrapes."

A smile appeared on the viscount's face. "I fear you're right, sir. And I shall tell you all about it, but first I must ring for a servant." Warrington went to the bell pull and quickly summoned the butler.

When the butler arrived, the viscount said, "Hayes, his lordship's fever has broken. Tell her ladyship and my sisters."

"Thanks be to God," cried the normally unemotional servant, who then rushed off to fetch his mistress.

"We were so worried about you," said Warrington. "You must rest and not overtire yourself."

"But I want to hear about you. Did you manage to live off the fifty pounds?"

The viscount smiled ruefully, "Actually, sir, some fellows robbed me of my money and my horse as soon as I set foot in Shropshire. And knowing that I mustn't reveal my identity, I had no recourse but to earn my bread like any common fellow. But I shall tell you more about it later."

At that moment Lady Gravenhurst and her two daughters came into the room. The countess threw herself on her husband's neck and began to sob. The doctor, who had arrived at the house only a few minutes before, pulled the countess away and seated her in the chair.

Then he examined the sick man and pronounced him on the road to recovery. This caused Lady Gravenhurst and her daughters to cry for joy. After many expressions of happiness at this news, the ladies and Warrington were ushered out of the sickroom so that the earl could have the opportunity to rest.

A sense of tremendous relief permeated Gravenhurst House and there was great rejoicing in the servants' hall when the earl's butler announced that Lord Gravenhurst would recover. At luncheon, Lady Gravenhurst and her children were exceedingly happy.

They sat at the table, their spirits and appetites restored by the good news. Warrington's sister Catherine's husband, Lord Ashbourne, had arrived to join them. An affable, pleasant young man, who dressed in the manner of the dandies, Ashbourne was very glad to hear that his father-in-law would be restored to health.

"And it is good that you are back in town," said Ashbourne,

looking at Warrington. "You missed some dashed good sport. The Prince Regent's horse did very poorly in a race last week. Devilish bad luck your missing that race, Warrington."

"Oh, I had sport enough in Shropshire," said the viscount.

"Shropshire?" said Ashbourne. "That must have been very tedious being there. I so hate the country. It is so very dull."

"I assure you, it wasn't in the least dull," said Warrington.

"Well, what did you do there?" said Ashbourne. "Where did you stay?"

"Warrington has been very mysterious about that," said Fanny, smiling mischievously at her brother. "He's scarcely told us anything and he was gone a month."

"Yes, you haven't said much about it, my dear," said Lady Gravenhurst. "Do tell us about your stay in Shropshire. Where did you stay?"

"At a house near Cawley for a time. And then I went to Shrewsbury."

"I don't believe I've ever been to Shrewsbury," said Lady Gravenhurst. "Nor can I see any reason for your having gone there. I was very vexed with your father for sending you off like that."

"Well, I'm dashed glad he did," said Warrington. "You see, while I was gone, I met the girl I shall marry."

"What!" cried Lady Gravenhurst.

Her daughters uttered similar cries, demanding that Warrington explain this startling pronouncement.

"I have become engaged to a young lady. Her name is Antonia Richards."

"Antonia Richards?" said Catherine. "But who is she?"

"Yes!" said Fanny. "Who is she?"

"She is the most wonderful girl. I'm sure you'll all like her very much."

Lady Gravenhurst frowned. "I thought you would marry Lady Sophie Parkenham."

"Mama, I never said I'd marry her," said the viscount. "On the contrary, I made it very clear that I had no wish to do so."

"Oh, dear, Warrington," said his sister Catherine. "I pray you aren't going to tell us that you intend to marry a provincial nobody."

"But who is she, Warrington?" demanded Lady Gravenhurst. "I don't know anyone named Richards."

"No, you don't know her, Mama. She is the daughter of a naval captain."

"The daughter of a naval captain?" said Catherine, regarding her brother with disapproval.

"It doesn't signify who her father is," said Warrington. "She is a remarkable young lady—intelligent, beautiful, kind, and talented."

"Indeed?" said Catherine. "It seems you've changed, Warrington. Why, only a few months ago you chided me for inviting Mrs. Rutherford to my dinner party simply because her grandfather was in trade."

"Perhaps I did," said Warrington, "but I do see things differently now."

"Where did you meet this Miss Richards, Warrington?" said Ashbourne.

"In Shropshire. At the country house where I stayed. It was called Larchmont."

"Then hers is a landed family?" said Lady Gravenhurst.

Warrington smiled. "No, Mama, Miss Richards was employed there as the governess."

"What!" cried the countess. "The governess!"

"Oh, Warrington!" exclaimed Fanny. "To think that you would wish to marry a governess! Oh, it is too funny."

"I cannot imagine how you could consider marrying such a person," said Lady Gravenhurst. "A governess! Oh, why did your father send you to Shropshire?"

"I'm sorry to distress you, Mama, but I shall marry Miss Richards. I have asked for her hand in marriage and she has accepted."

Lady Gravenhurst gave him a long, suffering look and reflected that after having just weathered one crisis, it was monstrous that her son had now presented her with another.

27

Antonia sat in front of the mirror while the hairdresser put the finishing touches on her coiffure. A finicky Frenchman who considered himself an artist, the hairdresser made a good many small alterations before finally announcing he had completed his work.

Studying her reflection, Antonia had to admit that he had done a splendid job. Her dark hair looked very attractive arranged high on her head with short curls surrounding her face. A garland of pink-satin flowers completed the picture.

Rising from her chair, Antonia smoothed the skirt of her gown. It was a lovely, high-waisted creation of pink satin, with a low-cut, tight-fitting bodice and dainty puff sleeves. Glancing into the mirror, Antonia was satisfied that she had never looked better.

Turning from the mirror, she took a deep breath. In a short time, she would be appearing before the very large audience that was now assembling in Crawford's Amphitheater. It was a rather daunting prospect.

There was a knock at the door. "Come in," said Antonia.

When the door opened, Jem entered the room. At his heels was Baldric. "Oh, Miss Richards," cried Jem, "you look beautiful."

"Thank you, sir," said Antonia. "You both look exceedingly handsome this evening."

"Baldric don't like his ruff overmuch," said Jem. " 'Tis far bigger than the other one. He thinks it silly. But Mr. Pickering says it looks very good, and Mr. Crawford, as well, so there's nought to be done but bear up as best as we can, eh, Baldric?"

Baldric cocked his head and looked at his young master as if trying to understand.

"Poor Baldric," said Antonia. "I hope it isn't too tight."

"Oh, no. And he can do all his tricks. And once he's in front of the audience and hears the shouts and applause, he'll be happy as a grig."

Antonia laughed. "I'm glad. And what about you? Are you nervous?"

Jem nodded. "A little. Are you?"

"Oh, I'm quite nervous, but like Baldric, I'll be fine once I begin. Or at least I expect I shall."

"Of course you will," said Jem. "You're always wonderful." He paused for a moment as if considering what to say. "I was thinking, Miss Richards. Do you think Mr. Bradford might be here tonight? I thought that maybe he was in London and maybe he would come to see us. Wouldn't that be splendid?"

Antonia frowned. She'd been trying hard not to think about Warrington. Of course, since coming to London five days earlier, she hadn't been able to think of much else. "Oh, I don't believe he will. I doubt whether he even knows we're here."

"If only we knew where he was," said Jem. "But I'm sure he'll come when he knows we're here."

"I don't know," said Antonia dispiritedly.

"Oh, I'm certain of it."

"Well, we must be going, Jem. Mr. Pickering will be wondering where we are."

Jem nodded and the two of them left the room.

Among the great crowd of people filling Crawford's Amphitheater that evening were two well-dressed young gentlemen. One of them was a handsome man, short of stature, with auburn hair and striking blue eyes. His companion was taller, with dark hair and eyes.

The shorter of the two men was well known to Antonia. Geoffrey Mansfield had arrived in London a week ago. He was staying with a friend, an old school friend named Cathcart.

Cathcart was a dissolute young man much addicted to drink and wild living. He and Geoffrey had been having a very enjoyable time in town, for Cathcart was doing all he could to keep his friend amused. They had spent most of their nights at gambling dens and bawdy houses. That evening Cathcart had suggested they visit Crawford's Amphitheater before proceeding to their usual haunts.

Although Geoffrey would have preferred to skip the exhibitions of riding skill and musical entertainments he knew were to be found at Crawford's establishment, he was willing to accompany his friend. As Geoffrey took his seat, he scanned the crowd for attractive females.

When they appeared to be in short supply, he muttered to his friend, "There's hardly a decent-looking girl in sight. Oh, wait, there's a pretty one. There in the blue dress."

Cathcart, with a bored expression, eyed the young woman. "Egad, Mansfield, what does it matter if they're ill-favored or beautiful? One woman's as good as another in the dark."

"That's true enough," said Geoffrey, ogling the girl in the blue dress, "but I'd sooner have a pretty one."

"Well, you'll see your share of beauties tonight. Crawford has a stable of fine-looking wenches."

"Good," said Geoffrey. Yet when the performance began, there seemed a dearth of female performers. Geoffrey had little interest in acrobats or jugglers. He perked up when a dancer called Princess Fatima appeared, and he cheered loudly at Tilly's performance.

When Jem appeared with Baldric, Geoffrey did not recognize his former servant. He was focused on the little dog and he laughed at the animal's antics. Since he had such an interest in horses, he also enjoyed watching a group of four perfectly matched gray horses that did amazing feats on command.

At the conclusion of this act, Geoffrey was ready to proceed to the next stage of the evening's entertainment, but Cathcart wanted to stay a little longer. Geoffrey, therefore, settled down as a diminutive young lady appeared with a stringed instrument of some kind.

"Good God!" muttered Geoffrey as Antonia began to sing.

"What is it?"

"That girl! I know her."

"Aren't you the fortunate one?" said Cathcart languidly.

"She was my sisters' governess."

"Governess?" said Cathcart, very much interested.

Geoffrey nodded. "That is Miss Richards. She was sent on her way for immoral behavior with a groom."

"Now that is interesting," said Cathcart, looking over at his friend. "I hope the groom wasn't the only one to benefit from her immoral behavior."

Geoffrey shook his head. "I never had my way with her. Not that I put any effort into it. And it was for the best. My father wouldn't have taken it well if he discovered that I'd seduced my sisters' governess."

Cathcart nodded. "Well, she ain't a governess any longer."

"That's true," said Geoffrey. "My stepmother will be very interested to hear what's become of her. I should like to have another try with her. I wonder if that groom is still hanging about her? By God, he was the most insolent, insufferable villain I've ever had working at Larchmont." Geoffrey appeared thoughtful. "Perhaps we can meet the wench after she's done singing."

"If you wish," said Cathcart. "She's a damned fine singer, I'll say that."

"Hang her singing," said Geoffrey. "I don't give two figs for that."

When Antonia was finished, the crowd roared its approval. She sang two encores, and then bowed and took her leave.

Geoffrey nudged his friend and the two got up and made their way out.

When Antonia returned to the dressing room she shared with Tilly, she found the dancer had changed from her near-Eastern costume and was attired in a dress and pelisse. " 'Ow did you do, Tony? Oh, I don't 'ave to ask. I could 'ear 'em cheering for you. I wish I could 'ave seen you, but I 'ad to 'urry. A gentleman is calling for me and taking me out to supper. We'll talk later, my dear."

And then, grabbing her hat, Tilly left her. Antonia was soon joined by one of the maids, who helped her out of her gown and then went to hang it carefully. Putting on her dressing gown, Antonia sat down at the table and began to take the powder and rouge off her face. As she did so, she began to think about Warrington, wondering where he was and if he was trying to contact her.

After a time there was knock at the door. "Yes, come in," said Antonia, thinking it would be Jem.

When the door opened and two men entered, she regarded them questioningly. Then recognizing Geoffrey Mansfield, her eyes widened in surprise and indignation.

"Miss Richards," said Geoffrey, coming forward and smiling affably. "Imagine my surprise when I saw you this evening. You were excellent. My friend thought so, too."

"Yes, you were wonderful," said Cathcart.

Antonia tried to remain calm. Although Geoffrey Mansfield was certainly the last person she wished to see, she resisted her impulse to jump up and push him and his companion out the door.

When she made no remark, Geoffrey continued. "May I present my friend, Mr. Cathcart? Cathcart, this lady is Miss Richards."

"Your servant, ma'am," said Cathcart, making a polite bow.

Antonia nodded coolly at the man. "Sir," she said.

"You have certainly made a success since leaving Larchmont," said Geoffrey. "But where is that fellow? What was his name? Oh, yes, Bradford. Jack Bradford." He turned to Cathcart. "The other servants called him 'Gentleman Jack' because, in their eyes, he acted like a gentleman."

Antonia made no reply, but continued to regard Geoffrey with an icy look.

Geoffrey grinned. "He's not here then? Well, he didn't seem the sort to stick with a girl. You're well rid of him, my dear Miss Richards."

Although she was doing an admirable job of controlling herself, these words made Antonia very angry. The sight of Geoffrey also brought back so many unpleasant memories that she experienced a tightness in her stomach.

"Mr. Cathcart and I would be very pleased to take you to dinner, Miss Richards," said Geoffrey. "Do say you'll go."

Antonia regarded him with an expression of incredulity. Did he honestly believe that she would accompany him anywhere? Yet there he stood, eyeing her with an expectant look as if she would be more than happy to go with him.

"No, thank you, Mr. Mansfield," said Antonia, trying very hard to restrain her temper.

"We'll be happy to wait for you," said Geoffrey. "Do come with us."

"I have declined, Mr. Mansfield," said Antonia. "Now if you would be so good as to leave, sir."

Geoffrey, whose view of Antonia in her dressing gown had made it hard for him to accept her refusal, continued in an insistent tone. "Now, Miss Richards, don't be so hasty. Mr. Cathcart and I will be very disappointed if you don't come with us."

"I cannot say it any plainer, sir. No, I do not wish to go with you." These words were said in a very firm voice. Yet, still Geoffrey stood there as if he didn't think she was serious.

Antonia was growing increasingly angry, and she was ready to call out for assistance. There were many people rushing about and Crawford employed a number of able-bodied men who would come to the aid of performers at such times as this.

Still, she was glad when Jem appeared at the door with Baldric. "Miss Richards?" he said, looking from her to the two men. Then recognizing his former employer and tormenter, he started.

"Good God!" exclaimed Geoffrey. "Why, it is Jem. So this is where you've gone to." He turned to Cathcart. "This lad was a stable boy at Larchmont. He ran off without so much as a word to anyone."

Jem looked at Antonia, who frowned. "These gentlemen are leaving, Jem. Perhaps you might find Mr. Crawford and have him send some of the men to escort them to the door."

Nodding, Jem scurried off.

"Good evening, gentlemen," said Antonia.

Geoffrey hesitated for a moment. "Very well," he said, "but I'll see you again, miss. That you can be sure of."

He gave her the cold, hard stare she remembered from Larchmont and she felt a mixture of revulsion and indignation. How dare the loathsome man come here, acting as though she would be glad to see him? She met his gaze for a moment, then replied in the tone of a queen dismissing a courtier, "Good evening, Mr. Mansfield."

Geoffrey frowned, but could think of nothing more to say. He turned, and then he and Cathcart left the room.

28

Now out of danger, the Earl of Gravenhurst began the slow process of recovering his strength. Warrington, who had been so relieved and happy to know that his father would be well, now had some disturbing news. The servant he'd sent with the letter for Antonia returned, saying that Pickering's Amazing Circus wasn't where his lordship had said it would be and no one knew where it was to be found.

Warrington decided that he must go find Antonia himself. In the morning, the viscount went to visit his father. Entering the sickroom, he found the earl sitting up in bed, drinking a cup of tea.

"You are looking much better, Father," said the viscount, sitting down in the chair next to the bed.

"I am better," said the earl. "I cannot say why that blasted doctor wants me to stay in bed for several more days."

"I'm sure it is only a precaution, sir," said the viscount. "You mustn't be impatient. It will take time until you are completely well."

"I imagine so," said Lord Gravenhurst, putting down his teacup on the saucer on the bedside table. "Now I have been thinking about you, Warrington. I've been wondering how you spent your month away from town. I confess I am pleased that I lost this wager of ours even though I would have liked very much to see you marry Lady Sophie. But you said you were robbed of your money. How the devil did you live?"

Warrington smiled. "Yes, I was robbed of my money, my horse, and my clothes, and was beaten soundly in the bargain."

"What!" exclaimed the earl.

"Yes, I fell victim to two notorious villains, known as the Scar and Ginger Tom."

"Good God, Warrington! Were you injured?"

"Well, I must admit I'd felt far better, but I recovered rapidly."

"You should have come home."

"What? And lose the wager?" said Warrington with a laugh. "I took care not to reveal who I was, and I discovered for the first time how inconvenient it is to be an ordinary person without money."

"But what did you do?"

"I took a position at a country house."

"A position? What do you mean?"

"A position as a groom."

"A groom!" spluttered the earl. "My son toiled as a groom!"

Warrington laughed again at his father's expression. "I know it was scarcely an occupation for a gentleman, sir, but I had to earn my bread somehow. Do not forget I couldn't reveal my name."

"This is extraordinary," said Lord Gravenhurst. "You worked as a groom."

"Yes, and then I left Larchmont and became a trick rider in a circus."

Warrington had expected this admission would astonish his father and he wasn't disappointed at the earl's reaction. Lord Gravenhurst gaped at his son. "What the deuce!"

"And I was thought to have an excellent future as a trick rider. Of course, I was only just learning, but Mr. Pickering thought me a promising subject."

"You have quite confounded me, Warrington," said Lord Gravenhurst, shaking his head. "I cannot say I'm pleased to hear how you spent your time, but I must say you had some interesting experiences."

"Very interesting, Father."

"And you didn't gamble?"

"No, Father," said Warrington. "Not a penny."

"Well, my boy, you have won the wager. I'll see that all of your debts are paid."

Warrington smiled. "Thank you, Father, and you will have no fear that I will incur more debts."

"Indeed?" said the earl, regarding him with some skepticism.

"You doubtless believe that the leopard cannot change his spots, but I'm not the same man I was when I left London."

"What?" said Gravenhurst in surprise.

"I know that I've been leading an idle, wasteful life. I swear to you that I have changed."

"Good God, my boy," said the earl, "what the devil has come over you?"

"My month in the country has taught me many lessons, sir."

"Did it, indeed?" Gravenhurst paused, fixing a hopeful glance on his son. "And did you also see the wisdom of making the Lady Sophie Parkenham your wife?"

"No, Father, I'm sorry, but I have no wish to wed the lady." He hesitated. "You see, I've met the girl whom I wish to marry. Her name is Antonia Richards and she is wonderful, Father. I fear my mother is very displeased because Antonia has no money and no connections. Her father was a naval officer who was killed in the Peninsular War.

"Tony, that is to say, Miss Richards, is a remarkable lady and I intend to marry her. I hope I will have your blessing, sir."

"But how did you meet this girl?"

"She was employed as governess at Larchmont. And then we joined the circus together. Tony is a wonderful singer."

"Good God, Warrington," said the earl, very much surprised at this information. "A governess and circus performer?"

"You are the one always telling me to see beyond such superficialities as rank and family."

"Am I?" said the earl. "But I didn't think that would be interpreted as leave to marry a circus performer. Marriage is an important step, my boy. I am glad that you wish to be married, but your wife will one day be the Countess of Gravenhurst. And one's own happiness is so dependent on one's choice of wife. I don't wish to see you marry some vulgar fortune huntress."

"Vulgar fortune huntress?" The viscount laughed. "Miss Richards is a true lady and, as to being a fortune huntress, she knows me only as Jack Bradford, a man without money who has worked as a groom and a rider in the circus. She loves me against her better judgment."

Gravenhurst seemed to consider this for a time. "And you told your mother about this girl of yours?"

"She was none too pleased."

"Well, I shall certainly incur her displeasure if I do not oppose you in this."

"I know that, sir."

"Well, you're damned lucky I'm such a broad-minded man, Warrington. I shan't object. It seems this young woman has been a good influence on you."

"Indeed, she has," said Warrington quickly. "Thank you, Father. But now I must leave London again. I must find Miss Richards. I'd sent Baxter with a letter to her, but he returned last night, saying he couldn't find her. I must be off to bring her to town."

"Very well," said the earl, and a very happy Warrington took his leave.

The next week passed quickly for Antonia. She was glad that she was very busy, for she had less time to brood about Warrington.

Things were going well for the former members of Pickering's Amazing Circus and Crawford was very pleased with them. He was especially thrilled with Antonia, whose wonderful voice delighted the crowds.

As the days went by and it grew unlikely that they would see Jack Bradford again, Michael Flynn grew more attentive to Antonia. Although she gave him no encouragement, the acrobat was undeterred. Flynn was determined that in time he would break down her resistance and convince her that he was the man for her.

Yet Flynn was not alone in his pursuit of Antonia. Her appearances in Crawford's Amphitheater inspired considerable masculine attention. She was soon receiving flowers and letters from admirers eager to further their acquaintance.

True to his word, Geoffrey Mansfield continued to make unwelcome appearances. However, his annoying visits were soon curtailed by Crawford and his burly employees.

Jem was thoroughly enjoying himself and would have been perfectly content, if only his friend Jack Bradford would appear. Unlike Antonia, Jem was still very certain that Warrington would arrive.

On one warm morning a week after they'd started performing at Crawford's, Jem asked Antonia if she'd accompany him on a shopping expedition. The following day was Jocko's birthday and Jem expressed his desire to buy him a gift.

Antonia readily agreed and the two of them set off. Jem was unsure what he might get the juggler. They visited a number of shops, with Jem studying the merchandise with great care. Although he came close to purchasing some handkerchiefs at one establishment, he then decided they wouldn't do. "I did want to buy something he would like," said Jem when, after finally rejecting the handkerchiefs, they left the shop.

Noting a bookseller's shop across the street, Antonia gestured toward it. "Perhaps a book. I dare say a Scotsman like Jocko might like a book by Robert Burns, the Scottish poet. Shall we go and look?"

Jem nodded eagerly, happy at the suggestion. They crossed the street and entered the bookshop. The proprietor was eager to wait upon Antonia, who looked very lovely in a wine-colored pelisse and bonnet. When asked if there were any works by the poet Burns for sale, the bookseller quickly led them to an assortment of books.

"Oh, I think he might like this one," said Antonia, selecting a small volume and handing it to Jem.

After studying it for a long time, Jem finally decided to buy it. While Jem was completing his purchase, Antonia looked at some of the other books. Her eye fell on a peerage book that had a coat of arms on the cover. Thinking of the crest that had been engraved on the back of Warrington's watch, she opened it and began to thumb through it, pausing to look at pages with drawings of coats of arms on them.

"Is there anything else I might help you with, madam?" said the bookseller, coming up to her once he had finished helping Jem.

"This book caught my eye," said Antonia, turning another page and finding more illustrations. Looking over the assortment of coats of arms, she saw a shield with the familiar crest, a stag beneath three diamonds. She eagerly read the name beneath it. "Fortescue, Earl of Gravenhurst." Then, turning to the bookseller, she pointed to the shield. "I saw this once. I wondered whose crest it was."

"Oh, the Fortescue family," said the bookseller. "The Earl of Gravenhurst. Such a distinguished family. Why, I often walk past his house on Grosvenor Square. He's been ill, you know, but I'm told he is now recovering."

Antonia closed the book and put it down. "I'm glad to hear it."

"Oh, yes, the earl is a fine gentleman. Are there any other books I might show you?"

Shaking her head, Antonia thanked the man. Then she and Jem left the shop. "What was that book, Miss Richards?" said Jem.

"Oh, it was a book about noble families. I was looking for the crest that was on Jack's watch. He said a gentleman gave it to him."

"Did you find it in the book?"

"Yes, I did." Antonia looked thoughtful. "It's the crest of the Earl of Gravenhurst."

"An earl?" said Jem. "Did Jack know an earl?"

"I don't know," said Antonia. "Perhaps."

"Does the earl live in London?"

"The bookseller says he does."

"Then could we not find the earl and ask him about Mr. Bradford? Perhaps he would know where we might find him."

Antonia laughed. "One doesn't just call on earls. Or one doesn't call on them and expect to be admitted."

"But couldn't we try?" said Jem. "What harm would there be in trying?"

Antonia paused. She had no wish to pay a call at the earl's home and she knew it would be pointless to do so. Still, if there was any chance at all that she might find out something about Jack Bradford, perhaps she should try. "I suppose there wouldn't be any harm in it. What is the worst that might befall us? That we will be tossed from the doorstep? Well, we've survived worse, haven't we?"

Jem laughed. "Yes, miss."

"Then I shall go ask the bookseller how one gets to Grosvenor Square, and then we will go call upon the Earl of Gravenhurst." They turned around and reentered the book shop. While the proprietor was surprised at the question, he was happy to give directions to the earl's residence.

Jem and Antonia then set off to Grosvenor Square, which was not so terribly far. It didn't take them long to get to the exclusive neighborhood with its grand homes.

It wasn't hard to find Gravenhurst House, for the bookseller had described the stately edifice very carefully. As they walked up to the door, Antonia felt rather nervous. She rang the bell and the door was opened by a somber-looking butler.

"I should like to see the Earl of Gravenhurst," said Antonia.

Hayes eyed Antonia and Jem appraisingly. While not dressed as well as many of the visitors who came to the front door, they looked respectable enough.

"His lordship is ill, miss, and cannot be disturbed. And Lady Gravenhurst has gone out. Would you like to leave your card, miss?"

"Oh, I don't have a card," said Antonia. "But do you think I might leave a note for his lordship?"

The butler nodded his assent and led them inside. Jem looked around, rather overwhelmed by the grandeur of the place as they stood in the vast entry hall with its large marble staircase. Hayes led them from the entry hall into a fashionably appointed room with mauve walls and classically inspired furniture.

"There is pen and paper there, miss," said the butler, motioning toward an elegant mahogany desk.

"Thank you," said Antonia, fixing her dazzling smile upon the servant. "You are very kind. I shall only be a moment."

Jem looked around the room while Antonia sat down at the desk and began writing. There were a number of paintings on the walls, portraits and landscapes. Suddenly Jem's eye fell on one and he let out an exclamation. "Miss Richards! There is Mr. Bradford! Look! That picture!" Jem hurried across the room to stand before a large portrait of a splendidly dressed young gentleman, his handsome countenance smiling down at them. It was, without a doubt, Jack Bradford.

Antonia stared at the painting in surprise. Jem had turned to the butler. "We know Mr. Bradford. Here is his picture. Do you know where he is?"

Hayes frowned at the boy. "You are mistaken, young man. That is a portrait of Lord Warrington, the earl's son."

"But it is exactly like Mr. Bradford," said Jem. "It *is* Mr. Bradford!"

Rising from the desk, Antonia went over to stand beside Jem and look at the portrait more carefully.

The butler, who found the visitors perplexing, frowned again. "The gentleman in the portrait is Lord Warrington. It is an excellent likeness painted three years ago on the occasion of his lordship's twenty-first birthday."

"Is Lord Warrington here?" asked Antonia, looking from the portrait to Hayes.

The butler shook his head. "His lordship left town a few days ago. I don't know when he will return."

"I see," said Antonia. "Do you know Mr. Bradford?"

"I don't know anyone by that name," said the butler.

"Is Lord Warrington's Christian name John?" said Antonia, staring back at the portrait.

"Yes," said Hayes, thinking he had answered too many questions already.

"I don't understand," said Jem, turning to regard Antonia with a bewildered look.

"Nor do I," said Antonia, taking the boy by the hand. "I think we should go, Jem."

"Would you like to leave the note, miss?" said the butler.

Antonia shook her head. "No, I don't think I shall leave a note. I do thank you. We will leave now."

Hayes escorted them to the door and watched them walk hurriedly away.

29

Jem looked over at Antonia with a pained expression. "It was Mr. Bradford. It looked exactly like him."

Antonia nodded. "I believe it was. Mr. Bradford is not who we thought he was. He is Lord Warrington." They continued on down the street, walking past the imposing homes of some of the town's wealthiest residents.

"But at Larchmont he worked as a groom! Would a lord do that?"

"A lord may do as he pleases," said Antonia grimly. "Perhaps he found it amusing."

Jem looked perplexed, but suddenly he brightened. "Mrs. Pickering said you would marry a lord. And so you will! What a grand house you'll live in."

"That is nonsense," said Antonia with unaccustomed sharpness. She stopped walking and looked at the boy. "Jem, I must ask you to say nothing more about this. I don't wish to speak about it. And you must promise me, on your word of honor, that you won't tell anyone."

"No, I won't say a word, Miss Richards."

"Good," said Antonia and they began walking again.

Warrington had first traveled to a village near Shrewsbury. Finding no trace of Antonia or Pickering's Amazing Circus, he had gone on to Shrewsbury. There he discovered that Pickering and the others had gone to London to perform at Crawford's Amphitheater.

The viscount had uttered a cry of frustration at hearing this news. Antonia was in London! She had been at Crawford's Amphitheater, a place he knew well and, indeed, had passed more than once during his days in town.

It had infuriated him to think that she'd been there and he hadn't known. And he'd traveled all this way to find her! After muttering a few choice expletives, Warrington had climbed back into his carriage and had instructed his driver to begin the journey back to town.

Tilly Blodgett couldn't help but notice that Antonia seemed even more depressed. Since they'd come to town, Antonia seemed unhappy and, knowing the reason for her gloom, Tilly found it understandable.

Yet that afternoon, when they gathered for tea in the dining room of the boarding house, Antonia seemed even more melancholy. When the two young women made their way to the amphitheater to get ready for the evening's performance, Tilly was determined to find out what was wrong.

When they entered the dressing room, the dancer turned to Antonia. "Whatever is the matter, Tony? You've been blue-deviled since we've come to town, but 'tis even worse now. What 'appened?"

"Nothing," said Antonia glumly.

"Nothing? Why, I can't believe that. It must be Jack." She nodded knowingly. " 'Tis Jack. That's clear enough. But you mustn't worry. 'E'll be back for you."

"He won't be back for me," said Antonia. "I know that now."

"Why? What 'appened?"

"Nothing. It's only that now I've given up thinking I'll see him again."

"I don't understand. 'Ow do you know that? It 'asn't been very long since we left Shrewsbury."

"I know," said Antonia.

"Well, I can't see 'ow you know that. I'll wager we 'aven't seen the last of Jack Bradford."

Antonia made no reply and Tilly decided that she'd better let the matter drop.

Some time later, Antonia stood waiting to go on and watching Tilly's performance.

"Miss Richards," came a masculine voice. She turned to see

Michael Flynn. The acrobat was resplendent in a new costume of peacock blue, with a cape of matching blue lined with ivory satin. The outfit revealed Flynn's muscular form to good advantage and he hoped that it would impress Antonia.

"Mr. Flynn," said Antonia.

"Dashed fine crowd," said Flynn, smiling brightly at her. "We've had fine crowds all week." When Antonia made no remark, he continued. "I love London. What good fortune brought us here."

Antonia still made no remark. She turned back to watch Tilly again, leaving Flynn to regard her resentfully. He was beginning to find her gloominess and lack of interest wearying. He wasn't accustomed to working so hard at winning a female. Usually, women were throwing themselves at him in droves. At that moment, Tilly completed her dance and took her bows, and Michael Flynn went out with his brother to have his turn at delighting the public.

It was growing late when Warrington arrived at his town house. He paused only to change his travel-stained clothes. He then called for another carriage to convey him to Crawford's Amphitheater. When he entered the vast auditorium, he found it very crowded. The audience was watching acrobats whom he immediately recognized as the Flynn brothers.

The Flynns were completing their performance. They acknowledged the enthusiastic applause of the crowd with low bows and then went bounding out.

The next performer was Antonia. Warrington smiled. Thank God, he thought. There she was. It would be only a short time until she'd be in his arms once again. She began to sing a slow, sad ballad, and with the rest of the audience, he marveled at the sweetness of her voice.

Antonia sang a number of songs and at the completion of each one, there was thunderous applause. She sang one song as an encore and then hurried away. Warrington left the audience, eager to be reunited with the woman he was going to marry.

As Antonia made her way to the dressing room, she felt despondent. One might have thought that the enthusiastic crowd would have cheered her, but Antonia had taken no solace from the applause. She was glad to have the performance over. She opened her dressing room door, expecting to find Tilly. Instead, she saw Geoffrey Mansfield sitting at her dressing table smoking a cigar.

"What are you doing here?" cried Antonia.

"Ah, Miss Richards," said Geoffrey, rising from his chair.

"How did you get in my dressing room?"

"Oh, I know you've told those thugs Crawford employs to keep me out, but it's easy to outsmart them."

"Well, I suggest you leave at once, sir."

"Come, come, my dear, aren't you tired of this little game we've been playing?" said Geoffrey. "It was wearisome at Larchmont and 'tis even more so here. I've come to take you to supper."

"If you don't go, I shall call for help. Get out!"

Geoffrey smiled and took a puff of his cigar. "You don't mean that, my dear." He started toward her. "I know you don't truly wish me to go."

"By God, she does!" said a masculine voice as Warrington appeared in the doorway behind Antonia.

Antonia turned in amazement. "Jack!"

"Bradford!" sputtered Geoffrey, eyeing him in surprise and noting that his former groom was now dressed in fine evening clothes.

"If you don't get out of here, Mansfield, you'll live to regret it."

Mansfield hesitated only a moment before hastily walking past the viscount and disappearing down the corridor.

"Tony, my darling!" Warrington took Antonia into his arms and hugged her tightly. "Thank God, I've found you! I cannot believe that blackguard Mansfield is still plaguing you."

Antonia pressed herself against him, scarcely believing he was there. "Jack, I thought you'd never come." She pulled away suddenly. "Oh, Jack, why did you come back? It would be better if you had stayed away."

"What? What do you mean?" He started to embrace her again, but she eluded his arms.

"No, Jack."

"What is it?"

"Oh, Jack, I know who you are! How could you have done this to me?"

"Done what? My dear girl, I don't know what you're talking about."

"You are Lord Warrington, the son of the Earl of Gravenhurst."

"Yes, I am, but what—"

She cut him off. "And it was some sort of game to you, playing at being poor and joining the circus. I shall never forgive you for leaving me as you did without a word."

"Without a word? My dear Tony, didn't you get my letter?"

"I don't know what you're talking about."

"Good God, you didn't get it! Damn the fellow! That morning I took Daphne for a ride. When she threw a shoe, I went to a blacksmith in Shrewsbury. There I read in the newspaper that my father was dangerously ill. I wrote you a letter which I entrusted to a man I met. He promised to give it to you."

When she regarded him skeptically, he continued. "It is the truth, Tony. I hated to rush off like that. I would have come and told you, but there was a man I knew from London, Sir Osbert Lumley, who'd gone to see Mr. Pickering. He would have recognized me."

"But why couldn't you say who you were? Why did you carry on that ridiculous charade, pretending to be Jack Bradford?"

"I didn't want to do so, Tony, but I'd made a wager with my father. I'd agreed to live on a small sum of money for a month, and I'd promised I wouldn't reveal my identity to anyone."

"But why?"

"My father thought me a frivolous wastrel. And, indeed, he was right. I was always gambling and wasting money. He wanted to teach me a lesson. And I shall always be grateful for him. I learned so much in that month. But even more important than that, my dearest Tony, I met you."

Tears began to fall down Antonia's cheeks. "Didn't you care about me? About breaking my heart? How could you propose marriage to me, knowing that it was impossible?"

"Good God!" exclaimed the viscount. "You think I didn't mean it? I want you to be my wife, Tony. And you agreed to marry me."

"I agreed to marry Jack Bradford, not Lord Warrington."

"My dear goose, we are one and the same. And I love you. I need you by my side."

"But your family! What will they say?"

"My father has already given his blessing."

"He has?"

Warrington nodded. "I confess my mother and sisters will need time to adjust to the idea, but I'm confident they will do so. Now, say you will marry me. It is your destiny, you know. Don't forget Mrs. Pickering's prophecy. You didn't realize what an amazing fortune-teller she is."

Antonia's blue eyes met his gray ones for a moment. She smiled, and then she threw herself into his arms. "Oh, Jack!"

The viscount eagerly covered her mouth with his own, kissing her passionately, causing Antonia to forget everything but her beloved Jack.

Epilogue

Although Lady Gravenhurst had been firmly committed to disapproving of his son's bride, she softened fairly quickly. She could not deny that Antonia was lovely, intelligent, and well-educated. The countess could also find no fault with her impeccable manners and ladylike bearing. A practical woman, Lady Gravenhurst soon decided that it would be better to accept her new daughter-in-law.

Warrington and Antonia were married in London in a quiet ceremony. And although Lady Gravenhurst was none too pleased that her son insisted on inviting a number of undesirable persons to the wedding reception, she was gracious to the Pickerings, the Flynn brothers, Jocko, and even to Tilly Blodgett, who arrived wearing a flamboyant pink outfit.

And surprisingly enough, Lady Gravenhurst grew exceedingly fond of Jem Perkins, who came to live with her son and daughter-in-law. She was often found strolling with Jem in the park, accompanied by the little black dog who did so many amusing tricks.

As might be expected, the viscount's marriage to a singer from Crawford's Amphitheater provoked a good deal of talk among London society. Yet as time went by, Antonia became a respected hostess and invitations to her musical soirees were eagerly sought.

When Geoffrey Mansfield visited London with his father and stepmother, Lady Mansfield obtained invitations for a ball that was to be attended by a great many of the great ladies and gentlemen of society. When Lady Mansfield and her stepson had heard the herald announce the arrival of Lord and Lady Warrington, they had eagerly craned their necks toward the new arrivals.

It was one of Antonia's fondest memories, which she often recounted in years to come, how they had passed by the Mansfields that evening. Lady Mansfield and Geoffrey had gaped at them in such great astonishment that Antonia had nearly burst into laughter.

Warrington had responded by giving them a brief disdainful glance as if such a lofty personage as himself would not deign to look at such provincial nobodies. Antonia had allowed a slight smile to appear on her face as they swept past; they had a most enjoyable evening.